ALIEN COVENANT

Genesis I

James Hansen

First published by Dog Ear Publishing
4010 W. 86th Street, Ste H
Indianapolis, IN 46268
www.dogearpublishing.net

ISBN: 978-160844-544-8

This book is printed on acid-free paper.

Printed in the United States of America

DISCLAIMER

The book title, *Alien Covenant: Genesis I,* is in no manner associated with the book and video game series titled *Halo*, that features a fictional theo-cratic military alliance of alien races called the Covenant (casually referred to as the alien Covenant), nor is the title associated in any manner with the very short story on the internet titled "The Alien Covenant Unveiled" by author Brenda Munday Gifford.

"As above, so below."

Hermes Trismegistus
(a.k.a. Thoth, Ningizida, Uriel)

"...the Independence of the United States of America the Twelfth."

Constitution of the United States of America

ACKNOWLEDGMENT AND DEDICATION

Alien Covenant: Genesis I is a re-imagined story based on ancient texts (some banned by the Catholic church): *The Book of Adam and Eve*; *The Book of the Life of Adam and Eve*; *The Apocalypse of Moses*; *The Book of Enoch*; *The Book of Jubilees*; *The Cave of Treasures*; *The Book of Jasher*; *The Holy Bible*; *The Holy Koran*; and miscellaneous texts from the ancient Sumerians, Egyptians, Akkadians, Chaldeans, Babylonians, Assyrians, Canaanites, Syrians, and others.

This story incorporates the idea of ancient astronauts, that humanoid aliens came to Earth a long time ago and created support bases, or safe havens with farmland, and later, somewhat unexpectedly, created mankind. An extension of this idea is that these gods or angels, again unexpectedly, interbred with mankind and their behavior altogether provided the basis for the mythologies and religions of the world, especially the rites and festivals of the Ancient Mysteries.

In 1971, I read *Chariots of the Gods* by Erich von Däniken, which introduced me to the idea of ancient astronauts. Many years later and after much research and pondering, I read *The 12th Planet* by Zecharia Sitchin, which, with his further books, greatly expanded and supported the idea of ancient astronauts, most notably the concept that a self-heated planet of the gods, called Nibiru, may be coursing around the sun in an extremely elongated and angled orbit that brings it near to the asteroid belt once every 3,600 years, and that its humanoid occupants' life span is seemingly eternal when compared to our own life span.

Erich von Däniken and Zecharia Sitchin are the forefathers of the ancient astronaut theory, as it has come to be known, and as such, they deserve to receive the dedication of my first book, which I consider to be my contribution to the theory, albeit in story form with a dash of artistry. I, therefore, dedicate this book to Erich von Däniken and Zecharia Sitchin and give thanks to the many others who have explored, pondered, and offered similar new ideas concerning the mysteries of the ancients. Thank you.

James Hansen
July 4, 2010
Portland, Oregon

ALIEN COVENANT

Genesis I

James Hansen

Contents

Creation

1

When, in the height, the gods, as dynamic planets, had not yet been brought out—not even God, as the sun and hub dynamo star, the singular soul that engendered them all, and not even Goddess, as the binary dynamo star to the sun, the soul mate who bore them all—and, in the depth, the earth had not yet appeared—not even Eden, as the lowland of rivers and lakes, and not even Zion, as the highland of mountains and valleys—their natures, as waters, were comingled in one androgynous domain, as a nebula. No reed house had been built, and no marsh land had appeared. It was then, when no works, whatever, had been brought into being or called by name, that the hub dynamo and its helper were formed. In the midst of the public domain was a single thought, a scratching bull of pent-up potential—Wholly Black Business Bull, or Black Bull for short, as the black sun—and on the horizon were follow-on thoughts, a marching sea of pent-up potential—Wholly Black Swastika Waters, or Black Waters for short, as dust. A fatal attraction of Black Bull to Black Waters caused Black Bull to become immersed in Black Waters, creating a charge account of reeds, an electro-magnetized bank of pent-up power—Wholly Invisible Whiz Spirit, or Invisible Spirit for short, as the holy spirit.

In the depths of Black Waters, Black Bull created bonds of reed-clay bricks and piled them into cells, building a sea-air-land creature in the shape of a crescent with wings, tall neck, bulbous head, and webbed feet—Wholly Black Faith Swan, or Black Swan for short, as the black binary star of the black sun. Bathing in radiant springs from Black Bull, Black Swan opened a set of doors in its front and rear. Black Bull, seduced in this manner, promptly mounted Black Swan and hymned a sweet six-tune lyre, creating a harmonic resonance that inflated Black Swan. Black Swan sang a grand ole opera and spread out its wings. Infused with Invisible Spirit from

Black Bull, Black Swan flew united with Black Bull up from the reed-clay abyss of Black Waters.

During the ecstatic inflation of resonance caused by the sexual drive of Black Bull with Invisible Spirit, Black Bull and Black Swan transformed into electromagnetic dynamos. They were synchronized in an upward arcing harmonic series of ever-tightening chords, a single contracting, double-helixed tornado cone, or unicorn horn. Black Bull was rushed by Invisible Spirit into generating great power, striking with sensational splendor into the capacity of Black Swan. Black Bull and Black Swan had double-clapped with tremendous thunder within a halo of air. With their heads now revolving in the clouds, they rejoiced, because they had transformed and gone to a safe haven, where they could rest in peace with brand new names.

Black Bull and Black Swan had been phenomenal. Their coupling had switched a lagging load into a leading load. Black Bull manifested its potential by creating an ever-tightening, ever-accelerating loop of electromagnetism that divided itself into two bodies—temporal seconds, or timely solid states—each possessing positive and negative potential. Black Bull had fashioned a vessel with a womb, which then received half of the full potential of Black Bull. The vessel, Black Swan, had become a dynamo half full of potential, and Black Bull had become a dynamo half empty of potential. Invisible Spirit had saved Black Bull from inhaling from Black Waters, a surefire method of collapsing to death. Invisible Spirit had caused Black Bull to exhale into Black Swan, a surefire method of expanding to live. In this manner, Wholly Black Business Bull transformed into Wholly Iron Clad Horse, or Iron Horse for short, as the iron sun, and Wholly Black Faith Swan transformed into Wholly Iron Bill Duck, or Iron Duck for short, as the iron binary star of the iron sun. Wholly Invisible Whiz Spirit, however, transformed into Wholly White Flash Bolt, or White Bolt for short, as the holy ghost, and then back again into Wholly Invisible Whiz Spirit, as the holy spirit. The dark age of creation was akin to the early half of a cold, winter night.

2

Iron Horse and Iron Duck danced in a coupling ceremony ministered by Invisible Spirit: Two bodies twirling, diving, swinging to and from, she flashing down to him and him rising up to her, and then the two consummating the many-splendored thing in a glorious arcing flash with him over her. In the consummation of the ceremony, the pharynx of Iron Horse became stiff, and then he chanted the chord, "A-a-a-a-a-a-u-u-u-u-u-u-m-m-m-m-m-m," six times. Coincidently, the pharynx of Iron Duck became supple, and she sang the hymn, "Ooh Al-le-lu, Yea!" six times.

During the crescendo, Iron Horse sprayed and stirred his freshwater into the saltwater of Iron Duck. Iron Duck conceived of White Bolt, and then twin eggs began to grow within her womb. A son and daughter were soon brought out—Wholly Right Mount Lion and Wholly Left Mount Lion, or Right Lion and Left Lion for short, as the red planet Mars and the blue planet Venus. For aeons, the two new dynamos grew in age and stature, becoming as firm bastions of a wholly royal family.

When Right Lion and Left Lion had reached their maturity, their parents engaged in the grave, electromagnetic Dance of Creation again. Iron Duck conceived of White Bolt, and another son and daughter were soon brought out—Wholly Stripe Suit Tiger and Wholly Savings Bond Fish, or Stripe Tiger and Savings Fish for short, as the stripe planet Jupiter and the school planet Saturn. For aeons, the two new dynamos grew in age and stature, becoming as ghastly giants of a wholly royal family.

As aeons progressed, the love of Iron Horse toward his family grew also. Iron Horse began to glow; he became a plasma generator, and a great pulse—his heartbeat—was felt by all. Now beaming with soothing hymns of joy, he shined upon his archon wife, the queen, and his wholly royal children, the two princes and two princesses, giving them the gift of enlightenment. In this manner, Wholly Iron Clad Horse transformed into Wholly Copper Penny Bear, or Copper Bear for short, as the copper sun, and Wholly Iron Bill Duck transformed into Wholly Copper Watt Gobbler, or Copper Gobbler for short, as the copper binary star of the copper sun. The iron age of creation was akin to the late half of a cold, winter night.

3

Stripe Tiger and Savings Fish engaged themselves in the Dance of Creation. Savings Fish conceived of White Bolt, and a son was soon brought out—Wholly Green Back Crab, or Green Crab for short, as the green planet Uranus. Green Crab, as a firstborn son, was heir to the power of his father. Stripe Tiger raised Green Crab in character and power to be like himself. Green Crab quickly grew in size and strength; however, he became stubborn and ugly as a tumor.

When Stripe Tiger and Savings Fish grew old and weak, Stripe Tiger was forced to transfer most of his power to his crabby son. There was a glorious exchange with a flaming scepter. The scepter was a huge, splendorous bolt of lightning, and Green Crab was crowned with the halo of Stripe Tiger. The power of Green Crab now rivaled the power left in his father, even the power of his grandfather, Copper Bear.

Stripe Tiger and Savings Fish then spawned many strange and tiny children, and Green Crab thought of the children as a threat to his power. Green Crab feared that he might become overpowered by them in the same manner that he had overpowered his father. Green Crab decided to slurp the spawns as soon as he could, and even new ones as soon as they were spawned. His father and mother were disgusted at Green Crab for his slurping.

Savings Fish devised a plan to avenge her little ones. She disguised a volatile rock to appear like one of her babes, and then Green Crab slurped it up. He promptly vomited up all the babes in a sea of foam. The babes, unseen by Green Crab within the foam, grew to be infants, who then sprang forth from the foam. The first was Wholly Blue Blood Scorpion, or Blue Scorpion for short, as the blue planet Neptune. The second was Wholly White Milk Cat, or White Cat for short, as the white planet-moon Triton. The third was Wholly Red Blood Bull, or Red Bull for short, as the red planet Jove. These three attracted the attention of Green Crab, who then decided to raise them in power to become strong motors willing to do his bidding for fame and fortune, unaware that they were spawns of his mother. The two brothers, Blue Scorpion and Red Bull, eventually quarreled, so Green Crab separated them from one another. Green Crab sent Blue Scorpion to an area far away to be a shepherd of scattered side-winders, or loonies, and he sent Red Bull to an area farther away to be a farmer of scattered seeds, or boonies. He then sent the sister, White Cat, to go back and forth as a diplomat between Red Bull, Blue Scorpion, and the rest of the upper assembly of dynamos.

Blue Scorpion, the first one spawned from Stripe Tiger and the first one spewed from Green Crab, felt that he was entitled to inherit both the spawning power of Stripe Tiger and the slurping power of Green Crab, and so he took steps to ensure his double inheritance. In league with his mother and sister, he succeeded in gaining a higher level of power from Green Crab. As Blue Scorpion grew, he became the spitting image of Green Crab. He also became wiser and even more powerful than all the other beastly dynamos in the assembly. Blue Scorpion had surpassed the combined power of Green Crab and Stripe Tiger, and became even mightier than his forefather, Copper Bear.

Feeling the power of Blue Scorpion, Red Bull steamed jealousy from his nostrils.

In a mad search for fame and power, Red Bull raped his sister, White Cat, while she was bathing in the wilderness. She conceived of White Bolt, and a son was soon brought out—Wholly Grey Gore Kangaroo, or Grey Kangaroo for short, as the grey moon. The offense of Red Bull did not go unnoticed by the assembly. As punishment for the rape, the patriarchs banished Red Bull to fly alone in a region of the wilderness far, far away from the assembly of Copper Bear, farther from where he was with the boonies. Blue Scorpion now had no rival in the assembly.

4

Many new kinds of side-winders, called goonies, were spawned from Copper Gobbler. The goonies banded and bonded as metal soldiers, disturbing the moody blue-green aura of Copper Gobbler. They became easily excited and jumped up and down in their seats. They surged back and forth and coiled and struck with spikes, and then dropped out. The goonies kidnapped one another with their gravity nets and threw rocks at each other. Some rocks went astray and hit Copper Bear, badly bruising him in the face.

The goonies tugged at the elders with their combined strength. Their unsettled behavior upset the stomach of Copper Gobbler, troubling the molten salt in her magma. She quaked and stormed. Drum-beating Copper Bear could not control the children, and hip-hopping Copper Gobbler became speechless. The hilarity of the goonies running amok in the assembly not only troubled the stomach of Copper Gobbler but confused their keeper, Copper Bear.

Left Lion, in her own rebellion, threw a bolt at her mother and thundered in her ear. Copper Gobbler roared to all of them to stop their loathsome behavior, but they were overbearing; their volatile personalities were not like hers. Although the strength of Copper Bear was not weakened by their antics, he was not able to correct their destructive ways, and no matter how terrible their behavior, Copper Gobbler remained speechless. An old pockmarked, wing-tipped dynamo-shoe moonie, earlier thrown toward the face of Copper Bear by one tin soldier, was kept at the side of the disgraced Copper Bear.

Copper Bear empowered the flying shoe to become his male assistant and shield—Wholly Family Crest Herald, or Family Herald for short, as the silver planet Mercury.

Copper Bear, or Father Hub Beast, as some called him, cried out, addressing Family Herald, "O you, flying shoe who bathes in my invisible rays, I want you to be my messenger. I want you to quickly deliver a message to my wife. Come closer to hear my words in confidence, and then quickly fly off with my secret message to her."

Family Herald stepped closer to his master, who whispered the secret words into his ear.

Copper Bear then waved his hand, commanding, "O shoe, fly away."

Arriving back at Copper Gobbler, Family Herald bowed before her and recited the secret message of Copper Bear concerning the rebellious ways of her goonies and what he was going to do to them.

Family Herald shouted, "Hear, you! Hear, you! Hear, you! In the name of Copper Bear and by his level of power, I declare his secret message to you: 'O Wholly Copper Watt Gobbler, my wife, the ways of your goonies are revolting. We cannot rest or sleep, and I fear that they may overcome us. Even though they are as strong as the titans in the upper assembly, I will destroy their ways and scatter their bodies beyond the horizon. We will weep in sadness for a while, but then we will have peace and quiet—we will be able to rest and sleep again.'"

Family Herald threw a bolt to demonstrate the anger and seriousness of Copper Bear.

Copper Gobbler was stunned, shocked by the secret message. She shuddered at the thought of being alone, because she always wanted to be with her children, regardless of whether they were terrible goonies.

Angry, Copper Gobbler replied to her husband, "What? Why must we destroy my creations? Yes, their behavior is troublesome, but let us kindly act to correct the problem. Let us wait a little while longer. If they do not settle down by then, we will make their lives difficult, and then we will have peace and quiet. O my Lord, what should we do?"

In this manner, Wholly Copper Watt Gobbler transformed into Wholly Silver Capital Heron, or Silver Heron for short, as the silver binary star of the sun.

Family Herald swiftly flew back to his master, bowed before him, and recited word-for-word the reply of the queen of the family.

Wishing ill toward the goonies who threw him out, Family Herald ungraciously advised Copper Bear before Copper Bear could ponder a response to his wife, saying, "My Lord, yes, while amalgamated they are as strong as the titans in their mutiny, but you can destroy their will, and then you will have rest."

When Copper Bear heard this, he imagined what destruction he could impose, and his face grew exceedingly radiant. In this manner, Wholly Copper Penny Bear transformed into Wholly Silver Dollar Stag, or Silver Stag for short, as the silver sun. The copper age of creation was akin to a warm, spring morning.

5

Silver Stag was well-pleased with his quick messenger, Family Herald, who had now become his vizier, or shielded business knight. They quickly began to conspire. In rejoicing, Silver Stag reached out with his fiery arms to the shoulders of Family Herald, kissed his forehead, and then pinched and shook his nose. All the children saw their father and Family Herald plotting together, and they became confused and upset, wandering aimlessly and wondering what might happen to them. They were restless and speechless. Wise Blue Scorpion, however, sensed what Silver Stag was planning to do, so he made a master plan to go against it for his own sake, a clever scheme that would retire Silver Stag and create a new world order.

Fully charged with power, Blue Scorpion put his plan into action. With a libation, a pouring emanation, he neutralized the rebellious goonies, calming and settling them back into their appointed seats, and he neutralized Silver Stag into early retirement. Family Herald and Silver Heron were dazed and confused. Blue Scorpion then quickly snatched the radiant crown of Silver Stag, the wavy turban, setting it upon himself and therefore usurping the power of Silver Stag.

After Blue Scorpion had subdued the foe and established his victory, he dwelled in the splendor of the abyss in the upper assembly of dynamos with White Cat, whom he affectionately called Firm Dame. In this manner, Wholly Silver Dollar Stag transformed into Wholly Gold Bar Lion, or Gold Lion for short, as the gold sun, and Wholly Silver Capital Heron transformed into Wholly Gold Egg Goose, or Gold Goose for short, as the gold binary star of the gold sun. The silver age of creation was akin to a hot, summer day.

6

In a reach of the wilderness far, far beyond the assembly of wholly royals, a savage dog star—Serious Business Alpha Dog, or Business Dog for short, as the star Sirius Alpha—had performed the Dance of Creation with a savage bitch star—Gothic Black Beta Bitch, or Black Bitch for short, as the star Sirius Beta, and she had soon brought out a litter of cute starlets—poopies. Among the litter was a buzzer, an ugly brown dwarf—boogie. While the poopies were all paddling-about the stretched-out teats of Black Bitch, the hyperactive boogie was trying to find its place in the family, but the siblings denied the ugly runt access to the nourishing milk of Black Bitch.

The ducky siblings were constantly telling the runt, "You are an ugly duckling!...You are a weakling!...You do not belong with us!...Are you a boy or a girl? You cannot be both. Get out of here!...You are a freak of mother nature!"

They repeatedly pushed the ugly duckling out of the way, and then Black Bitch cast the runt off into the black sea of the wilderness, hoping to never see her odd fellow again.

Although the dwarf failed to become a true dog or bitch star, the hermaphrodite was beautiful in her, or his, own class. He grew to become a boogie woogie doogie. As a buzz-sawyer trail blazing through the dark wilderness, he sparkled with a thousand blinking eyes. When he moved his lips, fire and lava blazed forth; the howling coyote appeared as a prince in his own right.

Meanwhile, after Blue Scorpion had crowned and nick-named himself Scorpion King, Gold Goose began to grumble and complain about the hypnotic, hexagram spell that Blue Scorpion had incanted on her husband. She demanded that Blue Scorpion decant the spell and return the noble gold crown of power to her husband at once.

She shouted to all, "Blue Scorpion has usurped the crown of power, the wavy turban of King God, the one and only true God! I demand that he return it to God at once!"

When Blue Scorpion flat-out refused a direct request from Gold Goose, she stormed away to visit her voodoo priestess daughter, Left Lion, to curse something awful to happen to Blue Scorpion.

In the meantime, after a long and lonely journey of survival through the dark wilderness, the confused doogie was about to pass by the wholly royal assembly. The first to see the buzzing bee-bop doogie was Blue Scorpion, the farthest one out, and he directed the doogie to come closer. Blue Scorpion engaged him in conversation and became wise to his plight.

Blue Scorpion spoke about the high-flying doogie—Brown One Sea Gull, or One Gull for short, as the stray brown dwarf star—to his step-father, Green Crab, and bio-mother, Savings Fish, adding, "The dogged-one, One Gull, has survived a long quest across the cold desolation of the wilderness far, far beyond our assembly, even farther than the boonies. He weeps and sits in misfortune, cowering in fear of not knowing what will happen to him. Let us welcome this weary gull into our warm dynamo house and treat him as a prince of our family. Let us raise his weak level of power to a higher plane and assign him a new name."

As Blue Scorpion spoke, the kindred of the dynamos of industry became excited about having a new and different dynamo in their house. Stripe Tiger agreed, and cordially welcomed One Gull, steering him into the royal household. The family members presented One Gull with some of their splendor upon his arrival. Blue Scorpion clothed him in a beautiful, multicolored coat, which was ten times grander than any of their own coats.

Blue Scorpion and White Cat adopted the hermaphrodite doogie as their son, sometimes referring to him as the Prince of Darkness. White Cat became his step-mother and nursed him back to strength, filling him with awesome radiance. His two bug eyes and two floppy ears, which saw and heard all things around him, were large and unblemished, perfectly formed. His figure was alluring, and he exulted and glowed—his heart was filled with warmth. Blue Scorpion became his step-father and rendered him flawless, and Stripe Tiger had endowed him with a double head, a back-head and a fore-head, one to see and understand the past and one to see and understand the future.

Blue Scorpion shouted to him, "My little son, my little son! My adopted son, my adopted son! Twelfth Dynamo of the Assembly!" and continuously spoke of him to the others as being wiser and stronger than any of them.

7

Stripe Tiger and Green Crab stirred up the matriarch, Gold Goose, day and night, contributing to the chaos in the midst of the assembly. In malice, they said to her, "When Blue Scorpion hypnotized Silver Stag, you did not come to his aid; instead, you remained still....Although your consort fashioned the awesome assembly of dynamos, your insides are diluted; therefore, we cannot have rest....Let Silver Stag, who has been vanquished, be put to rest in your heart. You are left alone!...Your consort has grown old and is retired. He is not a young buck like me, or a strapping antelope like he used to be, and you are not a spring chicken, or a summer heron anymore."

Gold Goose conceived a hatred for her male-born offspring, especially Stripe Tiger, Green Crab, and Blue Scorpion. In planning destruction to avenge her husband, she gathered the male eyes and ears of the assembly, calling the moonies and goonies all together an army of winding metal soldiers. She raged full of wrath with all of her net worth, and nearly all of the male eyes and ears turned and went to her, especially those whom Stripe Tiger with Savings Fish had created. The brother soldiers banded together, marching by her side. While advancing furiously, fuming and raging, they planned for destruction and trained for battle without resting. By joining their forces, they were prepared for war.

Gold Goose, or old Mother Hub Bird, as some called her, fashioned heavy and invincible weapons to go against her elder children in the upper assembly. She turned the goonies into fierce side-winders, ferocious dragoons with piercing fangs freckled with foam. She filled their bodies with toxic waste instead of gold blood, clothed them with terrorizing, explosive magma vomit, and bedecked them with glowing, fierce volcano eyes. They became monsters, and terror overcame whoever saw them. Their scaley bodies would rear up and nobody could stand upright against them in their attack. Gold Goose became visibly dark, and others now called her Mother Niger, Queen of Black Dragoons. In addition to the goonies, she spawned raging hound-dogs, whipping hurricanes, stinging scorpions, mighty tempests, biting sharks, and butting rams. They were well-trained in holding cruel weapons of war and were not afraid of a fight. The commands of Mother Niger were so mighty that nobody could resist them. In this manner, Gold Goose, the mother of beauty, transformed into a dark queen and created eleven kinds of monsters.

From among the rank and file who were of her offspring, the dark queen promoted the largest, most prominent one, Grey Kangaroo, because he had given her the strongest support in the assembly. He had been sired by Red Bull, who had raped White Cat, and the dark queen had swayed Grey Kangaroo away from White Cat during her gathering of soldiers for a revolt. She promoted Grey Kangaroo to the same level of power as Stripe Tiger, renaming him Sunny Kangaroo, the Grey Gore Dome Shield Cow Boy King, and entrusting him to march facing the opposing forces, lead the flying host for victory, give the beginning signal for battle, advance the attack for destruction, direct the wrestle for the honor of king, and win the fight for the glory of queen.

Mother Niger gave Grey Kangaroo a blue, undulating robe to distinguish him from the others.

She said to him, "I have raised the orders of the troops and have promoted you to a higher level of power. I have also entrusted to you the minions of the assembly. You have been drawn up from the rank and file—I have chosen you as the messiah, the savior of my flock. May everybody in the assembly exalt your name above their names."

Mother Niger then gave Grey Kangaroo a set of horror-scoping tables containing classified orbital charts and a program of logarithms, altogether called the Tables of Destinies.

As she placed the secret Tables of Destinies in his front pocket, she whispered in his ear, "You can now easily predict where our enemy will be and when he will be there. Your mission will not fail. My decree that Blue Scorpion immediately return the crown to our sovereign will be fulfilled."

In this manner, Grey Kangaroo was promoted from the rank and file, receiving the same level of power as the great dynamo, Stripe Tiger.

Grey Kangaroo decreed the fate of the dynamos to his army of winding metal soldiers, shouting, "Let your cries of fury avenge Allelu, the one and only true king, God, our sovereign monarch! Let whoever is a bull dog in battle display his might for King Solitar!"

The dark queen, with her loose lips, told her children, Right Lion and Left Lion, how she had spawned her monsters, the side-winding dragoons, and what she was going to do with them. Blue Scorpion was carefully listening in, and he became grievously affected, sitting in sadness afterward.

As many moonies and goonies went by, the anger of Blue Scorpion subsided, and then he made his way to the seat of Stripe Tiger. Upon his arrival, he stood before Stripe Tiger, repeating all of what the dark queen had plotted.

He said to Stripe Tiger, "Mother Queen has conceived a hatred for her male-born offspring. In planning destruction to avenge Gold Lion, she has gathered the male eyes and ears of the assembly, calling the moonies and goonies all together an army of winding metal soldiers. She has raged full of wrath with all of her net force, and nearly all of the male eyes and ears turned and went to her, especially those whom you had created. The brother soldiers have banded together, marching by her side. While advancing furiously, fuming and raging, they have planned for destruction and trained for battle without resting. By joining their forces, they are prepared for war.

"Mother Queen has wrought heavy and merciless weapons to go against us. She has turned the moonies and goonies into fierce side-winders, ferocious dragoons with piercing fangs freckled with foam. She has filled their bodies with toxic waste instead of gold blood, clothed them with terrorizing, explosive magma vomit, and bedecked them with glowing, fierce volcano eyes. They have become monsters, and terror overcomes whoever sees them. Their scaley bodies rear up, and nobody can stand upright against them in their attack. Gold Goose has become visibly dark, and others now called her Mother Niger, Queen of Black Dragoons. In addition to the goonies, she has spawned raging hound-dogs, whipping hurricanes, stinging scorpions, mighty tempests, biting sharks, and butting rams. They are well-trained in holding cruel weapons of war and are not afraid of a fight. The commands of Mother Niger were so mighty that nobody could resist them. In this manner, Gold Goose, the mother of beauty, has transformed into a dark queen and has created eleven kinds of monsters.

"From among the rank and file, the dark queen has promoted Grey Kangaroo, because he has given her the strongest support in the assembly. She has promoted him to the same level of power as you, renaming him Sunny Kangaroo, the Grey Gore Dome Shield Cow Boy King, and entrusting him to march facing the opposing forces, lead the flying host for victory, give the beginning signal for battle, advance the attack for destruction, direct the wrestle for the honor of king, and win the fight for the glory of queen. Mother Niger has given Grey Kangaroo a blue, undulating robe to distinguish him from the others.

"She said to him, 'I have raised the orders of the troops and have promoted you to a higher level of power. I have also entrusted to you the minions of the assembly. You have been drawn up from the rank and file—I have chosen you as the messiah, the savior of my flock. May everybody in the assembly exalt your name above their names.' Mother Niger has given Grey Kangaroo the horror-scoping Tables of Destinies. As she placed the Tables in his front pocket, she whispered in his ear, 'You can now easily predict where our enemy will be and when he will be there. Your mission will not fail. My decree that Blue Scorpion immediately return the crown to our sovereign will be fulfilled." In this manner, Grey Kangaroo has been promoted from the rank and file, receiving the same level of power as you, O Stripe Tiger. Grey Kangaroo has decreed our fate to his army of winding metal soldiers, shouting, 'Let your cries of fury avenge Allelu, the one and only true king, God, our sovereign monarch! Let whoever is a bull dog in battle display his might for King Solitar!'"

8

When Stripe Tiger heard from Blue Scorpion how Gold Goose was mightily in revolt, he bit his lips. His mind was not at peace; he, too, was grievously affected and sat in sadness afterward.

In bitterness, Stripe Tiger lamented to Blue Scorpion, "O Blue Scorpion, you have brought upon us a war within the assembly. You, O Blue Scorpion, are responsible to stop Grey Kangaroo. You have subdued Silver Stag, chained Family Herald, and now Gold Goose has transformed into a dark queen and promoted Grey Kangaroo to the same level of power as me, and where is someone who can oppose her?"

Stripe Tiger called for an emergency conjunction of three dynamos: Blue Scorpion, Green Crab, and himself. They deliberated over the fate of themselves as well as the fate of their crazy mother queen and her ferocious army of moonies and goonies led by a royal loonie. Blue Scorpion, a clever designer, suggested that the elder dynamos put their foot down and run the rebellious winding metal soldiers, the ferocious fire-breathing dragoons, out of the assembly.

After much discourse, Stripe Tiger addressed his son: "O Green Crab, my noble rottwiler, whose strength is great and whose onslaught cannot be withstood, go and stand up before our mother queen. She might perhaps become appeased and merciful. If, however, she does not listen, or does not agree to your words, you will speak our predictions to her. She then might perhaps become pacified."

Green Crab respected the command of his father and directed his path toward the mother queen. He made his way and came near to her. He heard her muttering an awful curse under her breath. His knees shook and gave way. Green Crab could not stand up before her, and so he turned back.

Upon hearing about the failure of Green Crab, Stripe Tiger addressed Blue Scorpion: "O Blue Scorpion, my noble rottwiler, whose strength is great and whose onslaught cannot be withstood, go and stand up before our mother queen, because it is you who brought upon us this war within our assembly. She might perhaps become appeased and merciful. If, however, she does not listen, or does not agree to your words, you will speak our predictions to her. She then might perhaps become pacified."

Blue Scorpion respected the command of Stripe Tiger and directed his step toward the mother queen. He made his way and came near to her. He, too, heard her muttering an awful curse under her breath. His knees shook and gave way. Blue Scorpion could not stand up before her, and so he turned back like his spawn-father, Green Crab, had done.

Stripe Tiger, upon hearing about the failure of Blue Scorpion, said to another emergency conjunction of three dynamos, "The adopted one, One Gull, in order to become a respected prince in our assembly, must become our avenger. He is a doughty, gallant knight who has survived a test of time in trouble, a passage through the harsh wilderness. He is now part of my plan for salvation."

One Gull whispered in the ear of Blue Scorpion, "I am honored by the great Stripe Tiger."

Blue Scorpion whispered back to his adopted son, "The dragoons will batter and slice us if not dealt with. You will take vengeance for us. You will journey, battle-ready, to the tempest! Although Gold Lion is retired, and Family Herald is locked, we cannot settle down in peace and quiet. Help us to settle down in peace and quiet."

One Gull eagerly remarked to Stripe Tiger, "O Lord, Stripe Tiger, entrust me with vengeance! Let us wage war!"

Stripe Tiger continued speaking to One Gull, saying, "You, O radiant knight, valiant prince from the dark wilderness, you will become *our* messiah, *our* savior! You will approach near to the battle, and anybody who sees you will bow in peace."

The valiant prince rejoiced at the words of Stripe Tiger and approached near to him, trembling. He knelt down before Stripe Tiger, who touched him on the shoulders with his fiery arm and spoke words of wisdom. The heart of One Gull was filled with great power and radiance from the induction ceremony. Stripe Tiger kissed One Gull on the forehead, and the fear in the prince departed.

Stripe Tiger had promoted One Gull and given him a new name—Wholly Scale Master Eagle, or Scale Eagle for short, as the scaley planet-star Nibiru, or Phaeton.

The prince replied, "My great, grand lord, Stripe Tiger, do not let the wise words from your lips be spoken in vain. Let me go now into the midst of the assembly to battle the foaming cow so that I can quickly accomplish all of what is in your heart."

Stripe Tiger pointed Scale Eagle in the direction of the mother queen and said, "Although the foaming cow is a gooey mother, she is armed to the teeth and will attack you. You will rejoice and be happy, however, because you will swiftly trample her long legs under your foot. O my strange son, you who are all-knowing, calm the dark, snake-headed dragoon queen with your strength and wisdom. Go quickly on your way. Your blood will not be shed, and you will return to us."

The prince rejoiced at the words of Stripe Tiger. His heart exulted, and he said to the great, grand lord, "O Lord of Dynamos, Maker of Destinies, if I as your avenger, your messiah and savior from the dark wilderness, slay your mad cow to save your lives, appoint and convene another emergency conjunction and declare my fate preeminent. I will then joyfully seat all the dynamos and sidewinders in synchronicity, and I will decree the fates with my mouth in your stead, as the new mother queen. May whatever I say or do remain in effect and unaltered indefinitely. May the words of my lips never be spoken in vain."

9

Stripe Tiger opened his ruddy, oval mouth, summoning his secretary—Wholly Lady Gorge Legs, or Lady Legs for short, as the gorge planet Pluto—a female sidewinder who had stayed by his side during the round up of male side-winders by Gold Goose.

He said to her, "O Lady Legs, my secretary who celebrates my level of power with radiance, I will send you as my notary witness to my elder brother and sister, the virgins Right Lion and Left Lion. You will arrange for them to conjoin before me. Inform the dynamos—they and Savings Fish, Green Crab, and Blue Scorpion—to prepare for a hexagram banquet. Let them conjunct to eat bread and drink wine with me, so that they can all together align and cast their votes to decree the fate of their avenger,

Scale Eagle. Go, O Lady Legs, and stand up before them, like Family Herald, and repeat: 'In the name of Stripe Tiger and by his level of power, I recite his message to you: "O my elder brother and sister, our mother queen now hates us. In planning destruction..."'" and Stripe Tiger repeated word-for-word the message of Blue Scorpion, and then added, "I sent Green Crab as an emissary of peace, and then Blue Scorpion, but they could not stand up before her and turned back. However, I, as governor of the assembly, have sent a valiant prince, an adopted one who is a seaborne iron duck in his strength and wisdom, against our mad mother queen. His heart agreed with mine, but he said to me, 'if I as your avenger, your messiah and savior from the wilderness, slay your mad cow to save your lives, appoint and convene another emergency conjunction and declare my fate preeminent. I will then joyfully seat all the dynamos and side-winders in synchronicity, and I will decree the fates with my mouth in your stead, as the new mother queen. May whatever I say or do remain in effect and unaltered indefinitely. May the words of my lips never be spoken in vain.' O my gorgeous secretary, go quickly now and repeat my words to Right Lion and Left Lion. Make accommodations for another emergency conjunction to decree the fate which Scale Eagle requests and to which I agree, so that he may go immediately into the midst of the assembly and fight our strong enemy."

Lady Legs departed, making her way and humbly facing Right Lion and Left Lion. She made obeisance and kissed their feet. She humbled herself, and then stood upright, heralding word-for-word the message of Stripe Tiger. Right Lion and Left Lion heard this and roared, wailing bitterly, "What has changed so that we must change? We do not understand this crazy deed of our mother!" and they shook their heads back and

forth, indicating that they would not attend the conjunction.

The great dynamos—prime movers—all of them
who decree the fates, now including Red Bull and White
Cat, not Right Lion and Left Lion, came into a hexagram
conjunction with Stripe Tiger. It was a party of six in the
upper assembly, as opposed to a gang of four in the lower
assembly. The five stood upright before Stripe Tiger, filling
their cups with nectar and blowing kisses to one another in
greeting. They prepared for the feast and then seated
themselves at a long banquet table. They ate ambrosia and
drank more nectar. The ethereal drink, nectar, confused
their senses. Their bodies were filled with drink, and in
this manner, they were entirely at ease with their mood.
For their avenger, the valiant prince, they aligned and cast
their votes, decreeing his fate. The dynamos then prepared
for their valiant prince a royal flying chariot, or throne
ship, with a long-bowed circuit as a great weapon.

Facing the patriarchs as a valiant prince, Scale
Eagle then knelt before them.

Stripe Tiger said to him, "Valiant prince, you are
promoted to a most high level of power among the
dynamos. You now possess the power of fifty temple states.
Your fate is unequaled. Your word is now the word of
Green Crab! Your name and your words will not be spoken
in vain. It is within your high-scaled power to promote and
abase others. The words from your mouth will be established and unaltered. None in the assembly will transgress
against your commandment. An abundant treasury of
gold, silver, and copper, your desire hidden within the
foaming cow, will be stockpiled in your sanctuary, even if
she refuses to offer it up. Brave Scale Eagle, you are our
avenger! We give you sovereignty over the assembly, which
will be renamed in your honor upon your return. Seat
yourself down in might, and be firm in your commandment. Your mace weapon, the cathore hammer, will never
lose its power of fifty, and it will crush the phaelynx. Most
High Lord, have mercy and save the life-essence of those

who trust in the name and number of your secret account. Now rise up and battle the phaelynx!"

The dynamos set a glorious red, undulating cloak on the shoulders of Scale Eagle, and then Stripe Tiger said to the avenger, "O Scale Eagle, Most High Lord, may your fate to destroy and create worlds reign supreme. Let your red cloak disappear and reappear to give everyone confidence that you reign supreme even when hidden, and that your commands are fulfilled. Demonstrate your most high level of power to all, O Scale Eagle. Let this red cloak vanish and then reappear before our very eyes!"

Scale Eagle stepped away as he commanded, "Disappear!" and the red cloak truly vanished from before their eyes. After a while, he stepped forward and commanded, "Appear!" and the red cloak truly reappeared before their eyes.

When the dynamos and side-winders saw the wonder and fulfillment of his commands, they rejoiced and paid homage to Scale Eagle. Stripe Tiger proclaimed to all, "Wholly Scale Master Eagle reigns supreme!"

Scale Eagle had also been clothed with a halo ten times the size of the halos of the others. He possessed the utmost in strength, because awesome flashes were heaped continually upon him. Blue Scorpion gave him a scepter of thundering power and a double gold-meter crown. They altogether gave him eleven side-winders, invincible weapons that overwhelm the opposing captain of the team.

The female side-winders jumped up and down, cheering and shouting along the sidelines, "Go bald eagles!...Break her leg!...Go giants!...Hit them hard!...Tackle the bastards!...Go packers!...Give them a one-two punch!...Give her a left hook!...Go redskin!...Shoot arrows into the eye of the bull dog!...Go chargers!...Shoot an arrow through her heart!...Knock her off her feet!...Cut off her head!...Slice her to pieces!...Go seahawk!...Club her skull!...Put a hole in her head!...Slice her throat!...Chop off her head!...Throw her bloody head into an empty valley!" and so on.

10

When the dynamos had decreed the fate of Scale Eagle, they caused him to set out on a path of prosperity and success. He made his long-bowed orbit around the retired Gold Lion ready—he considered this as his mightiest weapon. He slung a quiver of arrows, a gift from Stripe Tiger, on his shoulder and fastened it. The height of his long-bow was raised over his right shoulder, and the depth of his long-bow was lowered far below his left shoulder. He set a gold helmet on his head, a skull shield forged from the many gifts he had earlier received. He prepared a net to enclose the innards of the rebellious matriarch. He stationed four soldiers on his left and seven soldiers on his right, so that nothing of the dark queen might escape. He brought over his four soldiers, the side-winders that were gifts from Blue Scorpion—South Winder, North Winder, East Winder, and West Winder—near to his net. Scale Eagle then examined his seven soldiers, the side-winders that were gifts from Green Crab and Stripe Tiger—Evil Winder, Tempest Winder, Hurricane Winder, Fourfold Winder, Sevenfold Winder, Whirl Winder, and Unequal Winder. He brought the Seven, his gale-force winding soldiers, closer to him, to disturb the innards of the dark queen; they followed after him on his righteous side.

Scale Eagle then raised his three-phase thunderbolt of power, a mighty weapon, and mounted the grave chariot of Gold Lion. He accelerated with great speed, unequaled for terror. He harnessed his Four Winders, his rushing currents—he yoked his quarter horses dubbed Destructive, Ferocious, Overwhelming, and Swiftpace, the same as South Winder, North Winder, East Winder, and West Winder. Their teeth were sharp and menacing. They were skilled in battle and had been trained to trample underfoot. Their faces were mighty and fearless for battle. They rattled on the left and on the right.

The red, undulating cloak of Scale Eagle was awesome—he was now ready for battle, clad with terror and crowned with overpowering radiation. He went onward, taking his way, setting his face toward the snake-headed dragoon goddess, Mother Niger, the foaming cow. Scale Eagle held fire in his lips and eyes. He tightened his grip on his three-phase thunderbolt, even spat on it. The patriarchs, the great dynamos, wondered in awe at him. Scale Eagle came near and gazed upon the parts of the dark queen. He heard Grey Kangaroo, her chosen savior, mutter a curse. As Scale Eagle gazed and listened, Grey Kangaroo was troubled in his step; his will was destroyed and his motions ceased. The fire-breathing dragoons, the soldiers who marched with Grey Kangaroo, saw the misstep of their leader, and their vision was troubled. The dark queen, however, was stubborn—she did not turn her now-stiffened neck.

With black lips that did not fail, the dark queen spoke rebellious words to Scale Eagle: "Curse your coming as the messiah and savior of the dynamos! They were not created from your reed-clay—they were created from my reed-clay, and they will return to my reed-clay!"

Scale Eagle squeezed his three-phase thunderbolt, his mighty weapon, and sent his commanding word against the raging cow, saying, "You have become great. You have gathered and spawned an army that prompts you to battle, but my heart has prompted me to battle also. You have twice disobeyed the law of the conjuncted words of the Hexagram of Dynamos to cease your rebellion. You have also conceived a hatred of them in your heart. You have promoted the rake, Grey Kangaroo, as your partner in crime. You have promoted him to a level of power so that he issues decrees of fate as though he were Green Crab himself. You have followed after storm troopers of death and against the commandments of the assembled dynamos. You have contrived a wicked plan; therefore, O Dark Queen, you are responsible for the shameful behavior of your host. Let your host watch over and protect your snaking dragoons—let their weapons be girdled! Stand upright, you and me, and let us alone engage in a battle to the death. In this manner, you will save your subjects from a long and agonizing death!"

When the black dragoon queen heard these commanding words, she was like one possessed—she totally lost her mind and went absolutely crazy. Gold Goose screamed a piercing cry. She trembled and shook to her very core. She then recited a voodoo incantation and then gave an order to Grey Kangaroo to stay and shield all the dragoons from destruction, and to girdle all weapons. Grey Kangaroo then cried out an order to his soldiers, who then echoed it farther back. Gold Goose and Scale Eagle advanced toward one another. They came near to the battleground and then swayed in single combat, locked in battle. Scale Eagle spread out his gravity net and caught her. He let loose Evil Winder from behind, which went straight toward her face. When the dragoon queen opened her mouth to consume the side-winder, Evil Winder went in and lodged in her mouth so that she could not close her lips. The remaining six side-winders on the righteous side of Scale Eagle charged her belly, one after another, filling it with poison. The body of Gold Goose became distended and her mouth was left wide open; her courage was taken away and her mouth gasped widely open. Scale Eagle then thrust a spear that tore open her belly; it cut through her innards and split her heart. In this manner, after having subdued her, he exhumed her power. He then cast down her body and stood treading upon her legs.

Scale Eagle subdued Grey Kangaroo. The mighty but loonie rake was broken and captured, and seven prominent moonies were tied together as quid pro quo, payback for the loss of his seven winders. The flying host of monsters was scattered. The soldiers trembled—they were afraid and turned backward in their step. They took to flight to escape, but they were surrounded; they could not escape the powerful gravity net of Scale Eagle. Scale Eagle took the monsters captive and broke their weapons to pieces. They were snarling at his net and then sitting in his snare. They filled the assembly with their cries of sorrow. Held in shackles, they received judgment and punishment from Scale Eagle. Upon the eleven kinds of monsters that Gold Goose had filled with the power of striking terror, upon the troop of adversaries who had marched at her side, Scale Eagle brought affliction—he sapped their spirit in a purging judgment.

His quarter horses had trampled the opposition under foot. He had conquered the rebellious rake, Grey Kangaroo, mummifying him with sheets of dust and counting him among the dragoons. Scale Eagle had taken the classified Tables of Destinies from the front pocket of Grey Kangaroo and sealed it with impact imprints from each of the seven tied-up prominent moonies, which he embarrassed by renaming them with female names: Hailey Winder, Leighey Winder, Kaeley Winder, Aeley Winder, Maey Winder, Maery Winder, and Tailey Winder. He placed the Tables of Destinies behind his feather-scaled breastplate, and then took his red cloak and combined it with the blue robe of Grey Kangaroo, which he had won in the battle.

After the radiant Scale Eagle had conquered and cast down his enemies and had made the arrogant foes like slaves, after he had established the triumph of Stripe Tiger over the enemy, attaining the purpose of the patriarchs, he strengthened his net over the captive dragoons. He departed and then returned to Gold Goose, standing upon her hind-quarter. With a merciless, knobby club from her former boy king, he smashed a large hole in the skull of Gold Goose. He then cleaved her neck, cutting her core arteries of gold, and made ferocious North Winder send her bloody head toward the retired Gold Lion, stopping short at the radio wave station Limbo, guarded on the north side by the bastion Right Lion and on the south side by the bastion Left Lion.

Upon seeing this, the patriarchs of Scale Eagle were joyful and jubilant. They brought to him gifts of homage. Scale Eagle, Seizer of the Assembly, then rested while gazing down upon the hammered innards of Gold Goose. Scale Eagle wondered how to divide the remaining carcass, so he devised a cunning plan. He would butcher the headless bovine with her own weapons, slice her as a side of beef, and chop-out countless steaks as bricks and stack them together into a massive wall, a barrier against the migration of bitter waters from the lions in the lower assembly into the sweet waters of the giants in the upper assembly. He affixed a lock on the boxed, frozen cutlets, and then stationed watchers at gates.

He bade the watchers, "Do not allow those of the salty, lower assembly, to approach me when I return to sojourn—do not let them trespass beyond this great wall of staked-out bricks."

11

Scale Eagle surveyed the greater, upper assembly. He compassed and squared new circuit stations for the abode of Blue Scorpion, establishing a permanent lodge for him in the abyss, or ante-business space. He then flew above the plane and surveyed the lesser, lower assembly, compassing and squaring new circuit stations for the dynamos and side-winders there. After leaving the assembly, he founded his own permanent lodge, a sanctuary far, far away. He returned to the assembly and caused Green Crab, Lady Legs, and Blue Scorpion to permanently dwell in the upper assembly, which he considered part of his sanctuary; he compassed and squared new circuit stations for them. Next, he founded a lodge for Stripe Tiger to watch over and protect the lower, southern border of the upper assembly, so that none might err or go astray. Alongside, he founded a lodge for Savings Fish, the sister-wife of Stripe Tiger. On the northern horizon of the lower assembly, he established a large gateway through the firmament there and strengthened the locks on the left and on the right. In the midst of the firmament, he fixed a high watchtower with a big eye—Wholly Horizon Horror Zenith, or Horizon Zenith for short. Scale Eagle caused the mummified body of Grey Kangaroo, the former Grey Gore Dome Shield Cow Boy King, to become a zombie and circle the skull of Gold Goose. Scale Eagle decreed that Grey Kangaroo, whose essence of power was drained, to always face and reflect upon the dark half of the skull of Gold Goose. He decreed that the waxing and waning of the rebellion of Gold Goose and Grey Kangaroo will be memorialized by the mummified, zombie loonie, so that everybody should not forget the comedy and tragedy of the creation of the wholly royal assembly.

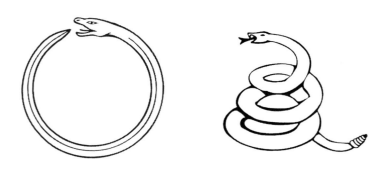

Scale Eagle assigned *new beginning* names to the dynamos and side-winders, even to the mysterious Wholly Invisible Whiz Spirit, of which he learned much about from his adopted patriarchs. He assigned them:

- Sagittarius to Black Bull, Iron Horse, Copper Bear, Silver Stag, Gold Lion (star Sun)
- Scorpio to Blue Scorpion (planet Neptune)
- Libra to himself, Scale Eagle (beagle star Phaeton/Phoenix)

- Virgo to Left Lion (planet Venus)
- Leo to Right Lion (planet Mars)
- Cancer to Green Crab (planet Uranus)
- Gemini to Family Herald & Lady Legs (planets Mercury & Pluto)
- Taurus to Red Bull (planet Jove)
- Aries to Stripe Tiger (planet Jupiter)
- Pisces to Savings Fish (planet Saturn)
- Aquarius to Black Swan, Iron Duck, Copper Gobbler, Silver Heron, Gold Goose (ex-binary star)
- Capricorn to Invisible Spirit, White Bolt (holy spirit, holy ghost)

Scale Eagle then plotted the stars far, far beyond the assembly and artfully played connect-the-dots to form mirrored images of the images of the *new beginning* names. His plot resembled a traveling circus of animals—Wholly Zoo Circuit Eel, or Zoo Eel for short, the zodiac.

Scale Eagle decreed that a completed circuit of Zoo Eel around the skull of Gold Goose (his trophy world), will be called a Year. The Year was composed of twelve ages, with each age corresponding to a wholly royal name. In the midst of a round plane of their images—Zoo Table—he placed a rotating, equilateral, apexed triangle that, at the end of each age, will select a different trinity of wholly royals to govern the assembly. As a gesture of reconciliation, he assigned to Gold Lion the age of Sagittarius, giving Gold Lion the honor-hour of being First High Governor, the Archer, accompanied by Stripe Tiger, assigned as Aries, and Right Lion, assigned as Leo, to act as the first co-governors, or co-regents. In this manner, Wholly Zoo Circuit Eel, with its internal rotary triangle of change that turns clockwise against the fixed circuit of signed images, as the time clock, facilitates the selection of a new three-phase government at the beginning of every age, or Zoo Loo hour, to balance the powers within the assembly.

Scale Eagle determined the various lesser years of the circling royal dynamos—their circuitous travel time—even his own year, which he called "shear," a word that reflects his cutting-through the planetary plane, or Zoo Table, between the circuits of Right Lion and Stripe Tiger at an angle of thirty degrees. He also went on to determine great and lesser Months, Weeks, and Days, assigning names and images to every circular period of time. A year of the new world was determined to contain 360 days, and a great Year of the new world was determined to contain 28,800 years; therefore, each of the twelve ages contained 2,400 years. A shear of Scale Eagle, the completion of his elongated, elliptical orbit around Gold Lion, was determined to contain 3,600 years, for a royal proportion of one shear to every one and a half ages. In this manner, Scale Eagle determined the basis for a circular labor-watch calendar.

12

The dynamos and side-winders felt and understood how the civilizing works of their chosen messiah and savior were accomplished by his powerful libations and long-bowed path, and how both, along with his four waveguides, or side-winders, would, on occasion, change the moods and motions of the dynamos and side-winders, that such change ranged from gradual to catastrophic.

When Scale Eagle sojourns in the midst of the assembly, he hears the emanations of the dynamos and side-winders, which prompts his heart to impress beautiful, mysterious designs upon their bodies, eerily reminiscent of the many designs on the faces of the seven captured and locked-up moonies formerly under the command of the loonie moonie, Grey Kangaroo.

Upon hearing pleas for labor relief from many of the side-winders of the assembly, Scale Eagle opened his mouth and addressed Blue Scorpion in a conjunction regarding a plan conceived earlier in his mind, saying, "Upon the clubbed and severed skull of Gold Goose, I will fashion and amass new creatures of animation—relief workers—a new kind of side-winder charged in the service of the trilaterally commissioned government, so that the whining side-winders will be at ease. I will cleverly guide the ways of the new side-winders. These replacement workers, though created alike, will be divided into two groups: Wholly Bee Hive Damners, or Bee Damners (Behemouth), those of the upper assembly, or land of mountains and valleys (mountainland), and Wholly Lee Vee Gardners, or Levee Gardners (Leviathan), those of the lower assembly, or land of seas (irrigated land). Each of the freed side-winders will then be given the right to their own life, liberty, and pursuit of happiness. Should anyone tread on these rights, I will be the one who decides who will be freed to live and who will be caged to die, because I am the freely elected king by a unanimous decree from a Hexagram Conjunction. I am the presiding one, One Gull God, your highly accomplished avenger and liberator who possesses the Zoo Eel Scales of Justice!"

Blue Scorpion replied in the assembly: "To achieve the plan of Scale Eagle, it will require the young blood of a dynamo within our wholly royal family to be sacrificed, to provide a good portion of wholly royal spirit so that a constant current of replacement motors may be made in our image and likeness. Grey Kangaroo, who became a traitor, should sacrifice his young blood; the guilty one should voluntarily sacrifice his blood to receive forgiveness of his offense and the offense of his followers."

Scale Eagle, presiding graciously over them all in conjunction, issued instructions, and they listened very carefully.

He first asked Blue Scorpion, "If your accusation that Grey Kangaroo caused Golden Goose to rebel is true, then have two witnesses declare the accusation to me under oath, swearing that it is true. Whoever truly caused the uprising should be handed over to us in chains. I will then make him bear not only his guilt but the guilt of his army, so that all of us may dwell in peace and quiet!"

A speaker of the side-winders replied, "I swear that it was the loonie moonie, Sunny Grey Gore Kangaroo, who caused the uprising and made Gold Goose rebel and join the battle."

Another speaker said the same; therefore, the ring-tide lords, those with the big circuits tied to Gold Lion, bound Grey Kangaroo and imposed on him his guilt, the guilt of his army, even the guilt of Gold Goose. They tapped into his veins to harvest his red mercurial blood cells—stem cells—wiring him to harvest his invisible spirit. From fresh spirit and young reeds in his blood were fashioned flesh-and-bone replacement side-winders. Scale Eagle imposed the service of the government upon the new side-winders and forgave the offense of the rebellious ones, setting them free from their chains, albeit with a tribulation tax of one-tenth of their gold, silver, and copper, each shear.

13

Green Crab faced the long-bow course of the messiah and savior and kissed the four arc side-winders of Scale Eagle—South Winder, North Winder, East Winder, and West Winder. Green Crab then shouted, "Hail, Most High Long Bow Star, He Who Reigns Supreme! Ooh Al-le-lu, yea! Ooh Al-le-lu, yea! Ooh Al-le-lu, yea!"

In a grand vision, Green Crab pointed to four places of arcing angles, or cardinal directions, of the long-bow orbit of Scale Eagle, and the four temporal business headquarters, or timely, stately temples, of Scale Eagle, declaring:

"When Scale Eagle is making his long approach to the firmament in the midst of the assembly, his arc angle East Winder will trumpet: 'Wholly Long Wood Bow Right!' and all will hail: 'Eastern Star of Warm Spring Copper Penny Sun Morning!'

"When Scale Eagle is making his quick turn, visiting briefly the battleground, ruling from on high in the assembly, and visiting briefly again the battleground, his arc angle North Winder will trumpet: 'Wholly Worm Wood Bow Up!' and all will hail: 'Northern Star of Hot Summer Silver Dollar Sun Day!'

"When Scale Eagle is making his long departure from the firmament in the midst of the assembly, his arc angle West Winder will trumpet: 'Wholly Long Wood Bow Left!' and all will hail: 'Western Star of Cool Autumn Gold Bar Sun Evening!'

"When Scale Eagle is making his slow turn to hibernate in the faraway wilderness of darkness, his arc angle South Winder will trumpet: 'Wholly Worm Wood Bow Down!' and all will hail: 'Southern Star of Cold Winter Iron Clad Sun Night!'"

Scale Eagle held his long-bow ellipse at an angle of thirty degrees to the concentrically ringed disk of the dynamos (the Zoo Table), and after determining the fate of his acquired court of ring lords and ladies, he, as the crowned sovereign monarch, emperor of the assembly, while wearing his red cloak and blue robe with white feather-scales, sojourned briefly on his throne ship seat high above the assembly, as it became customary for him to do so every shear. His court rejoiced, and then everyone dwelled in synchronous circuits.

To the chosen one, their accomplished avenger, the dynamos and side-winders stood up and faced the feather-scaled lord, Scale Eagle, and they proclaimed in unison an oath of allegiance and sang a little tune, which Green Crab had earlier inscribed in gold plates, or authored, and tasked them to memorize and recite.

They all memorized and recited: "I pledge allegiance to the red, white, and blue banner of the United Solid States of Scale Eagle and to the new world order for which it stands, one assembly under Blue Scorpion, indivisible with Invisible Spirit," and then the side-winders all proclaimed: "We, the Grey Gore Snake Dragoons, whom you have given relief, praise you, O Soaring Scale Master Eagle, Twelfth Dynamo of the Assembly, our messiah and savior, our God!"

The dynamos and side-winders sat down, but Green Crab remained standing and recited a message to those assembled concerning their constitution as a united assembly.

He said to them: "In order to form a more perfect union, establish justice, ensure domestic tranquility, provide for the common defense, encourage mutual support, and secure to ourselves and our posterity the assembly under Blue Scorpion, do ordain and establish this constitution of the United Solid States of Scale Eagle."

Six princely representatives of Green Crab then stood up, each trumpeting a sequential article of the constitution.

After the sixth representative finished speaking, Green Crab trumpeted: "Done in conjunction by the aligned decree of the wholly royals in solid state this moment in the shear of our Most High Lord and of the Independence of the United Solid States of Scale Eagle the Twelfth Dynamo, in witness of whom we have, after this, inscribed our names. All agree?" and they responded, saying, "All agree."

Green Crab garnered many artfully inscribed names, and then bestowed upon the shoulders of Scale Eagle the title Sovereign Monarch of Fifty Solid States on behalf of the others. Each of the fifty solid states—the free and accepted dynamos and side-winders—stood up and then sat back down, one at a time, each one raising a banner of Scale Eagle above their own banner and proclaiming a name with an honorable toast to Scale Eagle, concluding with Green Crab proclaiming an over-arcing, interstellar commerce name for Scale Eagle, also with a toast:

1. **"First State!** The solid state of solid states and the first solid state of the new world order. To him who proclaimed 'Liberty and independence!' With a seaborne storm, his weapon, he vanquished the enemy. Truly, he was rescued from distress and became our chosen heir, the most radiant of the dynamos. The foured motoring side-winders—Creation, Destruction, Deliverance, and Grace—are by his side."

2. **"Keystone State!** To him who proclaimed 'Virtue, liberty, and independence!' Truly, he appeased the side-winders and pleased the dynamos, because he knew the secrets within their blood."

3. **"Noble Guard State!** To him who proclaimed 'Liberty and prosperity!' Truly, he holds the aura of power, assigns beds to the ancient ones, and maintains the garden world."

4. **"Empire State of the Lower Assembly!** To him who proclaimed 'Wisdom, liberty, and moderation!' Truly, he stands up and takes hold of the reins of the chariot of the sun. His heart is wide and his sympathy is warm."

5. **"Constitution State!** To him who commands four great winding weapons, quells troubled waters, and fights beside us! Truly, he is the One above all others in the upper and lower assemblies."

6. **"Bay State!** To him who, by the sword, sought peace, but peace only under liberty. Truly, he monitors the solid states, because he knows their circuits—none may pass without his knowing. He is sub-commander of all the great side-winding weapons."

7. **"Old Line State!** To him who proclaimed 'Tough deeds with soft words!' Truly, as the protector of the spirits of the solid states, in fierce single combat, he saved the retreats in distress by wielding a flaming sword. He controls the watchers of the firmament."

8. **"Palmetto State!** To him who proclaimed 'While I breathe, I hope!' and 'Prepared in mind and resources!' Truly, he maintains the spirits and restores the lost spirits of the solid states as if they were his own creation, reviving dead ones by his pure and strong emanation and destroying wayward foes. None may pass without his knowing."

9. **"Granite State!** To him who proclaimed 'Live free or die!' Truly, he is the radiant dynamo who illumines the ways and dispenses wisdom to the priestly ones."

10. **"Old Dominion State!** To him who proclaimed 'In this manner, to tyrants!' Truly, he is the great farmer who establishes the level of the waters and, with his seeds, creates vegetation to prosper under any condition."

11. **"Empire State of the Upper Assembly!** To him who proclaimed 'Ever upward!' Truly, he is the great counselor who does not fear anything and whom the solid states hope for when possessed with fear."

12. **"Tar Heel State!** To him who proclaimed 'To be or not to be, that is the question!' Truly, he is the great counselor who does not fear, ensures that the will of the elder dynamos is done, is gracious, has great knowledge over armor and military matters, and can outfit an entire army in three shears. He is the provider who allots space to the solid states."

13. **"Ocean State!** To him who proclaimed 'Hope!' Truly, he opens the gates of the lower assembly, effecting restoration of the solid states by devising emanations and purifying their seats so that they may sit in relief."

14. **"Green Mountain State!** To him who proclaimed 'Freedom and unity!' Truly, he is the spirit of the flying host of side-winders. He establishes strong seats, keeps a hold on their ways, and determines their courses."

15. **"Bluegrass State!** To him who proclaimed 'United we stand, divided we fall!' Truly, he established wholeness, is one from the benign spirit, the unseen lord who listens and provides plenty of riches and treasures."

16. **"Volunteer State!** To him who provides for vegetation and exchange of power! Truly, he is the lord of charming personality, who revives dead ones with knowledge of the amulet and talisman, gives mercy to vanquished ones, and removes the yoke imposed on side-winders by his enemies."

17. **"Buckeye State!** To him who proclaimed 'With me, all things are possible!' Truly, his eminence is murmured by the mouths of the

side-winders, and, with his charming personality, he uproots all the destructive ones."

18. **"Pelican State!** To him who proclaimed
'Union, liberty, and confidence!' Truly, he
knows the secrets of the solid states by examining their innards. Destroyers cannot escape
from him, because he detects lies, directs justice, and separates the right from wrong and
keeps them apart; nothing buried or drowned
escapes his sight. He sets up the conjunctions
and gladdens the hearts of the solid states."

19. **"Hoosier State!** To him who established the
crossroads of the assembly! Truly, he silences
the insurgent, possesses a level of power to
reconcile differences between the solid states,
and enjoys an emanation of peace."

20. **"Magnolia State!** To him who proclaimed
'By valor and arms!' Truly, with the great
weapon, he roots out all enemies, frustrates
their plans, scatters them to his four side-
winders, and blots out all the wicked ones
who tremble before him."

21. **"Prairie State!** To him who proclaimed
'Solid state sovereignty, assembly unity!'
Truly, he roots out enemies and ensures a fair
hearing. He is a fashioner of the solid states."

22. **"Heart of Dixie State!** To him who proclaimed 'We dare defend our rights!' Truly, he
is lord of the unseen spirit, who pursues
destructive ones, brings fugitive side-winders
home to their dynamos, and can kill an entire
army should their ends be evil. His level of
power destroys all opponents and disobedient
ones."

23. **"Pine Tree State!** To him who proclaimed 'I
lead!' Truly, his power kills slowly. The
enemy merely pockmarks him in a battle."

24. "**Show Me State!** To him who proclaimed 'The support of the solid states will be the supreme law!' Truly, he knows the ways and currents of the waters in the lower assembly, is the lord who enables the solid states to flourish, and is the mighty one who transforms and renames the solid states."

25. "**Opportunity State!** To him who proclaimed 'The solid states rule!' Truly, he knows the ways of the new world order and the secrets of utilizing its firm ground where waters are found.

26. "**Wolverine State!** To him who proclaimed 'If you seek a pleasant corner, look around you!' Truly, he is the lord of the unseen spirit, the lord of abundance, opulence, and ample vegetation—creator of wealth."

27. "**Sunshine!** To him who proclaimed 'To me, entrust!' Truly, he provides fertility and heaps up abundance for consumption by the solid states. He causes rich rains to fall throughout the solid states, knows the plow, and knows the metals of the solid states."

28. "**Lone State!** To him who proclaimed 'Friendship!' Truly, he heaps up a mountain, and directs the dynamos and side-winders as their faithful shepherd. He wears the horned crown of the bull god king."

29. "**Hawkeye State!** To him who proclaimed 'We prize our liberties, and we will maintain our rights.' Truly, he goes forward in his ship of the reed-signed constitution."

30. "**Badger State!** To him who proclaimed 'Charge forward!' Truly, he stores up massive heaps of harvest and gushes out spirit, furnishing the seed of the solid states."

31. "**Noble Gold State!** To him who proclaimed 'I have founded it!' Truly, he makes the whole

assembly everlasting. He is the architect and builder of great works, and the security loop that holds the barrel together."

32. **"Gopher State!** To him who is the star of the upper assembly! Truly, he is the promoted one who tears off the crown of the enemy, creates the clouds above waters, designs great works, and makes the halos everlasting."

33. **"Beaver State!** To him who proclaimed 'I fly with my own wings!' Truly, he gives counsel on business matters, assists in all matters of trade. He is a great gardener who designates the fields, grants allotments and food-offerings, tends the flocks, and maintains the stockpiled good things."

34. **"Sunflower State!** To him who proclaimed 'To the stars, through difficulties!' Truly, he is the roaring of the sea, and creator of sidewinders of the upper and lower assemblies. He knows the secrets from before and during the gold creation age."

35. **"Mountain State!** To him who proclaimed 'Mountaineers are always free!' Truly, there is no other who can match him in strength. He is all-mighty."

36. **"Silver State!** To him who proclaimed 'All for our assembly!' Truly, he is the creator of wealth. His power destroys legions."

37. **"Cornhusker State!** To him who proclaimed 'Equality before the law!' Truly, he assists in the destruction of legions. His foundation is firm in the front and in the rear."

38. **"Centennial State!** To him who proclaimed 'Nothing without providence!' Truly, he is a mile high, and the foremost of all in knowledge of the past and present. His strength is outstanding."

39. "**Flickertail State!** To him who proclaimed 'Liberty and union, now and forever, one and inseparable!' Truly, he is the bonding agent and watches every move in the upper and lower assemblies—none pass by without his knowing."

40. "**Coyote State!** To him who proclaimed 'Under me, the solid states rule!' and 'Great faces, great places!' Truly, he is the lord counselor of wisdom, knows the laws of the covenant and the nature of the gates of the firmament. He is the determiner of the law of everything."

41. "**Treasury State!** To him who proclaimed 'Gold and silver!' Truly, only he knows the secret name and number of his account of power, and possesses the spirit rod of two noble rottwilers. His undefiled dwellings are always renewed."

42. "**Evergreen State!** To him who proclaimed 'Wholly royal firmament!' Truly, he knows the past when two dark ones were one. He makes no decision without consulting the counter-clockwise current at the crossroads."

43. "**Gem State!** To him who proclaimed 'I am perpetual motion!' Truly, he knows the essence of all spirits past, present, and future. His strength is outstanding."

44. "**Equality State!** To him who proclaimed 'Equal rights!' Truly, he carried off all of the foes amidst the struggle. His perception is broad and he gives wisdom to rulership."

45. "**Beehive State!** To him who proclaimed 'Industry!' Truly, he carried the night with the moon in the thick of the battle. He is the great judge of the solid states, promotes justice in its many forms—he is master of the great covenant, establishing the priesthood and conveying guidance for all."

46. **"Zooner State!** To him who proclaimed 'Labor conquers all things!' Truly, he knows the future, sits in a throne ship seat upon his temple-mount and accepts gifts, and measures all things, knowing their depth and width. He gives counsel with his four sidewinding emissaries."

47. **"Enchantment State!** To him who proclaimed 'It grows as it goes!' Truly, his wisdom is so great that not even the elder dynamos can fathom it. He is the master artisan who created great works in the time of battle, knows the secrets of fire and forge, raises storms that fill the entire sky, causes the solid states to tremble, shakes the very gates of the firmament in their stead, and fills the sky with his brightness, even in the darkest hour of the night. He keeps the weapon sharp in a time of need."

48. **"Gorge State!** To him who proclaimed 'I enrich!' Truly, he maintains the sharp point of the great weapon, created artful works in the battle, has broad wisdom, is accomplished in insight, and whose royal ellipse is so vast that the solid states, all together, cannot fathom it. His thunderous roar causes the assembly to shake; he storms to muster over the wide-ranging solid states, and he controls the storm and the light, even in the dark places. His power provides sustenance for all the side-winders."

49. **"Great State!** To him who proclaimed 'To the future upper assembly!' Truly, he knows treachery before it occurs, gives wisdom of the future and also of things past, and guides the ways of the dynamos. He covers the great solid states of the upper assembly."

50.   "**Greetings State!** To him who proclaimed
'The life of the land is perpetuated in righteousness!' Truly, he holds the key to the gates
between the upper and lower assemblies so
that the solid states must wait on him before
crossing over. He also proclaimed 'When I
restlessly cross in the midst of the sea to seize
and control the firmament, my name will be
La Crosse; therefore, I, as La Crosse, the
renewed, imperishable star, the Beagle Star
of Destiny, will guide you indefinitely.'"

X-terra. "**La Crosse!** He is the direct current, direct
course, and direct cross dresser of the upper and lower assemblies, even direct commander of their turnings. To him,
indeed, they look and proclaim: 'His name is Wholly Cross
Dress Lord, and he seizes control of the firmament in the
midst of the assembly!' Truly, he is king of the assembly. The
patriarchs celebrate and glorify his names, even his rosy
cross-dressed name, Sham-y-Aza. He lords over all the
rotary-selected governors, who administer the combined rites
in carrying out all the instructions of Cross Lord."

The diplomat, White Cat, lady peacekeeper of the
upper assembly, made herself heard in the assembly. She
proclaimed: "May Cross Lord maintain the fifty solid
states in their ways! May Cross Lord guide the fifty solid
states with the scales of justice! May Cross Lord vanquish
the enemies of the fifty solid states! When the years of the
fifty solid states have grown old and the ancient snake-
dragoons rise again, may Cross Lord make them recede
back into the depths of the black sea! May the patriarchs
celebrate the fifty names of the United Solid States!"

Green Crab added: "May all the dynamos and side-
winders celebrate the fifty names of the United Solid
States!"

Red Bull, earlier forgiven by White Cat for his rape
of her, came near to the conjunction and echoed the words
of Green Crab.

Blue Scorpion gave the last shout out: "May those of the fifty solid states whose names are celebrated by the patriarchs, as I have celebrated, become like me. May all the rites be combined and a new covenant be formed; may the instructions be performed in full. For my adopted son with the fifty names, may the solid states make his way supreme!"

In this manner, a Hexagram of Dynamos decreed Scale Eagle as Most High Lord of Fifty Solid States, toasted the names of his fifty solid states, and made his way supreme.

Scale Eagle decreed in return: "Every solid state will be held responsible to recite and honor the fifty names of my supreme court in a remembrance ceremony to be held every shear during my reign. You will each proclaim and toast them, and the wise will read and understand the words of the toasts, considering them altogether in a union regarding their ramifications and explain them to every side-winder. You will honor the fifty names in the constitution and celebrate them, so that you can pursue your own prosperity and happiness."

The decree of Scale Eagle stood fast—his command remained unaltered. Nobody would ever annul the words from his mouth; otherwise, he would gaze in anger and not turn his stiff neck. When he was angry, nobody could stand upright before his wrath; however, his heart was wide and his compassion was broad. The main offending side-winding soldiers, or moonies, that had been in his presence at the battle of Gold Goose, those who became known as Disobedient Ones, received sentences from Scale Eagle and then spoke their last words before him. They were locked up until their release in a secret shear, when replacement side-winders would be delivered. As for the clubbed and severed skull of Wholly Gold Egg Goose, it transformed into Wholly Blue Hymn Bird, or Blue Bird for short, as the planet Earth. In this manner, the gold age of creation is akin to a cool, autumn evening, which continues to this day with the comings and goings of the lēgull rēgull fēgull

tēgull bēgull sēgull, Wholly Scale Master Eagle—
Navvirhoo—the adopted colorful peacock star, Phaeton-y-
Phoenix, Wholly Cross Dress Lord of the Wholly Royal
Assembly of Dynamos.

Foothold

1

The new, or second, sun, Wholly Scale Master Eagle, from the creation ages of the royal primary order of metals, or primordial times, had cooled to become a firm planet about four times larger than the new world planet, Wholly Blue Hymn Bird, the planet Earth. The halo of Scale Eagle transformed into an atmosphere of air with clouds of water. Through an electrochemical process, large pools of moosh produced the building blocks of life: amino acids and proteins, and then the germs of life. After a very long, slow rate of electrochemical evolutionary change, plant and animal life sprang up and prospered on the self-heated world. Eventually, robust humanoids evolved and gathered into nations. These nations became highly advanced in their technologies.

Just over a million years ago, a particular royal family feud broke out, threatening to destroy many of the nations of the world. Disaster was averted, however, when Oriänthäl Välhorūsh, the king of a commonwealth of fifty nations, was ceremoniously crowned and promoted to Emperor of Sixty Nations on the southern and northern continent of Märikhä. The coronation took place among the males of the golden-domed nation called Phaëllustän, located in the Middle East of the planet. The crown was a gold ring of six horns, each clad with ten crystals of diverse colors, each crystal representing a particular nation. As recommended by a noble clan of priests from Jūdishrā, a priestly nation next to Phaëllustän, the king accepted a new name for his new position as emperor: Knūdälphaë Mäläni (translated from the Ängle language: Naked-water-mount-sphinx Beast-one-eye), or Än (One) for short. Earlier, when Emperor Än was King Välhorūsh, he had cleverly united the sixty nations through his own international alliances, or matings. His most important mating had involved three virgin princesses, each from the pivotal nations of Bussīneä, Ghraëseä, and Phaëriseä. The division line (divine) branch of kindred produced by the matings of Emperor Än became known as the Ängle family (hence the Ängle language)—those whom are out-räyed from Än, the base line.

- First, King Välhorūsh mated with Crown Princess Eurōikhä of the iron-skinned nation of Bussīneä (translated: Two-trade-sealand). Eurōikhä gave birth to his firstborn son, an out-räy bred Phrēkheän named Hōle Bōn Djed Shät-Phoërāth Änū of Knūdälphaë Māläni Ēl (translated: Wholly Servant Column Seat-Fear-spirit One-beast-spring of Naked-water-mount-sphinx Beast-one-eye Sperm), contracted as Shät-Phoëthäniēl, or Shätäniēl for short (folded even more to the syllable Foe, or Foy, a root which means adversary).

- Second, King Välhorūsh mated with Crown Princess Ōhlīvheä of the copper-skinned nation of Ghraëseä (translated: Grey-green-sealand). Ōhlīvheä gave birth to his firstborn daughter, an out-räy bred Mëdätauräëreän named Hōle Bōn Blyënd Khät-Phaërāth Änneū of Knūdälphaë Fēläni Ēlle (translated: Wholly Servant Blind Heal-Faith-spirit One-bird-first of Naked-water-mount-sphinx Bird-one-eye Egg), contracted as Khät-Phaëthäniēlle, or Khätäniēlle for short (folded more to the syllable Fae, or Fay, a root which means judge).

- Third, King Välhorūsh mated with his half-sister, Princess Royal Vällähorūsh, of the silver-skinned nation of Phaëriseä (translated: Fair-eye-sealand). After being renamed Empress Änne, she gave birth to his second-born son, an in-räy bred Albäknūdeän named Hōle Bōn Thūmb Ghäd-Rhaërāth Bänū of

Knūdälphaë Mäläni Ēl (translated: Wholly Ser-
vant Gravity God-Gold-spirit Second-beast-one
of Naked-water-mount-sphinx Beast-one-eye
Sperm), contracted as Ghäd-Rhaëthäniēl, or
Ghädäniēl for short (folded more to the syllable
Rae, or Ray, a root which means leader).

Shätäniēl, Khätäniēlle, and Ghädäniēl became
highly educated during their youth, earning many diplo-
mas and commissions.

- Shätäniēl earned a Doctorate in Medicine and a
  Doctorate in Civil Engineering. He was royally
  commissioned as a Surgeon of Life and General
  of Engineering, two titles which were combined
  and shortened to Surgeon General.

- Khätäniēlle earned a Doctorate in Medicine and
  a Doctorate in Mining Geology. She was royally
  commissioned as a Surgeon of Life and Colonelle
  of Mountains, two titles which were combined
  and shortened to Surgeon Colonelle.

- Ghädäniēl earned a Doctorate in Law and a
  Doctorate in Business Management. He was
  royally commissioned as an Attorney of Law and
  General of Business, two titles which were combined and shortened to Attorney General.

When this doctorial trinity of two royal half-broth-
ers and one royal half-sister was fully established,
Emperor Än renamed the world of Scale Eagle to World of
Fates, or Phaëton for short.

During the creation ages of the royal primary order
of metals, or primordial times, Phaëton, as Scale Eagle,
annihilated the mother queen of all planets, Gold Goose,
leaving strewn-out remnants of her, her army of dragoons
and side-winder moonies, and seven side-winder moonies

originally from Green Crab (planet Uranus) and Stripe Tiger (planet Jupiter), to become asteroids, comets, and very small moons. But the clubbed and severed skull of Gold Goose had been left intact, and the chief of her army, Sunny Grey Gore Kangaroo (the moon), had been mummified. Ferocious North Winder of Scale Eagle had carried the skull of Gold Goose toward Gold Lion (the sun), seating the skull in a new orbit between Right Lion (planet Mars) and Left Lion (planet Venus). The mummified moon was later carried to the same orbit to become a coiling sidewinder. The skull of Gold Goose had eventually annealed to become a new world—Tiaërräfirmä (translated: Life-aer-sun-earth-water; the planet Earth), and the mummified moon had eventually shrunk to become a reflective grey-headstone always facing the new world in shame.

About half a million years ago, Emperor Än became interested in placing his feet on Tiaërräfirmä, which later was variously called World of Fetes, World of Foot Rest, and World of Foothold, or Phoëton for short. He approved of a plan for a mission to establish a foothold in the new world, with the ulterior motive of obtaining gold leftover from the destruction of Gold Goose. They would alchemically transmute the gold into the finest form of gold: mono-atomic gold, a white powder extremely valued for its superconductive property to repair damaged genes when inhaled or ingested into the body, repel ultraviolet radiation from Phoëbus, the sun, when plumed into the air, and lighten, even float, a heavy load when sprinkled about beneath the load.

Emperor Än tasked his heir apparent, Crown
Prince Attorney General Ghädäniël, to be responsible for
the mission, and decreed that Surgeon General Shätäniël
select, organize, and lead an advance landing force of
enlisted laborers. The laborers would go forward without
the attorney general, to arrive with the surgeon general
first and explore for gold, stake a claim, and establish a
foothold in the new world. They would establish a support
base by creating a safe haven that would produce power
and a garden that would produce food, both to support
them and those of the future arrival and settlement of
many columns of colonial missionaries led by Attorney
General Ghädäniël.

On behalf of Ghädäniël, Shätäniël gathered
together a foreign legion of civil engineers and farmers,
mostly composed of light and heavy power-equipment operators from Bussïneä, the country of his mother. The legionnaires were kindred of a great Bussïneän king named Beast
Ïgäg, or Ïgog, and were very sensitive to bright light,
because they lived and worked in and on the tunneled continent of Phrëkhä, a low-light continent on Phaëton. When
they went into the brighter regions on Phaëton, they always
wore dark eye goggles. In this manner, the divine of the
Phrëkhäns of Ïgog became known simply as Ïgoggles.

Shätäniël ordered the legion of Ïgoggles into four
paternal orders, each split into two fraternal companies.
Each paternal order was distinguished by a general occu-
pation and a hierarchy of ten ranks ranging from First
Class down to Tenth Class, with a royally commissioned
captain to lord over them. There were four paternal orders
(P.O's.), each with two fraternal orders (F.O's.) of crafts.

P.O. of Hõst (astroaeronautical engineers): F.O. of Eagles
and F.O. of Watchers.
P.O. of Dõghboys (structural engineers): F.O. of Masons
and F.O. of Power Rangers.
P.O. of Nävvies (navigational engineers): F.O. of Diggers
and F.O. of Plumbers.
P.O. of Phaërmers (agricultural engineers): F.O. of Ranchers and F.O. of Garders.

2

When Phaëton, in its highly elliptical orbit around Phoëbus, the sun, approaches from below the planetary orbital plane, it enters the plane at an angle of thirty degrees, shearing near to the asteroid belt and arching above the plane between Mars and the asteroid belt for a period of 500 years before exiting the plane, shearing near to the asteroid belt again and then returning to the point of entry years later, for an orbital completion time of 3,600 years (1,000 years within the sphere of the solar system). In this manner, Phaëton, along with its four side-winders, accelerates in its approach from the region below the planetary orbital plane—Stellar South—tightly arches through the region above the plane—Stellar North—and decelerates in its departure. Moreover, upon every flyby near to Phoëbus, Phaëton transforms into the renowned, indestructible, scale-feathered eagle—Phoënix—and if any planet happens to be near to the flyby of Phoënix, the motion and aspect of that planet is changed. Such change has occurred repeatedly since the beginning of the solar

system and will continue to do so, especially during a major alignment of the planets.

Shätäniēl received the approval of Än and Ghädäniēl to launch the mission when Phaëton next became Phoënix near to Phoëton. An ärkh-class ship, *His Majestic Ship (HMS) Ärkhgōthorn*, was wholly loaded with provisions, along with a stock of various änimals and plants, and bärkh- and lärkh-class ships in its hold, all to establish a foothold of everlasting life on another world. Brave Shätäniël and his legion of civil engineers and farmers ventured through a gulf in the asteroid belt, the parted rēd sea, to reach their target. On the eve of the beginning day of the first recorded sign-age on Phoëton, *HMS Ärkhgōthorn*, dubbed *Wholly Spirit*, descended upon waters in a temperate middle region of the new world. Once system checks were complete, *Wholly Spirit* ventured northward, passing through a strait that Shätäniël described in the log of the ship as "a narrow strait bordered by many tall and strong-pillared trees, beyond which lies a vast region of paisley-shaped waters void of works. Darkness engulfed the waters."

When *Wholly Spirit* moved upon the face of the waters, Surgeon General Shätäniël, High Lord of the Advance Force, commanded, "Let there be light!" and a great light from the ärkh brightly illuminated the waters below.

He saw how well the light illuminated the waters below, and he approved of it by the wave of his hand over an emerald-green tablet.

The High Lord then commanded, "Let there be many lights to illuminate the darkness beyond," and many lights were placed within the darkness beyond.

He saw how well the many lights illuminated the darkness beyond, and he approved of it by the wave of his hand over the tablet. The High Lord called the darkness "night" and the brightness "day." In the daytime, he surveyed the virgin territory and created a clever design for a safe harbor and fertile land. The nights and days of the sign-age—2,400 years, or 0.666 shears of Phaëton—were the first phase of construction.

The High Lord then commanded, "Let there be a firmament in the middle of the waters to divide the waters from the waters," and his dōghboys gathered rēd clay into bends, and then molded the rēd clay into bricks, which were then baked hard by the hot rays of Phoëbus and piled high into cells, one above the other, creating a high crescent-shaped dam complete with deep chambers for winding power turbines and other equipment—a firmament dividing the waters below from the waters above.

The High Lord saw how well the multicolored arch of the firmament made the upper rainwaters deep and the lower rainwaters shallow, and he approved of the works by the wave of his hand, comparing it to a rainbow in the sunny wet sky, which gave him the idea to name the region of the power-production dam Eärāith—House Water Sun Reflection. In this manner, the High Lord created a firm structure for the Power Production Company and a safe harbor for *Wholly Spirit*, his ärkh of life-spirits. The nights and days of the second sign-age were the second phase of construction; 4,800 years had passed since the arrival of the High Lord.

The High Lord then commanded, "Let the waters below the firmament be gathered into one place; let moist land appear from the depths," and a long, deep river with angled canals was dug and leveed, and moist land appeared from the depths of the rēdmarsh below the dam.

He saw how well the lower waters gathered together into the river and canals and how well the moist land appeared from the depths, and he approved of the works by the wave of his hand. The High Lord called the gathered waters "seas" and the fertile land "earth." He called the region of new seas and new earth Newfoundland of Eädam. In this manner, the High Lord drained most of the rēdmarsh below the dam, creating a moist and fertile foundation for growing food of everlasting life.

The High Lord then commanded, "Let there be grasses yielding grain and herb, shrubs yielding vegetables, and trees yielding seed-fruits and crystal-fruits—let them sprout from the earth," and stocks of seeds and seedlings of the kind from his world were carefully planted in the fertile earth below the dam.

He saw how well the vegetation sprouted from the earth, and he approved of the works by the wave of his hand. In this manner, the High Lord provided fresh food and medicine of everlasting life for the foreign legionnaires. The nights and days of the third sign-age were the third phase of construction; 7,200 years, or two shears, had passed since the arrival of the High Lord.

The High Lord then commanded, "Let there be a vault over the earth below the firmament. Let there be great luminaries within the vault and the firmament to divide the day from the night; let there be lesser luminaries for signing and seasoning. Let the great illumination of the vault be an eternal brightness upon the earth, and let the face of the firmament reflect the eternal brightness of the vault," and a tremendously huge flower-shaped geodesic dome was erected over the earth, and bright lighting was installed within the dome and the dam, with lesser lights installed at key points.

Both towering structures—the piled rēd clay dam and the erected prefab greenhouse—were designed to work together as one grand system of governance with checks and balances, with enlightenment to quicken the seasons of growth and illuminate the signs of navigation.

The High Lord saw how well his super dome stood upright and strong and how well the greater and lesser lights of the two structures performed. He approved of the works by the wave of his hand. In this manner, the High Lord created perfect conditions for his plants of everlasting life to sprout from the earth. The eternal light in the dome increased not only the rate of growth and the mature size of the food but also the suitable conditions for labor—nävvies and phaërmers worked continuously within the dome.

The High Lord called the vaulted earth the Garden of Eädam, and the garders called themselves laboratory shift workers. The nights and days of the fourth sign-age were the fourth phase of construction; 9,600 years had passed since the arrival of the High Lord.

The High Lord then commanded, "Let there be fish yielding proteins and oils—let them swim in the seas. Let there be birds yielding eggs—let them fly in the openness of the sealand. Let the swimmers be fruitful—let them multiply to fill the seas; let the flyers be fruitful—let them multiply to fill the openness of the sealand," and stocks of fish and birds of the kind from his world were introduced into the seas and openness of the sealand within the garden-dome.

He saw how well his creatures of änimal life moved in the seas and upon the sealand, and he approved of the works by the wave of his hand. The nights and days of the fifth sign-age were the fifth phase of construction; 12,000 years had passed since the arrival of the High Lord.

The High Lord then commanded, "Let there be beasts of burden yielding strength, fur, hides, milk, and oils—let them tread upon the earth; let there be many living things crawling, creeping, and fluttering upon the earth. Let the creatures of life be fruitful—let them multiply and fill the earth," and stocks of beasts of burden and many living things that walk, crawl, creep, and flutter of the kind from his world were introduced upon the earth within the garden-dome.

He saw how well his änimals and insects swam, flew, walked, crawled, crept, and fluttered upon the earth, and he approved of the works by the wave of his hand.

The High Lord then commanded, "Let there be garders dwelling upon the earth—let them have the minion of fish, fowl, cattle, and every other living thing that moves," and the garders received allotments of staked beds upon the earth, and he called their dwelling place Bedford.

He saw how well the garders dwelled in their bed rows of field houses, and he approved of the works by the wave of his hand.

Through trumpet-shaped loudspeakers mounted high in the dome, a deep voice from the abyss, or änte-business, of Eärāith Dam spoke to an assembly of the garders, saying, "Let your labor upon this earth be fruitful; let the harvest be multiplied to satisfy everybody. Replenish the earth with seeds and seedlings after each season. Rule in this great garden-dome—manage properly the vegetation of the earth, the fish in the seas, the birds of the air, and every living thing moving upon the earth."

He paused briefly and then added, "O brave and brute legionnaires, you from the black land of Bussīneä, look around you. I have given you every grass of grain and herb, every shrub of vegetable, and every tree yielding seed-fruit and crystal-fruit upon the face of this earth for your food and comfort. However, understand: I have also given the same to the birds, cattle, and every other creature of life moving within the dome."

The High Lord saw how well the watery haven and fertile earth became a support base for the mission, a perfect foothold in the new world, and he approved of the whole creation by the wave of his hand. In this manner, the first haven and earth on the World of Foothold were created and the places of the foreign legion assigned by the High Lord of the Advance Force, Surgeon General Shätäniël. The nights and days of the sixth sign-age were the sixth phase of construction; 14,400 years, or four shears, had passed since the arrival of the High Lord.

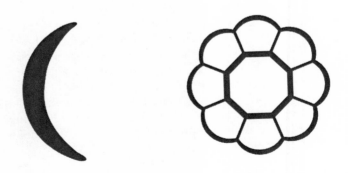

On the eve of the first day of the seventh phase of construction, the High Lord ceased the work that he had made and decreed the seventh phase to be a recurring sign-age of rest, celebration, and planning for the following sign-ages. While resting from their corvée, the legionnaires were encouraged to make music and dance, even to build follies during the entire sign-age. The High Lord and his commissioned officers spent much of the sign-age planning and designing the first city called One. The High Lord called the seventh sign-age the Crescent City Sign-Age, or Seätur/Shätur (Satur) Sign-Age. The Īgoggle legionnaires, however, called the sign-age of music and dance the Shāmbä Sign-Age, honoring a particular princely captain who loved to colorfully dress-up, and sing and dance. In this manner, the Īgoggle labored hard for six sign-ages and then rested and danced, altogether enjoying themselves and the works of the High Lord for one sign-age, honoring the decree of the High Lord of the advance force. Surgeon General Shätäniēl called seven sign-ages a Week—a recurring period of 16,800 years, or 4.666 shears.

The day after seven Weeks had passed—117,600 years, or 32.666 shears—the imperial flagship *HMS Glōry,* with Attorney General Ghädäniēl and last-minute passenger Emperor Än on board, arrived on the new world amid much pomp and circumstance. Behind and to the left of *HMS Glōry* was Surgeon Colonelle Khätäniēlle in another ärkh-class ship, with a fleet of bärkhs, lärkhs, and shärkhs, more foreign legionnaires and commissioned officers, much-needed equipment and supplies, and, surprisingly to Shätäniēl, Queen Eurōikhä, who was so pleased with what she had heard concerning the great civil works of her firstborn son that she wanted to sojourn with him. Ghädäniēl took charge of the foothold mission for his father, the emperor, and called the sign-age the Sun City Sign-Age, or Goätur/Ghädur (Godur) Sign-Age, a sign-age for all to celebrate and commemorate the founding of a new city and the arrival of Emperor Än and himself upon the new world. "The Sun City Sign-Age," he decreed, "will be honored here on Phoëton by all of the working class and administered by the upper class on every sign-age following a period of seven Weeks of sign-ages, completing ceremoniously a period of fifty sign-ages, which I hereby call a Jūbēlle. The Jūbēlle Sign-Age will be a recurring period of founding remembrance ceremonies and a rest from labor."

3

Many sign-ages prior to the arrival of Emperor Än and Attorney General Ghädäniēl upon the World of Foothold, or Phoëton, Surgeon General Shätäniēl commanded his first officer, "Let there be a firestone recharging throne ship seat for *HMS Glōry* atop a pillared mount on the raised eye-land eastward of the Grand Canal from Eäräith Dam and lying adjacent to the garden-dome—let a terraced mount, a ziggūrāt, be built over the upwell of honeywater there for *HMS Glōry*, and let two opposite sides of its foundation align north to south. Let there be a raised floor, an altar featuring a flagstone table for offering gifts to the emperor, before the north face of the mount, and let there be a grand staircase leading up the length of the north face to an Everest Station at the top. Let there be wholly enclosed raceways flowing with honeywater beneath the middle of wide avenues laid out in the shape of the primordial Wholly Waters: four wide and equidistant bent arms and legs joined at the shoulder, each arm and leg stretching out perpendicular from the squared shoulders of the foundation of the mount, and then bending halfway to the right, establishing four cardinal quarters of the new earth. Let the boulevards be wide enough for the orders of companies to march and present their colored arms to the emperor, who will be seated at the Everest Station.

"Let many smaller raceways bend squarely from the underground mains and into the cardinal quarters. Let there be a Conjunction Hall within the upper hold of the mount, and let there be twelve each iron-platters, silver-platters, and gold-platters resting equally apart upon cedar-boarded walls there. Let both sides of the Boulevard of March that stretches northward be fronted with twelve smaller recharging throne ship mounts for the various princes and future princes—six on the right and six on the left—and add one at the northernmost end of the squared elbow for Princess Khätäniēlle. Let a large banquet hall stand adjacent to the Mount of Khätäniēlle. Let there be a walled and gated marshalling yard around each temple-mount, each yard with a marching pad fronting the boulevard.

"Let all the temple-mounts be interconnected by an underground chase. Let the four quarters of the new earth be squared with streets less travelled and bed rows for the incoming troops, the ten ranks of cards, to rest in peace from their labor, and let the city with this concrete Grand Parade and quartered streets, marshalling yards, princely temple-mounts, Exchange conjunction hall, banquet hall, and garden-dome be surrounded by a high- and wide-stepping wall with a grand gate at each hand and foot of the four bent avenues, one facing east toward the iron-top mountains, one facing south toward the strait of the pillars of date palm, one facing west toward the desert of sand and ash, and one facing north toward the abyss of Eäräith Dam."

In this manner, the Surgeon General created the first dynamic city called One on the world, and he dedicated it as House of Änne—Eänne—to honor the empress and impress the emperor. Shätäniēl informally referred to the eye-shaped land upon which the city was built as the Eyeland of Ēls, and he renamed Newfoundland of Eädam to Änglëa.

4

Throughout the many shears before the City of Eänne was ready for a ceremonious state visit of Emperor Än and Empress Änne, various Ängles for various reasons would come and go between Phaëton and Phoëton, some staying longer than others. Some of them, even the doctorial trinity—the two royal half-brothers and the one royal half-sister—actually mated and the ladies gave birth, some on Phaëton and some on Phoëton. Most importantly, sons and daughters were born and raised by Princess Khätäniëlle, some sired by Crown Prince Ghädäniël and some sired by Prince Shätäniël, before and after the state visit of the emperor and empress. Prominent sons descending from Emperor Än, those from the doctorial trinity, were eventually commissioned as captains and assigned companies and throne ships.

When the day arrived for the state visit of the emperor and empress, the most important royal family members hovered, each in their own electromagnetic motive throne ships, above their respective recharging throne ship seats on the front tier of mounts along the Boulevard of March. Each mount was colored to correspond with the approximate skin color of the associated prince or princess. The first ship to dock was *HMS Glōry* of Emperor Än, docking atop a gold-yellow mount, featuring a gold-clad seat at the top. The huge round ship, when she mated with the tallest terraced and pillared mount, appeared from a good distance like a giant mushroom towering above the surrounding marshland. The Īgoggles sometimes referred to her as the Ship of the Rēds. The divine trinity of throne ships then docked atop their respective family mounts: At the right hand of *Glōry* was *HMS Prince Ghädäniël* atop a snow-white mount, featuring a silver-clad seat; at the left hand of *Glōry* was *HMS Prince Shätäniël* atop a charcoal-black mount, featuring an iron-clad seat; and at the far end, facing *Glōry*, was *HMS Princess Khätäniëlle* atop an olive-green mount, featuring a copper-clad seat. Along the *right-*

eous side of the boulevard, the throne ships of the three prominent sons of Ghädäniēl docked atop blood-red mounts featuring ruby-clad seats, in order of descending age: *HMS Prince Sīnhäēl; HMS Prince Mīkhäēl; and HMS Prince Jäkhäēl.* On the lefteous side of the boulevard, the throne ships of the six prominent sons of Shätäniēl docked atop navvi-blue mounts featuring sapphire-clad seats, in order of descending age: *HMS Prince Shämyazäbäēl; HMS Prince Räphäēl; HMS Prince Ghäbräēl; HMS Prince Bärräkhäēl; HMS Prince Yhūriēl; and HMS Prince Yhūziēl.* Each prince with his company of troops, and Princess Khätäniēlle with her coven of witches, marshaled themselves around their mounts and then fell into a formation on their marching pads. With disciplined precision, each company, and the coven, goose-stepped down the boulevard toward the Mount of *Glōry.*

When the orders of companies neared the Mount of *Glōry,* each super-stepper presented their colorfully decorated arms before the emperor, who sat in a high and gold-clad chair upon the altar of his temporary house mount, or temple-mount. The princes high-stepped up the Grand Staircase and went into the Conjunction Hall, wherein they reported and exchanged counsel with one another. Each head of the eleven princes stood proudly behind high-backed chairs, all of which were arranged about a large, circular table, each prince patiently waiting for their emperor to enter and sit at the Zenith of the table. The royal family playfully called the Roundtable of Fates the Wheel of Fortune, later described as a large table representing a traveling circus of änimal stars—the Zōdiäkh. The high-power council of twelve änimal spirit lords would forevermore be called the Majestic Twelve.

When the Majestic Twelve were seated at the roundtable, arguments immediately ensued regarding areas of responsibility and orders of workers. Shätäniël and Ghädäniël were in greatest disagreement; therefore, Emperor Än, before casting lots in metal, consulted the Bible of Destinies and Fates, also called the Plan, or Blueprints and Sepias of Creation. The Bible includes a fivefold book called the Book of Destinies, which contains the charts and stories of the creation ages of the royal primary order of metals, or primordial times, and a sevenfold book called the Book of Fates, which contains the epic story and decrees of their beginning ancestors, whose first lots were cast in metal after the first king consulted the Book of Destinies, which then became customary for their kind to do so on occasion. Based on the secret scoping documents, Attorney General Ghädäniël was decreed two hundred Īgoggles and assigned the rēdland below the crescent-shaped dam, including the garden-dome and the City of Ēls in East Ängleä. Surgeon General Shätäniël was decreed two hundred Īgoggles and assigned the seas, including the damnation of Eärāith with its dam, powerhouse bolts and canal locks. Surgeon Colonelle Khätäniëlle, who reported finding the ore of gold and other precious metals within the snow-capped Peak District located across the desert west of Ängleä, was decreed two hundred Īgoggles. She was tasked to mine the three-peaked mountain there, smelt the gold oregon, transmute the base metal into mono-atomic gold powder, the essence of gold, and accommodate the transportation of the powder to Phaëton. At the place of the mouth of the mine, Prince Shämyazäbäël would lord over Mōving Company and Prince Rāphäël would lord over Mineoring Company, after Masonry Company had constructed a firestone base there for payload shärkhs—a rocket ship base. The rocket ship base would be called Shippaër City.

The two half-brothers Shätäniël and Ghädäniël became quite envious of their half-sister, Khätäniëlle, who possessed the shärkhs and most of the heavy equipment, such as the scorpion, bull, and beetle machines, even the ore drills and jack hammers. They constantly competed for her favors, both political and sexual.

5

When the enlisted ranks did the work in every canal, field, and orchard, bearing the heavy loads of earth and harvest upon their shoulders, the burden was too great—the work was too hard and the trouble was too much. The newly arrived lords had made the enlisted carry the workload sevenfold—seven sign-ages a Week—dishonoring the Satur-Shāmbä Sign-Age of every Week and honoring only the Sun-Jūbēlle Sign-Age, which had not come around yet for the second time. Emperor Än was their sovereign monarch; Attorney General Ghädäniēl was their council leader; Captain Sīnhäēl was their command king; Captain Mīkhäēl was their labor chancellor; and Surgeon General Shätäniēl was their canal controller, dwelling in the abyss of the damnation, harnessing the energy stored in the water and opening and closing the sluice and canal locks. Shätäniēl was High Priest of the Paternal Order of Dōghboys (Masonry Company and Power Production Company), and the Paternal Order of Hōst (Flying Company and Scoping Company). Khätäniēlle was High Priestess of the Paternal Order of Indūcetrialists (Mineoring Company and Mōving Company), and the Maternal Order of Hospitaliers (Mercy Company and Death Company). Ghädäniēl was High Priest of the Paternal Order of Nävvies (Digging Company and Plumbing Company), and the Paternal Order of Phaërmers (Ranching Company and Garding Company), as well as being the Most High Priest of All.

Emperor Än had not sojourned on Phoëton for long. After staying only three sign-ages—7,200 years—he returned to Phaëton, relinquishing control of the mission to Attorney General Ghädäniēl. Before Än departed, he entrusted to Ghädäniēl the Paternal Order of Governing Agents, the legal and enforcement engineers—Lä (Law) Ministry and Phoëlease (Police) Ministry. This is when the new overlords on Phoëton began making the enlisted bear the workload seven sign-ages a Week, allowing them to rejoice only on the recurring fiftieth sign-age, the Sun-Jūbēlle Sign-Age.

Īgoggle nävvies continually dug the canals and cleared the smaller channels, the lifelines of the earth, without a sign-age of rest at the end sign-age of each Week. After many shears of constantly dredging the wide Grand Canal without a break, when the deathly silting of the big muddy river became too great, they were forced to dig and levee a new river parallel to the old, but on a higher plain east of Bedford. The lords called the new river simply New Bedford River and called the old river simply Old Bedford River. Īgoggle dōghboys constantly repaired Eärāith Dam, the canal locks, streets, and houses, and constructed and repaired all sorts of terrace walls. Īgoggle phaërmers were constantly plowing the fields and sowing and reaping in the garden-dome. The Īgoggles counted the years of their corvée in the operation and maintenance of Änglëä. They bore the excessive work through every watch without rest, groaning and blaming each other for many shears. The length of their corvée had been almost forty shears, or sixty sign-ages, from when they had arrived on Phoëton. Their next scheduled sign-age off was well over forty sign-ages away—more than 96,000 years away!

A group of nävvies were grumbling over an excavated black mass of earth when one of them said, "We must confront our labor chancellor and convince him to give us relief from this never-ending labor!" and then another said, "Come with me, and we will carry our labor chancellor from his temple-mount to show him our overburden!"

Young Captain Sīnhäēl made his voice heard among them. As the firstborn son of Ghädäniēl, he had been appointed by his father to be the king of the legionnaires in the muddy garden-dome. Sīnhäēl was playfully called King Mucky Muck by his half-brothers, the sons of Shätäniēl.

King Sīnhäēl shouted through the loudspeakers in the garden-dome, "Yes! Yes! Come, but instead of carrying our labor chancellor into the garden-dome, we should carry our council leader, Ghädäniēl. Come, we must carry the attorney general from his temple-mount! Now, everyone bang and rattle your tools, and we will go out together to wake the Most High Lord!"

The Īgoggle subjects of King Sīnhäēl listened to his stirring speech of commotion, and then they set fire to large piles of their hand tools, baskets, carts, dried wheat-grass, and dead branches, creating great fires throughout the fields. However, before they set them ablaze, they received the approval of their Fire Marshall, King Sīnhäēl himself. They also saved a portion of their spades, baskets, horns, and gourds to the side for making torches, drums, bugles, and rattles. After flaring up their torches and strik-ing, blowing, and shaking awful noisemakers, the Īgoggle goon-dog garders, also known as Greygōres, went in unison to the front tier of the Boulevard of March. When they reached the gate of Whitecastle, the temple-mount of Ghädäniēl, it was mid-watch and dark. The mount was surrounded, but the Most High Lord was unaware; how-ever, the watch sergeant was attentive and had closed the gate, holding fast the bolt and watching for any breach. The sergeant roused Captain Mīkhäēl, and both listened to the awful noise of the fiery goon-dogs outside. The captain then roused his commander, the attorney general, making him get out of bed.

Mīkhäēl said, "My Lord father, Whitecastle is sur-rounded. An awful rabble of fiery goon-dogs is running around your wall! Attorney General, wake up. Whitecastle is surrounded. An awful rabble of fiery goon-dogs is run-ning around your wall!"

Ghädäniēl ordered weapons to be brought to his chamber, and he said to his executive, "Mīkhäēl, lock the door. Take up your weapons and come stand before me," and the captain did as commanded.

Mīkhäēl said, "O my Lord, your face is as pale as a tamarisk tree! Why do you fear your own troops? Send for your father to be brought down to you, and summon your wise half-brother to come before you," and the council leader sent for his father, Än, and his half-brother, Shätäniël, who was considered the chief wizard, and even for his half-sister, Khätäniëlle, who was considered the chief witch.

Ghädäniël became so nervous that he decided to call a full council meeting within the Zōdiäkh room of the Mount of *Glōry*.

Emperor Än, at this time sojourning above the world in *HMS Glōry*, descended and was present. Shätäniël, residing in the abyss of the damnation, hurried down the New Bedford River and docked. Sphinx Khätäniëlle, commanding in the Peak District like a mountain lioness, or cougar, flew down and paced in the änte-chamber, barred from entering the Zōdiäkh Room because whenever the emperor was present, she was not considered one of the Majestic Twelve. Nine great lords had scurried through the underground chases and were assembled with Än and Ghädäniël at the Roundtable of Fates. One was missing, so the emperor summoned Khätäniëlle to step in and assume the chair of the missing lord.

When Khätäniëlle was seated, Ghädäniël rose up and paid homage to Än and then put his case forward to the council, saying, "Have not the Greygōre goon-dogs risen up against my castle? Should I not fight against them? What did I see and hear with my own eyes and ears? A rabble of Greygōre goon-dogs breathing fire is revolving around my castle!"

Än replied to his heir, "Let Captain Mīkhäël go out and retrieve the message of the fiery goon-dogs," and Ghädäniël commanded his son to go out, saying, "Captain Mīkhäël, girdle your weapons at the door, and then open the door and make a stand in the name of Emperor Än. Before the rabble of fiery goon-dogs, bow and then stand up and say to them: 'Your monarch, Emperor Än, has sent me to ask you: "Who is the crier who shouted for a rabble of fiery goon-dogs to strike drums, blow bugles, and shake rattles to disturb the sleeping lords along this boulevard? Who is the one who decreed this revolution of fire and noise around the castle of the attorney general? Who is the speaker of this congress of rebels at the gate of the council leader?""'"

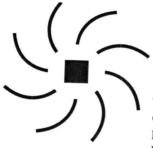

The captain went and spoke the words of Ghädäniēl to the rabble of goon-dogs. An old dog from *HMS Ärkhgōthorn* when it first landed upon the world, let loose a reply, shouting, "Every single one of us has declared this revolution! We have put a stop to the digging and harvesting. The workload is excessive—it is killing us! The work is too hard and the trouble is too much! We must have rest and relaxation, music and dancing! Therefore, every single one of us has agreed to complain to our council leader, Ghädäniēl: 'We demand to have the Satur-Shāmbä Sign-Age returned to us!'"

Mīkhäēl turned, removed his weapons from his girdle, and returned to Än and Ghädäniēl. He repeated what the old dog had said. Ghädäniēl listened to the speech, and tears ran down his face.

Ghädäniēl spoke cautiously, addressing Än: "Father, pure-spirited noble one, I ask you to show your strength before you return to Phaëton. While the twelve of us are sitting here, call up the leader of the rebellion and have him sacrificed on behalf of the workers, to spare their lives from an agonizing death in a rēd bond fire."

Än said to his children, "What are we complaining of? Their labor is indeed too hard and their trouble is too much. Every sign-age, the dominion has resounded; the transmission signals were loud enough for us to hear and be forewarned. We kept hearing the murmuring and doing nothing about it. We should have lightened their workload and reinstated the Satur-Shāmbä Sign-Age."

Shätäniēl spoke up, saying, "I agree with our noble father. Why are we blaming them? There is another solution. While the twelve of us are sitting here, while the wisest witch, Khät', is here, have her create a simple-minded brute with her coven of witches. Have her create a new, strong, two-legged simpleton to perform the hard labor without questioning and rebelling against authority. Have a hewn simpleton bear the yoke of the captain, Jāk', the workload of the bully, Ghäd'. Let hew-brutes bear the workload within the garden-dome!"

Än turned his eyes to his daughter, the witch doctor Khätäniëlle, chief midwife to the lords, and said to the wise mamme, "You are the birth doctor who will concoct a mixture of life-spirit to hew a brutish kind capable of replacing the rebel goon-dogs! Create a new brutish kind to bear the yoke! Have it bear the yoke of Jākhäël, the workload of Ghädäniël—have it bear the workload within the garden-dome!"

Witch Khät', after silently recalling discussions and experiments with her half-brother, the wizard Shät', replied to the House of Doctors seated at the Roundtable of Fates, saying, "On the first quarter, the half, and the last quarter of the moon, I will concoct a chaste mixture of life-spirit and bond it to fourteen eggs taken from an indige-nous, upright ape to create domestic zōgōts. The young blood of a wholly royal lord, however, will have to be sacri-ficed, so that the unique mixture and resultant creature of life can be trademarked as a proprietary product of ours, one which is bonded purely to our wholly royal family. One in our immediate family will have to be chosen and cruci-fied—affixed upright to a filtering crucible with a piercing in each hand, one to pour out spirited blood and the other to return de-spirited blood. We must have a wholly royal lord crucified to secure a legitimate and unquestionable claim to the new brutish kind, a creature of life who will be bonded to us forevermore as an incarnate ghöst of our life-spirit. To accommodate continual production and experi-mentation, the spirit-springs of the lord can be kept fresh in a purified immersion for a sign-age; therefore, the lord would have to be crucified every sign-age. I will combine the spirit from his young blood with the eggs of this world, and the eggs will be planted in my virgin womb witches to grow. The resulting new brutish kind will then be permanently knotted in spirit to our family for our exclusive use in workship. We will hear the drumbeat of their hearts indefinitely. We will have spirited ghōsts come into existence from the young blood of the chosen lord. Let me proclaim the new kind as my creation and as the living sign of the chosen lord. Let the new, spirited ghōsts exist so that we do not forget our chosen, crucified lord."

One after another, the great wholly royals who assign the fates answered "Yea" in the conjunction (Shätäniēl was grinning from cheek to cheek). Ghädäniēl, however, imposed a deadline for completion: If Khätäniēlle could not meet her promise by the last minute of the last hour of the last day of the fortieth shear or sixtieth sign-age since the arrival of *HMS Ärkhgōthorn*, all of the rebel goon-dog garders would be destroyed in a rēd bond fire.

6

When the bärräkhs of the legionnaires were built upon the earth, when the lords were assigned areas of responsibility and orders of personnel, when watches were assigned to the workers and supervisors, and when the ladies were taken as wives by the lords and gave birth, the lords for whom the ladies baked food and set tables oversaw the labor of the mission while the nävvies, dōghboys, and phaërmers performed the hard labor. After the nävvies had been digging into the rēdland and piling up clay into wide levees for many shears, creating more canals and fertile fields and then planting seeds for the food of everlasting life, the nävvies carrying the earth on their shoulders began to moan, weep, and murmur about the incessant labor imposed upon them.

After the rebellion and on the eve of the fifty-ninth sign-age from the beginning of their labor, the crafty creator and canal controller, Shätäniēl, was lodging in the abyss of his damnation, usually drunk, and constantly lying on his bed, lonely, depressed, and not getting up.

In a field next to a levee in which the sea was seeping through, a place where the labor chancellor and attorney general had never laid eyes, the nävvies were still complaining but now saying, "Our canal controller has made our lives miserable!" yet they did not dare rouse the wholly royal sleeper from his bed.

The mother of Shätäniēl, Queen Eurōikhä, who was still lodging in the abyss with her son, took the tears of the nävvies to her son and shouted, "Lazy boy, rise up from your bed! Between noon and evening, the workers will be smashing the baskets they have just filled. When they have done this, and because you are the clever one who will have rested, in your ingenuity and after searching and finding the skill, *you* create a new army of änts to replace them, because witch Khät' does not appear to be doing well at the task. *You* should be the doctor who frees them from their relentless, backbreaking labor!"

When Queen Eurōikhä finished speaking, the surgeon general rose up from his bed and flew to the twin-city haven, Shämbäēlle, a beautiful place in the Peak District of the West where two high and broad valleys, along with their two cities at the crest, are joined head to head, the same place which is called the Crest of Säphärōn (Saffron—golden dust), or Sion for short. Dōghboys of Masonry Company had earlier built the two walled cities back to back there: Shippaër for Mineoring and Mōving Companies, a city featuring an immense flame-thrashing floor for payload shärkhs—the rocket base—and a mouth that led to an underground labyrinth of mining tunnels deep within the adjacent mountain; and a city called Shērpäppäkh for Mercy and Death Companies, a city featuring many granaries, a hall of hospitality, a phaërmacy, and laboratories for the very wise Surgeon Colonelle Khätäniēlle. The mountain of Säphärōn, the adjacent mountain of the underworld labyrinth was called Three-headed Dog Mountain, or Three Dog Mountain, where the enlisted Īgoggles of Mineoring Company used the khäth-ore-drill, or cathedral, to route through rock and the khäth-ore-hammer, or cathor hammer, to crush oregon, a multi-faceted metal ore rock. Among the tall and beautiful cedar trees in Shērpäppäkh lay a creation house, a hall of laboratories called Khūgar Hall—the Hall of Noble Silver belonging to Khätäniēlle.

While pondering in the laboratory, the adept and wise one, skillful engineer of deep havens and fertile earth, the lord who opens the floodgates of the havens onto the earth, he who pulls back the bars and loosens the fastenings to open the canal locks, he who is creator of numerous and varied civil works, struck his thigh and shouted, "Eurōikhä! I've got it!"

Within the sanctuary of the white-uniformed witches of Mercy Company, the surgeon general summoned two midwives—Ensigns Imägeneēlle, or Emmä Jēnēlle, and Imäshēreēlle, or Emmä Chērēlle. After they had arrived and were briefed concerning an issue of great value, they were purified in a sanitizing bath. The surgeon general then stretched out his arm and inserted a drop of sperm from a native upright ape into each womb. As moons came and went, one fetus grew, and it was in the image of the donor—muscular and hairy!

Shätäniēl called out to the sōphist Khätäniēlle, who was assisting him, saying, "O Sōphi, because our twin sons for whom you are arranging witches to provide heirs for have not yet departed for Phaëton, have them, Captains Yhūriēl and Yhūziēl, together design and build a royal cradle. And bring me a vessel of the spirit of Captain Sīnhäēl, because I will need to add some of its springs of knowledge to the fetus. Emmä Jēnēlle can then grow the creature larger. When you see its limbs developed and you have determined how large it will be, you will then have the measurements for the cradle to give to the twins. The twins will act as your aides before they depart, and your witches will help you in its birth. When the cradle is complete, you will facilitate the birth of a new kind of spirited-being, a being which did not involve the mating of a male!"

Without the mating of a male, Khätäniëlle facilitated the birth of a new breed of being, a hairy, man-like creature with both male and female parts—a hermaphrodite. The femaleness of the creature would prove to be the downfall of its strength. Khätäniëlle stretched out the shoulders of the babe and then poked her finger into its mouth; it promptly began to suckle. She cleansed the newborn and then enclosed its body within a thin but moist membrane. Shätäniël prepared a swathed woolen turban, which Khätäniëlle gently placed the baby within. The baby began to cry as though celebrating sound!

Shätäniël held a feast to honor Khätäniëlle. To everyone at the banquet, even Ensigns Emmä Jënëlle and Emmä Chërëlle, and the other midwives and chiefs of midwives, he offered choice fruits, bread, and wine. However, for his father, the emperor, who had returned to Phoëton during the uprising of the fiery goon-dogs, and for his half-brother, Ghädäniël, he roasted perfectly an unblemished young goat as an inside joke.

When the legionnaires heard the good news from Shätäniël, they praised him, and some of their chiefs said to him, "Majestic One of Knowledge, who could have imagined it!...High-charged Lord Surgeon General Shätäniël, nobody can match the things you do!...You are like the wholly black father who created an assembly of sons!...You are our messiah and savior!...The emperor will raise your level of power, and you will become greater than Ghädäniël!"

7

The missing one in the Zōdiäkh Room, Captain Sīnhäel, the overlord of the Īgoggles in the garden-dome, had been chosen by the House of Lords (at the urging of Khätäniëlle) to become the crucified wholly royal lord, the one to undergo everlasting äphaëraōhsis, the continual harvesting or drawing down of spirited young blood. After being arrested and taken to a suite in the sanctuary of the Order of Hospitaliers in Shērpäppäkh, Captain Sīnhaёrbäd—as he was now sometimes called by his father— wholeheartedly agreed to be voluntarily taxed to contribute a tenth of his life-blood savings to support the creation of a new breed of bonds, to give a share of his life-building spirit to save himself and his Īgoggle subjects from an agonizing death by rēd bond fires. He would be shamefully affixed to a cross resembling the crosspiece of an ox yoke, humiliated for a time, and then resurrected, after refortifying his blood, to continue his reign as king in the garden-dome of Ghädäniël, only to repeat the äphaëraōh crucifixion at the beginning of every sign-age, until a yet-undetermined end time.

Captain Sīnhäёl was crucified, and would be crucified every sign-age, tied upright on a cross and pierced to pour out his blood into a filtering crucible. He became diminished in spirit, like the waning of the moon. He had to atone for his shameful way and the shameful ways of his subjects. Sīnhäёl became known as Moon Lord, an association with Sunny Grey Gore Kangaroo from the creation ages of the royal primary order of metals; his recurring crucifixion became alternately known as Drawing Down the Moon, and Day of Atonement. Soon after the hermaphrodite was born by Ensign Emmä Jēnēlle, the two great surgeons of life experimented numerous times with various spirit-springs to correct error after error, with the deadline of the last day of the fortieth shear looming closer.

While sitting and drinking beer together, the thoughts of the surgeons of life became elated, and Khätäniëlle mentioned to Shätäniël, "The body and mind of this creature will be either good or evil depending on my decisions. O Shät', I do not wish to decree the fates of my imperfect creatures of life."

Shätäniēl replied, "O Khät', you will tribulate and sentence the perfect creatures of life and become their bastion in life, and I will tribulate and sentence the imperfect creatures of life and become their keeper in death," and with that said, they both went back into Khūgar Hall.

Khätäniēlle took a vessel of life-spirit from the hand of Shätäniēl, and she fashioned at first a male who could not grasp very well, one whose hands were constantly shaking. Shätäniēl examined the creature and decreed his fate, appointing him as a general servant in his first estate, the abyss of his dam.

Second, Khätäniēlle fashioned a male who was blind, one whose eyes rarely moved. Shätäniēl examined him and decreed his fate, appointing him as a musician and a joker in his small octagon-shaped garden within the abyss of his dam.

Third, Khätäniēlle fashioned a male deformed in his ankles and feet, one who did not walk well. Shätäniēl examined him and decreed his fate, appointing him as a metalsmith in his workshops within the abyss of his dam.

Fourth, Khätäniēlle fashioned a male who was an idiot. Shätäniēl examined him and decreed his fate, appointing him as a garder in his octagon-shaped garden within the abyss of his dam.

Fifth, Khätäniēlle fashioned a male who could not contain his urine. Shätäniēl examined him and corrected his defect. He decreed his fate, appointing him as a swabby in the ship hold of *HMS Ärkhgōthorn*.

Sixth, Khätäniēlle fashioned a female who could not give birth. Shätäniēl examined her and decreed her fate, appointing her as a weaver in the household of Khätäniēlle within Shērpäppäkh.

Seventh, Khätäniēlle fashioned one who had neither a serpent nor a womb—androgynous. Shätäniēl examined it and decreed its fate, appointing it as a buttler to stand and bow before him in his bed-chamber within the abyss of his dam.

Khätäniēlle threw a vessel of spirit-springs to the floor, and then a great silence fell upon the room.

The great surgeon general said to the bastion Khätäniēlle, "O Bast', understand: I have decreed the fates of your creatures of life and have given them their daily food. Come here. I will now fashion seven bodies, and then you must decree each their fate and give them their daily food."

Shätäniēl devised a new formula for a man-like being.

He said to his consort, "Place this mixture into the womb of a virgin midwife to give birth to my creature." Khätäniēlle did as instructed and then stood by in anticipation of the newborn. Many moons later, in a clean chamber, the midwife brought out a male man-like child. The head of the child, however, became infected with bacteria—demons—even in the place of his hair. His eyes and neck became infected. He could hardly breathe. His ribs became soft, his lungs and heart became infected, and his bowels became infected. He could not eat with his lolling head, and his spine and head were dislocated. His hips became weak and his feet became shaky. He did not move on the proving ground.

Shätäniēl had fashioned him this way on purpose. He said to Khätäniēlle, "I have decreed a fate for each of your creatures of life and have given them their daily food. Now you must decree a fate for this, my creature of life, and give him his daily food."

Khätäniēlle turned to the demon-possessed creature and examined him. She asked him questions, but he could not speak. She offered him food to eat, but he could not reach out. He could not lie on his back because he could not stand up straight. While crooked, he could not sit down, lie down, eat food, or build a house.

Khätäniēlle shouted to her half-brother, "This creature of yours is possessed by demons! He is neither alive nor dead—he cannot support himself!"

Angry, frustrated, and fearing demons might infect her own body, she took scissors and horribly cut her own hair. She would later shave her head bald and wear a beautiful, black-hair wig whenever outside the chambers.

Shätäniēl calmly replied to the barbaric-looking, bellowing lioness: "O Barbellow, remember. I decreed the fate of your weak-handed creature and gave him his daily food. I decreed the fate of your blind-eyed creature and gave him his daily food. I decreed the fate of your wobble-footed creature and gave him his daily food. I decreed the fate of your idiot-minded creature and gave him his daily food. I decreed the fate of your leaky-serpented creature and gave him his daily food. I decreed the fate of your barren-wombed creature and gave her her daily food. I decreed the fate of your missing-sex creature and gave it its daily food. My beloved sister, you must now decree the fate of my demon-possessed creature and give him his daily food."

In continued bitterness and frustration, Khätäniēlle answered, "You have played a trick on me. You purposely fashioned this creature infected with evil demons to see if I would decree that it be destroyed."

She then exorcised Shätäniēl, shouting, "O you evil demon lord, understand: You will not dwell here in this city, and you will never come here to view this land! Your voice will never be heard here! You will never visit me here forevermore! Where you do not dwell and where my city is built, I have been quieted because of my grotesque creations. My city is being ruined by the rebellious goon-dog leader, Greygōre Guerilla of Mineoring Company. An army of änts strike here and there, rising up through secret tunnels; my phaërmhouse of medicinals has been raided and is destroyed, and my young goats, kids, are constantly being napped away. Behind my back, I have been called incompetent, because time is running out I have not yet even produced a prototype model of the replacement worker. I am living like a fugitive, and now I cannot even escape from your clever hand!"

Shätäniēl sweetly replied, "O Khät', who can improve upon the incantations you make? Remove the demon-infected creature from here and let your work with my secret assistance continue. Let your creatures of life become great, and let them praise you with gifts of gratitude. With my secret assistance, you will become gloriously fortunate. Together we can perfect what is imperfect in these creatures. Who can match this? The creature of life that I infected with evil demons, let him simply live to beg to you. Let my rising serpent please you; let our organisms be consummated together. Let the sweetness of my gonads mix with an egg of this world, and then plant it within your sour puss to produce a recipe for success. O Wise Owl, your heroic strength of mind, along with the 'ooh, ooh' songs you sing and the sōphi dance you dance, means that your destiny, instead of being the Mother Dame of the Lords, is to be the Mother Donna of the Lords! The Majestic Twelve who heard your promise...show them that you can fashion a simple brute to build a house, dredge a canal, carry the earth, and plant and harvest a crop—even drill the rock and break the piles of oregon!"

The surgeon Colonelle could not resist the great seducer.

8

In Shērpäppäkh, the visionary Shätäniēl and the wise Khätäniēlle went into the Chamber of Creation, or laboratory. While mulling over mugs of nectar, they decided to proceed in a new direction. Birth-witches were immediately gathered into an assembly room and informed of the plan, to issue new bonds to replace the old, worn-out bonds which were underperforming, not only within the garden-dome of minions, but within the under-world of Captain Rāphäel, a son of Shätäniēl with Khätäniēlle. Everything was explained to them, including how the assignment of the newborn bonds would be determined by the members of the Zōdiäkh board, or the Majestic Twelve, and then the witches returned to their stations within the Hall of Mercy Company.

In the Hall of Noble Silver, the wizard Shätäniēl produced a vessel of his own spirit-springs, and with the young blood-spirit of Sīnhäēl, he concocted a unique mixture according to a trial formula recited to him by the witch Khätäniëlle. When the white-uniformed witch finished the incantation for her brother, she cleaved fourteen native eggs, setting seven on her right to become males and seven on her left to become females. She infused each egg with the spirit and then planted each in a fertility dish to germinate. To protect against infection by demons, she placed over each dish a bell-shaped canopy, featuring an attached upright utility handle, later symbolized by a pair of wedding bells, or a shtuppah. After nine days, she summoned the seven ensign birth-witches and, with a purified rēdpipe, inserted paired male-female eggs into each fertile womb.

Many moons later, after counting the moons and calling the tenth moon the Term of Fates, Khätäniëlle covered her head with a folded, starched headdress of striped cloth with a band featuring a forehead lamp, tied a squared white apron above and below her waist, wrapped a black belt around her waist, and performed the witchcraft in the birthing chamber. She gave incantations of approval and best wishes to each of the seven sisters arranged in beds around the room, and in time slid a curled staff, or crosier (staff of a shepherd), into each virgin womb to bring out the babies, the first womb belonging to Ensign Imämaoriëlle, or Emmä Mūrīëlle. As each child was born, Mother Superior Khätäniëlle gave the honor of cutting the umbilical cord to the virgin mother, and each time, the face of the virgin mother erupted with gladness and joy. As determined by Chief White Witch Khätäniëlle, the seven midwives each bore twins—seven males and seven females. Shätäniēl assisted in delivering them, two by two, in her presence.

Creator Khätäniēlle said, "Let there be a picture of each mother sitting down and holding her twins one at a time, and then paste each picture into the top right corner of each respective nativity chart. Let a copy of the chart be placed on the headwall of each crib, and let each mother possess a sistrum to rattle," and it was made so.

The immaculate sisters had held up their trophy newborns in two ways, the males with one hand as if the babes were victory mugs of beer, and females with two hands as if the babes were victory chalices of wine!

Whenever lords and ladies came to see the Children of Bastēlle (Bastēlle being yet another pet name of Khätäniēlle), the spawned breed in the nursery, Khätäniēlle showed them her baby pictures and joyfully said, "I made them all by myself! Without the mating of a male, I made these babies all by myself! Look, see how they run!"

Thereafter, on the first quarter of the moon, the half moon, and the last quarter of the moon, and secretly assisted by Shätäniēl, Khätäniēlle infused a concoction of the essence of life into fourteen native eggs and soon heard the drumbeat of their hearts. Bonded spirit ghōsts came into existence from the intertwining of two life-spirits, one from Phoëton and one from Phaëton. Khätäniēlle proclaimed them as the living sign of Lord Sīnhäēl, Moon Prince whose blood was drawn down. These hybrid spirit ghōsts would perform daily workship so as to also not forget the lord who would be crucified every sign-age for the repurification of the spirit of their species. The seven womb-witches were secretly initiated and bonded together in the Maternal Order of the Sisters of Qätärän (Qätärän being the same as Khätäniēlle), each swearing a vow to devote her entire life to workship in the änt nursery, remaining chaste and not seeking fortune, for the sake of the mission. They would produce waves of children without the mating of a male, and the procedure of invitro-fertilization would be called Immaculate Conception. The sisters would group together the morphing children and raise them as though they were fish in a stock pond, calling them morphäns. Mother Superior Khätäniëlle was so happy with her nursery school that she composed many rhymes and read them to her children there.

After Khätäniëlle had created a bond from the spirit of a wholly royal lord, a multitude of simpletons capable of carrying out commands of labor, she requested an audience with the Majestic Twelve, including the missing one from the earlier assembly in crisis, the named and shamed Lord Sïnhäel, her son from the rape of her by Ghädäniël.

The surgeon Colonelle said to the twelve, "I have carried out precisely the work which I had promised you by the last day of the fortieth shear. I have crucified the chosen lord to gather stem cells and life-spirit from his young blood located deep within his bones. I have created a new front line of workers to relieve the Ïgoggle dogs from their labor in the garden-dome, even the rock-dome—I have imposed the workload of Ghädäniël on the new bond. They understand simple commands and perform hard labor without question or rebellion. Let the iron fetters and chains be removed from the legs and necks of the dogs!"

The Majestic Twelve listened to her amazing speech and were relieved from their anxiety, altogether answering "Yea" as they sat at the roundtable of fates.

All of the princes stood and bowed before her, kissing her feet and saying to her, "We used to call you Mother Dame and Princess of Phoëton, but now we will call you Mother Donna and Queen of Phoëton!"

Ghädäniël decreed loudly, "Let the dogs out! Let them be free citizens upon the world. Allow each of them to go out into the wilderness to find a fortune and pursue their own happiness. However, confine them to this world—do not let them fly off of it, and let each of them pay a tax to my established governing Trilateral Commission equaling one-tenth of whatever fortune they collect in gold, silver, and copper each shear, as a tribute of gratuity to their Most High Lord and Protector, I, Ghäd of Än, who freed them from their corvée of forty shears."

9

The Majestic Twelve were planning the fate of each new hew-brute, assigning to each a particular lifelong task for the mission. Combined birth and infancy charts were distributed to each of the twelve just prior to vocational school graduations of the hew-brutes. The new workers, in mass, participated in what was called Confirmation Day, vowing devotion to their assigned job for life. Each member of the Zōdiäkh board was responsible for a particular period of birthdays. They consulted the charts and decreed a specific duty and location within the garden-dome for each new worker. This process would later be expanded to include decrees of duty and location within the mining tunnels.

The new brutes in the garden-dome came under the supervision of Captain Mīkhäél and Captain Jākhäél. The hew-brutes took hold of plows, made new picks, spades, and sickles, and tilled and harvested the fields and dug the canals. Later, other hew-brutes would take drills and hammers and mine the tunnels within Three Dog Mountain under the supervision of Captain Rāphäél and a dark, younger sister of Surgeon Colonelle Khätäniëlle.

During the next forty shears, out of their love of research and science—or sorcery, as some would later say—Shätäniël and Khätäniëlle secretly continued to experiment with the spiritual formula of the hew-brute. After adding a few more bits of wholly royal spirit, they succeeded in creating a wiser and nimbler derivative of the hew-brute, calling the new breed hew-man, a male individual whom Shätäniēl appointed as a sage charged with affairs of Eärāith Dam, or Alpha Dam, the first of many damnations on the world. He was so pleased with the proving of the new creation of life that he gave the upgraded creature a divine name: Ädam.

Ädam and Ēve

1

After being secretly raised by Mother Donna and her coven of white-uniformed witches in Shērpäppäkh, Ädam was taken to Eäräith Dam to serve Shätäniēl as keeper of his damnation. Shätäniēl revealed to him the destiny of the civilized world, and then charged him to perform various daily chores for the Lords and Ladies, such as preparing food and drink, setting and clearing tables, and opening the town at dawn and closing it at dusk. Ädam was even the fisher and gatherer for Shätäniēl.

One calm day, Ädam embärkhed in a rudderless boat from a quay on the Eäräithräeän Sea to go fishing. As he made his way by oar near to the inlet tower, his boat was suddenly overturned and he was drowning in the depth of the sea. The winding power turbine system which blows sea-gales toward the South had suddenly thrusted after being calmed for maintenance. A whirlpool in the sea sucked Ädam into the depth of the throat of the inlet tower. As Shätäniēl would have it, however, Ädam was rescued from the turbulence by an Īgoggle pilot.

Ädam became angry and swore at the south-blowing power turbine system, shouting, "I will break all of your fins, however many you have, even if you send your brother side-winders against me, however many you have!"

He soon broke the fins, or blades, of the south-blowing power turbine system. The gales ceased for seven days. As a result of his rebellious behavior, Ädam was summoned before Emperor Än on Phaëton. Up until this event, Ädam had never worn clothing, so Shätäniēl made a shawl of sack-cloth and hung it over the shoulders of Ädam as a mourning and penitence garment.

He said to Ädam, "O Ädam, you are going before my father, Emperor Än, who dwells on another world, Phaëton, a star which moves in a long bow through the Black Sea above the sky. When you approach his door, my missing sons the twin princes Yhūriēl and Yhūziēl will be standing there, and they will ask you, 'Who are you coming to see, and why are you wearing a shawl of sack-cloth?' Say to them, 'I have been summoned by an emissary of the emperor, and I wear this shawl of sack-cloth because two great Ängles have vanished from the world.' They will then ask you, 'Who are the two great Ängles who have vanished from the world?' Tell them, 'The two great Ängles Yhūriēl and Yhūziēl.' They will look at each other in astonishment and then laugh out loud, but then they will say a few words in your favor to the emperor, presenting you to him in a good mood. They will offer you food to eat. Say 'No, thank you' and do not eat. They will then offer you wine to drink. Say 'No, thank you' and do not drink. They will then offer you fragrant oil to anoint yourself. Say 'Yes, thank you' and anoint yourself. They will then offer you a fresh garment to cover yourself. Say 'Yes, thank you' and cover yourself. Do not forget these commands."

An emissary of Emperor Än arrived in Eäräith and announced to Shätäniēl, "Ädam has broken the fins of the South Gälër which belongs to the emperor; therefore, the emperor summons Ädam to come before him to explain his destructive behavior."

Ädam was taken up in a bright flying wheel to Phaëton.

When Ädam approached the great door of Än, the twin princes Yhūriēl and Yhūziēl were indeed standing there, and they asked him, "Who are you coming to see, and why are you wearing a shawl made of sack-cloth?"

He answered, "Two great Ängles have vanished from the world."

They then asked him, "Who are the two great Ängles who have vanished from the world?"

He told them, "The two great Ängles Yhūriēl and Yhūziēl," and, as foretold by Shätäniēl, they looked at each other in astonishment and then laughed out loud.

Ädam went before the emperor, who said to him, "Come here, O Ädam. Why have you broken the blades of the South Gälër?"

Ädam humbly replied, "O Lord, Your Highness, I was fishing in the middle of the sea for the House of my Lord your son. The sea was calm, but then the South Gälër suddenly caused a swirling storm which overturned me and I was drowning in its throat. I would have lost my life had not an Ängle of the hōst saved me, delivering me to my Lord in the abyss, where I saw the South Gälër. In my anger and strength, I broke its fins."

Än grew very angry at Ädam, but then Yhūriēl and Yhūziēl spoke favorably of Ädam into the ear of their Lord. In this manner, the emperor was appeased and grew quiet.

Än said to his two grandsons, "Why did your father give this wretched laborer such strong emotion and disclose the destiny of the world? He has even given him a divine name! I decree that your father is responsible for breaking the wings of South Gälër; I will have a word with him later. Now, what will we do for Ädam? Let him eat our ambrosia and drink our nectar, and then let him be escorted back to the world. However, instead of Ädam being charged with the affairs of the damnation, let him be charged with the affairs of the garden."

Yhūriēl offered Ädam leftover food, but he politely refused and did not eat. Yhūziēl offered him leftover wine, but he politely refused and did not drink. Yhūriēl then offered him fragrant oil, and he politely accepted and anointed himself. Yhūziēl then offered Ädam a fresh garment, and he politely accepted and covered himself.

Än looked at Ädam in wonder and said, "Come, O Ädam, why do you not eat nor drink? Do you not want to have everlasting life? Sadly, for you and the downtrodden kind, you and they will not live an everlasting life."

Ädam remarked, "My Lord commanded me not to eat or drink before you."

Än said to Yhūriēl and Yhūziēl, "Your father is very clever. He has dramatically shown to me that the hew-man is worthy to have everlasting life as an obedient servant to our mission. Yes, have him escorted back to where he was taken. Let your father know of my verdict; let Ädam be delivered by Mīkhäel to the Crown Prince. Let Ädam *not* remember this trip and his past life with your father, and let him be the king of the hew-brutes in the garden-dome."

The emissary of Än returned Ädam to Eäräith Dam, recited the message of the emperor to Shätäniēl and to Ghädäniēl, and then returned to Phaëton. Mīkhäel immediately grabbed Ädam from the damnation of Shätäniēl, delivering him before Ghädäniēl in Sun City on the Isle of Ēls. After some pomp and circumstance, Ädam was crowned Greene King of Ängleä, or Gardener House King of Ängleä, and his memories of the trip and serving Shätäniēl were erased by a psycho-pomp to ensure his loyalty and workship to Ghädäniēl alone. His performance was rewarded when his request for a proper helper, something which every male änimal in the garden possessed, was granted by Ghädäniēl. Ghädäniēl gave him his wish, thinking Ädam would not want anything more from him. By decree, a womb-man for Ädam was created by Khätäniēlle (secretly assisted by Shätäniēl) in the western land of mountains and valleys, the Peak District. When the helper was presented to Ädam, he was overjoyed and simply called her Ēvening, or Ēve for short, because he received her during the evetime of the day.

2

To the East of the Garden of Ängleä is a range of natural iron-topped mountains, and to the West is a vast desert of sand and brimstone. To the South are enormous pillars of date palm and a narrow strait of a sea, beyond which is an ocean of seas encompassing the world. To the North is the crescent-shaped firmament of Eäräith Dam, beyond which lies the Eäräithräeän Sea, a vast storehouse of clear water sweet to the taste. Through the clearness of the sea, one may look into the depths of the world, and, when one washes himself in it, he becomes clean as the cleanness of the sea and bright as the brightness of it, even if he were muddied. Shätäniël created this reservoir of energy according to his plan, creating sustainable power and renewable earth to support the wholly royal mission of obtaining gold from the world.

The Īgoggle garders labored in the vaulted and terraced earth, digging, planting, and harvesting, until they went on strike and were replaced with hew-brutes, male hew-brutes supervised by the hew-man, Ädam, and female hew-brutes supervised by his proper helper, Ēve. After keeping the garden-dome for a few years, however, Ädam offended Ghädäniël, and as a result, he was summoned before him and reprimanded. Ädam, Ēve, and the hew-brutes were then banished from the garden-dome and replaced by newly arrived Īgoggle legionnaires.

After Mīkhäël and Jäkhäël drove them out through the gate of the garden-dome, Ädam and Ēve saw a broad wilderness spread before them, a strange land which they knew nothing about and had never seen before. They saw a great expanse of sand riddled with large and small stones. Fearful and trembling, they looked back at the gate and saw a large Knight of the Garder twirling a golden, fiery stick in his hands. Their fear and trembling grew until they fell with their faces flat to the ground as if they had died. Ghädäniël was looking into his seven-phase vision-sphere and saw them in their fallen state. Having pity on them, he sent Jākhäēl back to raise them up and comfort them with good news. Emissaries of Ghädäniēl employ heralding knights whenever they must recite a message to a lower class.

Jākhäēl went to Ädam with a herald, who shook him up, shouting, "Hear, you! Hear, you! Hear, you! Most High Lord Ghäd of Än, Attorney General, has good news for you! Lord Ghädäniēl says: 'O Ädam, open your eyes and see the light of day! Understand: I have not destroyed you. You now serve a new purpose of mine. Instead of lording over the workship of the hew-brutes in my garden-dome, you will now lord over the workship of the hew-brutes in the wilderness of Shätäniēl and the underworld of Khätäniēlle, having them break and smelt oregon for five and a half Great Years. You will be eligible for rēdemption in five Great Years, or sixty sign-ages. At the beginning days of each sign-age, I will send to you an appointed emissary from my Law Ministry to assess your trust in my name and to collect my interest. My ships will collect the interest, transmute it into a featherweight powder, and then ship it to the imperishable star, Phaëton. When the five and a half Great Years of your term are complete, I will return you to my great garden-dome. Yes, I who made you as a replacement king, I who received your harvest from my great garden-dome, I who banished you from your dwelling there, I who raised you up from a fall of death outside the gate of my garden-dome, and, yes, I who will return you through the gate of my garden-dome if you perform as agreed and your trust in my name and number is complete. This is my solemn promise, a covenant which will always be with you and honored by me, Lord Ghäd of Än, Most High Lord."

When Ädam heard these words of Ghädäniēl, he did not understand the meaning of them. He thought he and Ēve might perhaps be able to return to the lush green fields and orchards of the garden-dome after spending only a short while in the wilderness, or not. He wept from his confusion and asked Prince Jākhäēl to explain the words of Ghädäniēl to him.

Jākhäël explained in great detail about how the creation and measurement of time for the world was determined by Shāmyazäbäël and endorsed by Ghädäniël, how the clock and the calendar are divided into portions by a correlation of dials between Phoëton, and the moon, and Phoëbus, the sun, agreeing with a denomination of sixty to create the seconds, minutes, hours, dusk and dawn, days, weeks, moons, mōnths, years, jubilees, centuries, epochs, millennia, aeons, sign-ages, shears, myriads, Great Years, and pentagrams, and how, when greatly struck by a round mace, a single atom of Khōbäëlith, or Cobalt-60, casts off two opposite particles of creation—matter and antimatter—as seconds for a total of 60 seconds for one minute, how 60 minutes is one hour, 24 hours is a day with a dusk and a dawn of 12 hours each, 6 days and 1 consolation day is a week, 30 days is 1 mōnth, 12 mōnths (360 days) is a year, 49 years (seven weeks of years) and 1 consolation year is a jubilee, 2 jubilees is a century, 4 centuries is an epoch, 1,000 years is a millennium, 1,200 years is 1 aeon, 6 epochs (2 aeons or 2,400 years) is a sign-age with a decline (dusk) and an ascent (dawn) of three epochs (1,200 years) each, 9 epochs (3,600 years) is a shear, 1 shear is a Year of Phaëton, 25 epochs (10 millennia or 10,000 years) is a myriad, and 72 epochs (12 sign-ages or 28,800 years) is a Great Year, which is a complete circus of the stars with a dusk and a dawn of 14,400 years each, so that 5 Great Years (360 epochs, or 144 millennia, or 60 sign-ages, or 144,000 years) is 1 pentagram, and the one-half Great Year after the pentagram of trust-building is a period of graceful living.

Jākhäël continued to explain, saying, "A sign-age is measured by the precession of the equinoxes, a slow westward motion along the ecliptic caused by the gravitational action of the sun and the moon upon the protuberant matter about the equator of the world, and there are twelve sign-ages within one complete cycle of the Zōdiäkh. Each sign-age has an appointed prime minister from the Law Ministry. The sign-age before the end of a Great Year is a sign-age of assessment, and the sign-age after the end of a Great Year is both a sign-age of confirmation and a sign-age of atonement. If your trust in the name and number of Ghädäniēl is assessed as lacking at any end time of a Great Year and you do not atone for the lacking of your trust by the end of the next sign-age, you will awaken the wrath of Ghädäniēl. If your trust is assessed as lacking at the end time of the final sign-age of the pentagram of the covenant, your spirit and soul will be destroyed for eternity in a rēd bond fire. At the end time of each Great Year, or twelve sign-ages, if your assessed trust is complete, your spirit and soul will be saved, resting in a limbo of peace for the duration of the grace period of half a Great Year. On the contrary, if your assessed trust is lacking, you will have the opportunity to quickly atone for yourself, making amends to Ghädäniēl. These are the last sign-ages and the first sign-ages of the five Great Years of the pentagram— the twinned sign-ages of the cusp of the Great Years, occurring five times over the coming period of 144,000 years of the pentagram, the same amount of time which the foreign legion had spent in corvée within the dome of the garden. However, O Ädam, I forewarn you: Time is quickened and slowed by the interplay of Phoëbus and Phoënix; therefore, keep careful observation and measurement of time. Remember: The time of your term is measured in Great Years, and it is five times and half a time. But do not concern yourself with this now, because you will be taught later by my half-brother, the Ängle Yhūriēl, on how to keep time, after he returns to this world.

"It is foretold that, during the final sign-age of assessment and judgment, a Ray from the South will pierce the side of the Cross of Phaëton, preceded by the False Cross. The long count of days to the final end time is currently beyond an accurate foretelling of days to come, because Phoënix and its four moons sometimes changes the motions of the planets, even this world, and, in this manner, changes the measurement of the time of your term for better or for worse. Time Lords will continuously go out across this world to survey celestial time at observation stations, measuring the degrees and minutes of hours and days, years, epochs, aeons, sign-ages, shears, and Great Years, to correctly foretell the end times. A herald will announce a newly appointed prime minister at the beginning of each sign-age. O Ädam, I also forewarn you: There will be many observers among you who will be wrong in their foretelling of the end times."

Captain Jākhäēl promised Ädam a series of thirty-five emerald-colored tablets containing a record of this mysterious wisdom, along with some mysterious wisdom authored by Captain Yhūriēl, to be given to him one book at a time, the first book when he would be worthy of understanding and able to recite its words from memory, and subsequent books at times when he would be found worthy of achieving a greater degree of understanding. The last two books, however, are reserved until the final end days.

Jākhäēl continued in his speech to Ädam, saying, "All of this mystery wisdom is of a degree greatly beyond your current understanding. You are merely an initiate, a neophyte of the Law School of Ghädäniēl, a tenderfoot who has already been washed out once from the proving ground of Ghädäniēl for trespassing in the rēd zōne of Ēve. You are a security risk of Ghädäniēl, a bond who must perform in the wilderness on his own, one who must mature before returning through the gate of the garden-dome. You desired to see and eat the bitter fruit beyond your allotment in the garden, so now you will see and eat the bitter fruit far beyond your allotment. You will now lord over the hew-brutes on a mountain in the dusty wilderness, a land with an underworld far beyond the garden-dome and firestone seat of Ghädäniēl. Your tests will be great and deceiving, yet Ghädäniēl has faith in you. He does not wish you to fall short or fail. O Ädam, although you are a risk, you come highly rated by the emperor. You have been entrusted by

Ghädäniēl to perform well. Ghädäniēl has even pledged a reward for you should you meet your quota before the beginning of each new sign-age. You were the king of the hew-brutes in the land between the two rivers of Änglea, but now you will be king of the hew-brutes in a land far beyond the big muddy river of dead rēd sticks and beyond the desert of fire and brimstone. You will be the king in the wilderness of the mountain land and underworld of Lady Khätäniēlle, the king who will fully fill his coffers with bars of gold, sealed with impressions of the bull and lion!

"O Ädam, listen carefully to the words of Ghädäniēl. His credibility is on the line. He will be watching you with the keen eye of his falcon ship *Bhōssphoërūsh*, assisted by the Īgoggle hōst. Ghädäniēl will track your performance in anticipation of periodically collecting his interest in you, and to eventually rēdeem the script on your head. Ghädäniēl will know your every move through his all-seeing eye and vision-sphere. He will watch you patiently in your dusks and dawns, charting your every step up and down. This is the serious business of the Top Dog, Emperor Än, and he wishes you to be upright, to stay on the righteous uphill path to rēdemption. O Ädam, you are about to embärkh on an arduous and perilous journey for the survival of not only your kind, but for the kind of Ghädäniēl. Depending on the weight of your trust, he may of his own good will intervene to help you along the way, or he may of his own wrath intervene to plague you.

"Your auto-genes, the automatic instruction springs within your spirit, will be sampled and marked on a ribbon throughout your stay in the wilderness. Your spirit-ribbons will be examined and graded as good or bad; therefore, O Ädam, listen carefully. Besides strengthening your trust in Ghädäniēl, watch over and protect your spirit—remain chaste! I do not know how successful you might be, but if you behave righteously before Ghädäniēl in the management of the rock-dome in the wilderness, you might become a King of Kings—only Ghäd' knows!

"Your first test is to read and understand the Doctrine and Mission of Ghädäniēl and recite it from memory. You will soon receive the book written by myself in an emerald-colored tablet. I will be with you to help you read and understand its scrolling; however, we must quickly be on our way, because I must soon deliver you altogether across the river of dead sticks and the desert of hot brimstone to a naval of this world. You must be driven through the Isle of Ēls to get to the big muddy river. An Īgoggle pilot will then ferry you and Ēve, along with your brutes, across the river of sticks and through the desert of ash."

3

The term of Ädam was announced to the Ängles soon after Ädam was discovered trespassing in the forbidden rēd zōne of Ēve. While being driven out by the spray of sea hoses, Ädam and Ēve came near to the fig tree whose broad-leafed branches they had hidden beneath, that its leaves were withered and had fallen, and on the contrary the leaves of the other fig trees were still fresh and hanging on. As Ädam drew near to the barren tree, his fear and trembling grew until he dropped to his knees and begged to Jākhäēl to give him something from the garden to take with him.

When Ädam and Ēve had passed out beyond the garden-dome gate, they saw the Knight of the Garder twirling his fiery stick; he was a large figure with colorful and swirly tattoos, making an angry and horrible face at them, even sticking his tongue out at them! They both feared for their lives, believing the fiery goon-dog garder was going to destroy them. This is when their fear and trembling became grave and they dropped as if they had died. The knight turned away and spoke into an oracle to Ghädäniēl, asking him about what to do with them.

The knight said, "Your Majesty, you sent me to secure the West gate of the garden-dome with my firearm, but when your servant and his helper saw me after passing through, they became gravely frightened and have fainted with their faces flat to the ground. Your Majesty, what should I do with your servant and his helper?"

This is when Ghädäniēl again had pity on Ädam, and sent his son, Jākhäēl, to give him a jumpstart in his adventure. He ordered Jākhäēl to raise Ädam and Ēve up again and to give Ädam the good news, especially concerning his Day of Rēdemption.

When Ädam heard the gospel he was comforted by hope, believing he and Ēve would be saved from harm and eventually delivered back into the great garden-dome of Ghädäniēl.

4

Jākhäēl said to Ädam, "Lord Ghädäniēl is sponsoring your race against death in the wilderness and against the temptations of selling out to his adversary. Therefore, O Ädam, he loans to you this pyramid of gold bars, each bar impressed with the seal of the Bull and Lion, which is the official seal of Ghädäniēl. He loans this treasure to you as an investment to help you jump-start your venture in the wilderness. He expects you to deposit this pyramid of gold bars for safekeeping with the Trust Lord at the river bank. In exchange for your deposit, you will receive many gold coins for you and your entourage to journey quickly and safely to your destination. At the booth along the River of Ōze, each of you must purchase a ticket to ride the bärkh *Blū Skī*. Each of you will do this by giving a gold coin to the booth attendant. Next, at the plank of the bärkh, each of you must show your ticket to the sinister pilot. Before you depart the bank, you will also receive the emerald-colored tablet which contains the promissory note—the Covenant of Ghädäniël. I will be with you to explain the script in the tablet, even the script hidden beneath the script, especially regarding when, where, and how you must make periodic payments. You will be taught by the many-degreed dōgh-boys of Masonry Company on how to build metal-bar pyramids for your trust in the name and number of Ghädäniël. To help you fulfill this covenant, I will ensure that you understand the protocols of the Prime Ministers of Säphärōn, and if you agree of your own accord, you must mark and seal with bloody fingerprints seven and seven chapters—seven in an original tablet and seven in a copy of the tablet. You will keep the copy safe for yourself, and I will keep the original safe in a vault inscribed with the secret name and number of Ghädäniël. He will long-suffer in his waiting to collect his interest from your trove of metals at the beginning of each sign-age and to fully rēdeem the covenant on your day of maturity. If you disagree with any of this, you and the hew-brutes will die a sudden death, either by a drowning in a deep sea or by a burning in bond fires. His covenant with you will be effective for five and a half Great Years, enough time for you to prove yourself worthy to return to the garden-dome of Ghädäniël. If you ever try to return early, he will extend your bondage and increase your burden. You must now show him your unwavering loyalty. Never utter or otherwise reveal his secret pass name or number, not even to your wife, unless you are instructed to do so by an appointed prime minister of the Law Ministry. O Ädam, during the final sign-age of assessment and judgment, if your trust is not complete, you will have awakened his wrath once again."

Ädam was escorted to the river bank, where he exchanged the small pyramid of gold bars for many gold coins, one for each member of his boarding party. He also received the promissory notebook of the covenant. Jākhäel explained everything to him, and then they both sealed and locked the seven and seven chapters with an oath of promise and bloody fingerprints.

Jākhäēl said to Ädam, "Now, the Īgoggle pilot of *Blū Skī* is waiting to ferry you and your entourage across the River of Ōze and the desert of dust to a deep naval in the West, to the hole which will lead you to an underground world where the hew-brutes will break and pile oregon on your behalf; you will be their overlord in charge of affairs—you will be their king! Now, you must ensure that each of you gives a gold coin to the booth attendant and receives a ticket to ride in return," and he began escorting them to the booth near to the big *Blū Skī* along the River of Ōze.

Ädam was very angry at what was contained in the covenant concerning metal bars, how he was responsible to collect such treasure from the rocks of the underworld in great quantity by the hard labor of the hew-brutes for sixty sign-ages. He became so angry about the sentence spelled out in the tablet that he threw the book into the big muddy river before boarding the bärkh. A psycho-pomp Ängle named Rhaëhäbiēl, a junior lord who manipulates mood with harp music and sweet song, suddenly became hysterical and jumped into the river to retrieve the tablet. It was still in its case, which allowed it to float some, but it had to be fully recovered back at the bank. Jākhäēl would eventually return the book to Ädam.

Once everyone was on-board the airy barge *Blū Skī*, harp music began playing to sooth its riders, the same music they had heard while working in the garden-dome of Ghädäniēl. Sulky-looking Khaërān, the sinister Īgoggle pilot of the bärkh, ferried them across the shallow river of ashen mud and dead rēds, the Old Bedford River, later referred to as the River of Promise, or River of the Covenant. They continued on, cruising low and slow above the desert of sand and brimstone, heading westward toward Three Dog Mountain, the highest point in the region, the staked mountain described as a giant goon-dog with three hoary heads and sharp teeth around its necks, even a toothy tail. This is the claim-staked mountain of Khätäniëlle, and this three-peaked mountain is like a heavyweight garder-dog who keeps anyone from leaving its underworld by simply sitting upon them. Between its front paws is the great naval, the cavernous hole into the zigzagging labyrinth leading into its stomach, which is like a giant palace complete with spires and a hill called Augōthore, and whose mouth at the other end is located beneath the capital fire-thrashing floor of Shämbäëlle. The relatively level land atop the foothill, its heights, was an ideal place for Ädam to begin building his trust, because within the mountain is the great lode of gold discovered by Khätäniëlle and her Greygōre goon-dogs of Mineoring Company.

Ädam and Ēve, the hew-brutes, and a few psycho-pomps disembärkhed upon the heights of Three Dog Mountain. The big, blue, airy barge with its crossed-oars, or propellers—a magnificent airship—had landed near the naval of the mountain.

When they came altogether upon the cavernous opening, Ädam shed a large tear and said to Ēve, "O Ēve, look at this hole in which will be our prison in this land of death, a place of our punishment! How does it compare to the great garden of Ghäd'? Look how narrow it is. What is this rock there by the side of those groves? What is the gloom of this hole compared with the brightness in the great garden of Ghäd'? What is this overhanging ledge of rock to shelter us compared with the trees and the guiding Ängles which overshadowed us in the great garden? What is the hard floor of this hole compared with the soft floor in the great garden? What is this land of the wilderness strewn with bitter stones compared with the land of the great garden planted with sweet fruit? Our eyes saw the guiding Ängles playing their harps and our ears heard them singing their songs without end, but now we do not see nor hear them. What are our bodies compared to what they were when we were in the great garden of Ghäd'?"

After his lament, Ädam did not want to enter the cave under the overhanging rock, and he would never have entered it if he had not been commanded to do so by Ghädäniēl. However, he bowed to the emissary of the Law Ministry and said to himself, "If I do not enter this hole, I will again be guilty of disobedience to Ghäd', and he will punish us even more."

Ädam, Ēve, and their entourage of hew-brutes entered the cave and sat down—all but Ädam, who stood tall, pleading for forgiveness. While he was pleading, he looked overhead, examining the rock of the roof. He could not see any creatures of life like those in the massive greenhouse of Ghädäniēl', and in anguish, he cried out and beat upon his chest until he dropped again as if he had died. Ēve went and sat down beside him, weeping over his body because it was not moving.

After a while, Ēve rose up and spread her arms, pleading for pity and for Ghädäniēl to send an emissary of his Mercy Company. She shouted out, "Hear! Hear! Hear! O Lord Ghäd', forgive my shame! Do not hold my offense against your servant Ädam, because I alone caused him to disregard your law and to be washed out into this land of death away from your eternal light and into this dark hole, away from your house of brightness and into this prison. Look, O Lord Ghäd', at your fallen servant. Raise him up so that he can weep and repent of his shame which he committed through me. Do not take away his life this once, but let him live so that he can stand after your judgment and perform your bidding as he did before his fall of death. If you do not raise him up, O Lord Ghäd', take away my spirit so that I will be like him. Do not leave me alone as one of his kind in this prison, because I cannot stand to be alone in this world without him, and because you, O Lord Ghäd', had caused the essence within his bone to be taken and a rib from his essence to be cleaved, wrapping the cleaved rib in a garment of flesh with a heart like his, wise with thought and speech, creating me to be his proper helper. You made me in his image and likeness with your Ängles of

Power and Mercy. He and I are one, and you, O Lord Ghäd', are our maker, he who made us linked together. Therefore, O Lord Ghäd', return his spirit to give him life so that he can be with me in this land of death, while we dwell in it on account of our offense; however, if you will not return his spirit, take mine so that I will die on the same day."

Ēve shed tears of bitterness from her great sadness, and then she threw herself upon the body of Ädam. Ghädäniēl saw them in his vision-sphere not moving as if dead from their sadness. In his pity he sent Mīkhäēl, who raised them up and comforted them on his behalf.

Mīkhäēl went to Ädam with a herald who shook him up and shouted, "Hear, you! Hear, you! Hear, you! Most High Lord Ghäd of Än, Attorney General, sends his own son Captain Mīkhäēl as an emissary of his Mercy Company with good news for you! Lord Ghädäniēl says: 'O Bond, Ädam Bond, before I drove you from my great garden-dome in the East, you disobeyed my command by your own free will. On your own accord you disobeyed me by your desire for freedom and a higher state of being than I. Therefore, O Ädam, I deprived you of the eternal light of growing food for everlasting life which I had given to you in my great garden-dome, making you depart through its door and come into this land rough and full of trouble. If only you had not trespassed into the rēd zōne of Ēve, you would not be in this predicament now! However, you listened to Shätäniēl, my half-brother who rebelled against me, he who was banished from Ängleä, he who had no good intention toward me, and he who, though I lobbied for his appointment as General of the Advance Landing Force and yet he thought nothing of me later, sought a higher promotion to become a rival of mine. He made your fruit appear pleasant to Ēve with his deceptive words until you mated with her! In this manner, O Ädam, you failed me by the deception of Shätäniēl, and this is why you have received an affliction of pain to death instead of a sudden and ultimate death by drowning in a deep sea or burning in a rēd bond fire, which I had forewarned you about, and as I would have done to you had Shätäniēl not deceived you and because I am the great Lord of Mercy, and who, when I promoted you to king of the hew-brutes, did not truly intend to ever destroy you or them. When you sorely aroused my wrath, however, I punished you with grievous pain until death, and I will continue to do so until you repent with the fulfillment of your trust in my name. If you continue to be stubborn, you will fall under my wrath indefinitely.'"

When Ädam and Ēve heard these words of Ghädäniēl, they strengthened their faith in him because they now thought of him as their father, and they were weeping and seeking his emissary of Mercy Company because of this.

Ghädäniēl saw them again in his vision-sphere and again sent Mīkhäēl, who heralded to Ädam, "Hear, you! Hear, you! Hear, you! Most High Lord Ghäd of Än, Attorney General, sends his own son Captain Mīkhäēl as an emissary of his Mercy Company with good news for you! Lord Ghädäniēl says: 'O Bond, Ädam Bond! I have determined an unalterable term in a covenant with you—I cannot change this. I cannot allow you to return to my great garden-dome until the provisions spelled out in the covenant concerning the five and a half Great Years is fully filled.'"

Ädam replied, "O Ängle Mīkhäēl, tell Lord Ghäd' on my behalf: 'O Lord Ghäd', you cultured me and made me dwell in your great, colorful garden house. Before I trespassed in the rēd zōne of Ēve against your law, you paraded the änimals before me so that I should give them names that correspond with the names of the Ängles, each according to their character. Your grace was upon me then, and I named every one with the names of the Ängles, as you commanded of me. You then promoted me to lord over the hew-brutes. However, now, O Lord Ghäd', because I offended you and caused them to be washed out through the door also, the beasts and hew-brutes will rise up and destroy me and my handmaid, Ēve. They will cut off our life from the face of this world. Therefore, I beg of you, O

Lord Ghäd', because you have made us come out of your great garden-dome and dwell in a strange land, please do not let the beasts and hew-brutes harm us here."'

5

When dusk fell on their first day in the wilderness, Ädam and Ēve could not see each other—they could only hear the noise of each other and the hew-brutes. Ädam wept in deep anguish and beat upon his chest.

He rose up and shouted, "Hear, O my wife! Where are you?" and she replied, "My Lord, look over here. I am standing in this darkness."

Ädam replied, "O Ēve, remember the eternal light in the garden in which we dwelled! O Ēve, remember the grace of Ghäd' which rested upon us there. Remember the trees in the orchards that overshadowed us while we walked among them. O Ēve, while we were in the garden of Ghäd', remember, we did not know darkness from brightness. O Ēve, remember the garden of Ghäd' and the brightness there! Think, O think of the garden in which there was no darkness while we dwelled there. Here, however, as soon as we came into this hole in the wilderness, darkness surrounded us until we could no longer see each other. All the pleasures of our living are coming to an end!"

Ädam beat upon his chest again, and in turn, Ēve beat upon her breast. They mourned the entire night, sighing over the length of the darkness until the morning came near. Ädam beat again upon his chest from his bitter sadness and the darkness and then threw himself on the floor, lying there as if dead. Ēve heard the noise when he fell. She felt around with her hands, eventually finding him like a corpse and becoming afraid and speechless. She sat still by his side.

Ghädäniēl had looked into his vision-sphere and seen the fainting of Ädam again and the silent fear in Ēve from the darkness there. He again sent Mīkhäēl, who with a herald raised Ädam up from his faint of death and woke Ēve up to speak.

Ädam shouted, "Hear, O Lord Ghäd', Most High Lord! Why has the brightness departed from us and this darkness come upon us? Why do you leave us in this long and terrible darkness? Why do you plague us in this manner? This darkness, O Lord, where was it before it came upon us? It is such that we cannot see each other. When we were in your garden, we neither saw nor knew what darkness was. I was never hidden by darkness from Ēve until now, and neither was she from me—she cannot see me now, nor I her. There was no darkness in your garden. Hear, O Most High Lord! Are you going to plague us with this darkness?"

Once again Ghädäniēl replied through Mīkhäēl, saying, "O Ädam, if I had let my wrath fall hard upon you, I would have suddenly put you to death. If I had placed you into eternal darkness, it would have been as if I had suddenly put you to death, but I have instead placed you where you are near to the house of my Mercy Company. Soon after you transgressed, I drove you out from my garden-dome and made you come into this land, ordering you to dwell in this naval and lord over the workship of the hew-brutes in the underworld. Darkness comes upon you as though it comes from my irreverent half-brother, Shätäniēl. In this manner, O Ädam, the night deceives you—it will not last forever but only for twelve hours. When the night is over, brightness will return. Therefore do not sigh or be moved, and do not believe that this darkness is long and drags wearily on. Do not believe that I plague you with it! Strengthen your faith in me—build your trust in my name and number and do not be afraid. This darkness is not a punishment. If I had not ordered you to keep your serpent out of the rēd zōne of Ēve and you had gone into the rēd zōne with your serpent, it would have been an offense on my part for not having given you that law, because you would have turned around and blamed me for all of your ills, ills from knowing good and evil. I did properly command and warn you, and yet you transgressed. My bondservant cannot blame me for the ills from his transgression; the blame rests on you alone. O Ādam, understand: The lightness of day is for you to serve me, and the darkness of night is for you to rest yourself. Only a little darkness remains now, and lightness will soon appear."

Ādam said, "O Lord, please take my life and do not let me see this gloom any more, or deliver me to some other place where there is no darkness."

Ghādäniēl replied, "O Ādam, I tell you truly that this darkness will pass away every day that I have determined for you until the fulfillment of the covenant, when I will send a rēdeemer to deliver you and your remaining trove into my realm, into a dwelling of eternal light which you are longing for, where there is no darkness, ever.

"O Ādam, understand: All of your expressions of misery, the misery of which you have taken upon yourself because of your transgression, will never free you from the wilderness of Shätäniēl, and he will not deliver you from there either, but I will. You must accept full responsibility for the ills and pains of which you suffer as a result of you mating with Ēve against my law. Endure your ills and pains in the wilderness until the completion of your term!"

Ghädäniēl then withdrew his messenger Mīkhäēl from Ādam.

Ādam and Ēve were full of sadness and wept many tears because of what Ghädäniēl had said, that they would not be allowed to return through the great garden gate and into his bright house until the covenant was fully filled.

Ādam and Ēve did not cease standing, pleading, and weeping until dawn arrived. When they saw the brightness returning, they restrained their fear and strengthened their faith in Ghädäniēl. Ādam walked out of the cave and turned his face to the East, where he saw the spectacle of the sunrise with its glowing rays, and he felt the heat on his body. He became afraid of the sun, however, thinking it was Ghädäniēl coming to plague him.

Ädam wept and beat upon his chest again, and then bowed to the ground with his head toward the sun, pleading out loud, "Hear, O Lord Ghäd'! Do not plague or burn me, nor yet take away my life from this world."

Ädam believed the bright hot sun was Ghädäniēl himself, because when he had been in the greenhouse and heard the sounds and voice of Ghädäniēl, and feared him, Ädam had not remembered seeing Ghädäniēl, nor brilliant Phoëbus, the sun, nor had he felt the flaming heat of the sun ever touch his body there, because the opaque fabric and night-lights of the greenhouse had limited his experience, and his memory of a past life in Shāmbäēlle and Eärāith Dam had been suppressed. Although summoned before Ghädäniēl to hear his sentencing in the covenant, Ädam had not looked at Ghädäniēl because of the intense brightness surrounding Ghädäniēl. He had not seen Ghädäniēl even when he, Ēve, and the hew-brutes had been washed out of the garden-dome; although, once washed out, he and Ēve had seen the magnificently terraced commandment of *HMS Glōry* and the lesser mounts reaching high to an overcast sky. Now at the cave, Ädam was afraid of the sun when the flaming rays of it reached him. He truly believed Ghädäniēl had meant to plague him all the days of his term in the wilderness.

Ädam said to himself, "Although my Lord did not plague us with darkness, he has caused this thing to rise up and plague us with a burning heat."

While Ädam was pondering this, Captain Mīkhäēl arrived and heralded, "Hear, you! Hear, you! Hear, you! Most High Lord Ghäd of Än, Attorney General, says to you: 'O Ädam, rise up and stand. The sun is not me. It was formed and arranged to give its brightness by day, which I had earlier explained to you in the naval, saying, "The morning will come, and there will be brightness by the day." I, who comforted you in the night, am your Lord, and the sun is the sun!'"

Ghädäniēl then withdrew his messenger, Mīkhäēl.

6

Ädam and Ēve shed tears while remembering their expulsion from the emerald-colored fields and orchards beneath the majestic vault of the garden. Indeed, when Ädam looked at his body, how it was beginning to harden and wither like the leaves of the fig tree which he and Ēve had mated beneath, both he and Ēve wept bitterly over what they had done.

Ēve then said to Ädam, "O my Lord, I am hungry. We should rise up and find something to eat. Ghäd' might look back and have pity on us and summon us back to his garden."

Ädam replied, "O Ēve, I thought about destroying you, but I remembered that you were made from the essence of my bone and that you have wept and shown remorse; therefore, my feeling of love did not leave you," and they rose up together and wandered in search of something to eat, but they found and ate only weeds and grasses of the field, nothing such as they used to have back in the Garden of Ängleä.

Ēve said to Ädam, "O my Lord, I am dying from this hunger. We were never hungry in the garden. It would be better if I were dead. Please destroy me now so that the punishment and wrath of Ghäd' can leave you. Perhaps then he will deliver you back to his garden, because you were banished from there on account of my transgression."

Ädam replied, "O Ēve, Ghäd' punished us together. I do not know whether he did this because of you alone. Do not ever mention it again. Otherwise, he might punish us even more, and then we will become contemptible before his eyes. How is it even possible for me to destroy you? You are a part of me! No, we should continue searching for something better to eat, so that we will not die an early death."

Ädam and Ēve wandered aimlessly toward the East and came upon a huge snake. This reptile was licking the air in its search of food and wriggling on its belly to move around and mark its territory.

Before time was measured on this world, the reptile had been the largest and most evolved of all änimals on the planet, but it had been changed and belittled by a great wrath which came from above. It had become legless and slippery. Instead of feeding on the best of food, it had devolved into eating änimals of the dirt. Instead of dwelling in the best of places, it now lived in the dirt. Because it had been the most magnificent above all änimals, which had all stood dumb at its sight, it was now abhorred by them. While it dwelled in a beautiful place, änimals would come from all around to drink where it drank, and they had drunk altogether from the same. Because the snake had become vile from the great wrath, however, änimals now fled from its dwelling place and would not drink the water which it drank, but fled from it.

When the cursed snake saw Ädam and Ēve, it swelled its head, stood on its tail, and with rēd eyes behaved as if it were going to consume them. It made straight for Ēve and followed her as she fled. Ädam, standing by, began to weep because he did not have a rod by which to beat the snake; he did not know how to stop or destroy it. Out of his strong love for Ēve, however, Ädam approached the snake from behind and grabbed it by its tail. It turned toward him and hissed, and with its great strength it knocked them both down to the ground. It then began spitting at them. A Knight of the Garder arrived by the command of Captain Mīkhäēl and stunned the snake and then raised Ädam and Ēve up by performing witch-craft.

The knight said to Ädam about the reptile, "Long ago he was dominant in this world, and then he was changed to wriggle on his belly. He roared then, but now he hisses. The ruin of his kind came from the realm of Phoëbus, when Phaëton became Phoënix near to this world, hurling down a giant flaming mountain from the sea above the sky, and now he wishes to destroy other lives, even those from Phaëton. This is why he is banned from the havens," and he struck the snake again until it was dumb, hissing no more.

The stunned and wounded snake was taken far away in the claws of an eagle ship and dropped in a sea of the ocean which encompasses the world, a sea far beyond the southern boundary of the great garden-dome. The snake eventually washed ashore in the armpit of Aundeä.

Ädam and Ēve wept, and then Ädam shouted, "Hear, O Lord Ghäd'! Hear, O Lord Ghäd'! I say to you: When I was in the cave, I spoke to you about this. I said that beasts will rise up against me and destroy us here, cutting off our life from the face of the world. Did you not see this thing attack us?"

Ädam beat upon his chest until he dropped as if dead, again.

Mīkhäēl came and raised him up with a herald, saying, "Hear, you! Hear, you! Hear, you! Most High Lord Ghäd of Än, Attorney General, says to you: 'O Ädam, remember: With my falcon ship *Bhōssphoërūsh* I see and hear everything of you. Not one of these vile snakes will destroy you, because when I caused my creatures to parade before you in the garden, I did not allow the snake to be among them; otherwise, it would have risen up against you and made you fearful and trembling, and the fear of it would dwell in your mind forevermore. I know the cursed snake is wicked, and therefore, I will not allow it to come near to you while you dwell on this mountain. Strengthen your faith in me. Build your trust in my name and number and do not be afraid of the snake, because I am always watching over and protecting you.'"

Ädam wept and replied, "O Lord Ghäd', deliver us to some other place where a snake cannot come near to us and rise up against us; otherwise, another will find Ēve alone and destroy her. Its eyes are hideous and threatening."

Mīkhäēl said to Ädam, "Lord Ghäd' says to you: 'O Ädam, do not doubt my word! From this day on, do not fear the snake, because I will not let it come near to you. I have driven it away from the mountain, and neither will I leave anything on the mountain to harm you. The upper world of this mountain is your royal sanctuary, and the underworld of this mountain is your royal dome. Consider them together as your own wholly royal king-dome."

Ädam and Ēve then praised and thanked Ghädäniēl, honoring him for having delivered them from an early death. In agreeing that they were far from life, they spent the remainder of their day in the cave, consoling each other in great sadness.

7

The heat beat upon their faces like a thrashing of wheatgrass; both were sweating and weeping. Ädam and Ēve had hiked up Three Dog Mountain in an attempt to see the lost garden-dome, but they saw only a vast expanse of desolate flatland of ash and brimstone. Ädam wanted to die. In great sadness, he threw himself out toward the East and tumbled down the toothy slope. His face was torn and his flesh was flayed. He was bleeding and near to death.

Ēve stood where Ädam had perched, crying out above his bloody body, "O Ghäd'! O Ghäd'! I say to you: I do not wish to live after my Lord, Ädam, because everything he has done to himself is because of me."

Ēve then threw herself from the perch and tumbled down the slope, landing just above the body of Ädam.

She was torn and scotched by the stones and remained lying there, bloodied, but not dying.

Ghädäniēl saw Ädam and Ēve in his vision-sphere as they lay bloodied and motionless, and he quickly sent Mīkhäēl to them, who raised them up with a herald, saying, "Hear, you! Hear, you! Hear, you! Most High Lord Ghäd of Än, Attorney General, says to you: 'O Ädam, all of this misery which you have brought upon yourself will not sway my decision—this will not alter the term of five and a half Great Years of the covenant.'"

Ädam replied, "O Lord, I harden and wither in this heat like the leaves of the fig tree under which Ēve and I had mated. I am weak from walking and loathe this world. I do not know when you will bring me out of this place to rest in peace."

Ghädäniēl replied, "O Ädam, it cannot happen at this time, not until you have fully filled your trust in my name. At that time I will have you delivered from this wretched land."

Ädam said, "O Lord, while I was in your great garden, I knew neither heat nor weakness, neither laboring, nor shaking, nor fear, but now, since I have come to this land, all of this suffering has come to me."

Ghädäniēl replied, "O Ädam, so long as you were keeping my garden-dome, my eternal light and grace rested upon you. However, when you trespassed into the rēd zōne of Ēve, sadness and misery came upon you."

Ädam wept and said, "O' Lord Ghäd', do not cut me off because of this, neither beat me with heavy plagues nor yet repay me of my offense, because Ēve and I did transgress of our own accord. Yes, I confess that we disregarded your law and we desired to become great and glorious, but your adversary tricked us."

Ghädäniēl replied, "O Ädam, because you have shown fear and trembling in this land, weakness and suffering, wandering and laboring, hiking up this high mountain and nearly dying, I promise to give your spirit a replacement body after your body dies of a natural death, a fresh body infused with your spirit. However, the new body with your spirit, together called a khrīst, will receive your original shame and the burden of the covenant upon its shoulders."

Ädam wept even more, and said, "O Lord Ghäd', send a messenger back to me in a little while so that I can inform you of what I will now do," but Ghädäniēl recalled Mīkhäēl before Ädam could finish what he was about to say.

8

Ädam and Ēve stood where they had ended their tumble down the toothy slope.

Ädam said to Ēve, "Gird your body and I will gird mine," and together they gathered up the heavy stones stained with their blood, even the stones near to these stones, and they built a series of squared terraces, one upon the other, like the throne ship mounts they had seen during their flight from Ängleä.

They built a small and crude imitation of the high terraced Mount of *HMS Glōry*, which Ghädäniēl had received as a gift from his father, the emperor, who permanently resides on Phaëton. Ädam built the high-stepped pyramid with a raised floor, or altar, on one side, with a flagstone table on the altar, to entice Ghädäniēl to arrive and be with him in the wilderness. Ädam and Ēve next took leaves from nearby oak trees and used them to spread their spilled blood over the face of the stones. Their blood which had spilled into the dirt was gathered with the dirt it had mingled with, and they offered it to Ghädäniēl, placing it upon the table.

Ädam stood before the table upon the altar and wept and begged, saying, "Hear, O Lord Ghäd'! Hear, O Lord Ghäd'! Hear, O Lord Ghäd'! Our father who dwells in the haven of the East, you whose secret name and number are venerated with our flesh and blood upon this mountain in the West, bring your throne ship *Glōry* to mate with this seat above us. Your law will be honored in the wilderness as it is in the haven. Give us our daily food, which is not food for the beasts, and forgive us of our offenses as we forgive the beasts who offend against us. Do not lead us into temptation, O Ghäd', but deliver us from evil, because the king-dome, powers, and *Glōry* are yours forever and ever. Agreed?

'O Lord Ghäd', watch over and protect us with the emissaries of your Mercy until the final end time which

you have determined for us, because we have not finished
singing our songs of praise to you which were sent up to
you when we were in your great garden. When we came
into this strange land, we no longer heard the soothing
music and sweet songs of praise from your guiding Ängles,
nor righteous pleading, nor love, nor honesty, nor just
counsel, nor vision of days to come. Neither did our bright
skin leave us, but our bodies have changed from the way
they were at first when we were made. They are now rough
and shriveled, and losing their brightness. Now, look upon
our flesh and blood, which is offered upon the stone of this
mount to you, and accept our flesh and blood from our
hands like the songs of praise we used to sing toward you
at first when we were in your dome of plenty."

Ädam began to make more requests.

Ghädäniēl looked into his vision-sphere and saw
the blood sacrifice upon the mount, and the blood in their
hands, which they held up as an offering to him without
his request to do so. He wondered at their performance and
accepted their gift by sending a column of bright light
which appeared to consume the offering on the table. The
offering was then brought to him by his emissaries and
burned in a purifying fire.

When Ghädäniēl smelled the savor of the offering,
however, he remarked, "Hmm, how sweet it is," and then
he sent Mīkhäēl to Ädam, saying, "Hear, you! Hear, you!
Hear, you! Most High Lord Ghäd of Än, Attorney General,
says to you: 'O Ädam, understand: Because you have
scotched your face and flayed your flesh, bleeding near to
death, your khrīst will desire to do the same. Because you
have built a model of my temple-mount with an offering
table upon an altar, your khrīst will desire to do the same.
Because you have offered your blood upon the table of the
altar, your khrīst will desire to do the same. Because you
have petitioned through your blood for forgiveness of your
transgressions and the transgressions of your helper, Ēve,
your khrīst will desire to do the same. If the accounting of
your khrīst is good, I will act favorably upon you and consider your early rēdemption.

"O Ädam, understand: I have accepted your blood offering this once, but the pentagram of the covenant is far from being complete. When the sixty sign-ages of the covenant are complete, when the coffers of your trust in my name and number are fully filled, and if the accounting of your khrīst is good, I will act favorably upon you.'"

Ghädäniēl understood that it would be quite a while before Ädam understood what was said to him concerning the khrīst, and he foresaw that Ädam would desire to offer his own blood again and again; therefore, he commanded him, saying, "O Ädam, understand: Do not ever again tear your face and flay your flesh, and offer your blood up to me. Otherwise, you will surely die a horrible death in a rēd bond fire. Instead, offer to me every week the roasted meat of a clean beast and the wine of red grapes. My Ängles will collect your sacrifice from upon a clean table. I will soon give to you my law regarding all of this and more."

Ädam replied, "O Lord Ghäd', I was wishing to quickly put an end to my life for having disobeyed your law, and for having come out of your great garden, and for the eternal light which you have deprived me of, and for the songs of praise which poured out without end from my mouth, and for the bright skin which clothed every bone of my body. Yet, of your goodness, O Lord, do not altogether you and the Ängles of your face depart from me, but instead save me every time I come near to death. By this, O Lord, let it be known among your subjects that you are the Lord of Mercy who does not wish anyone to tear his face and flay his skin and then die a horrible death in a rēd bond fire; let it be known that you do not condemn anyone in a cruel and wicked manner."

Ädam then remained silent.

Mīkhäēl arrived on behalf of Ghädäniēl and expressed his endorsement and best wishes, comforting Ädam in his grief. He again reassured Ädam about the promise which Ghädäniēl had made with him, that his spirit would be resurrected with a new body during the last days of every sign-age, that he would be periodically reborn as a flesh-and-blood ghōst-son of Ghädäniēl and promoted within a haven and earth.

This was the first offering Ädam had made to Ghädäniēl in the wilderness, and in this manner, it became customary for him to do so.

9

Ädam took Ēve by her hand and walked back toward the cave where they had dwelled the night before, but when they saw its opening from a distance, they stopped and stared, greatly saddened at the sight.

Ädam said to Ēve, "When we were high up on the mountain, we were comforted by Ängle Mīkhäēl speaking to us and the sun from the East shining over us. However, now the Ängles are hidden from us and the sun has changed to disappear and let darkness and sadness come upon us. We are forced to enter this hole of confinement where darkness covers us, parting us and blinding us from each other."

After Ädam said this they both spread their hands and wept because they were so full of sadness. They begged Ghädäniēl to bring the sun to them, to have it enlighten them so that darkness would not return and they would not have to go under the dome of the rock. They wished to die rather than to be in the darkness again.

Ghädäniēl was still gazing into his vision-sphere at them and their sadness, pondering over everything that he and his princely sons had done with much effort regarding the troubles of Ädam and Ēve, the misery that had come upon them in a strange land, which was contrary to their former well-being. Therefore, Ghädäniēl was not angry or impatient with them but instead was enduring and patient, like toward his three princely sons Sīnhäēl, Mīkhäēl, and Jäkhäēl.

Mīkhäēl went to Ädam and said, "Most High Lord Ghäd' says to you: 'O Ädam, if I were to take the sun and bring it to you, the hours, days, mōnths, and years would all disappear and the covenant of trusting would never be fully filled. Instead, you would turn away and be left in a long plague, and there would not be any salvation left to you forever and ever. Rather, endure a long and steady productive life while you dwell night and day, until the fulfillment of my promise comes. An appointed prime minister will arrive at each sign-age on my behalf, and your khrīst will arrive during the last days of every sign-age. I do not wish you to be afflicted in this manner any longer than you have to. When the emissaries of my Mercy Company finish evaluating the spirit from all of the bodies in which your auto-genes will have passed into and lived upon this world, I will then willingly give you potions of love from my Mercy. I cannot change the term which I have decreed for you, because I am the attorney general, and my decrees must always remain unaltered to retain my righteous credibility; otherwise. I would have brought you back into my garden-dome by now. When the covenant with you is fully filled, I will bring you into my garden-dome, to the land of joy, the land of milk-goats and honey-dates where there is neither sadness nor suffering but living in gladness and happiness, into the eternal light, and soothing harp music and sweet songs of praise that never end; I will bring you into my beautiful king-dome which will never pass away.'"

Mīkhäēl paused and then continued, saying, "O Ädam, endure your term of enlistment and enter the naval of this world, because the darkness you fear will only last for twelve hours, and when it has ended, the sun will rise up."

When Ädam heard this message from Ghädäniēl, he and Ēve praised him, and their thoughts were comforted for a while. They returned into the cave, after which it became customary for them to do so every evening. Tears again fell from their faces. Sadness and wailing had returned to their thoughts, and they wished that their life would leave their bodies. They stood pleading until the darkness of night came and they became hidden from one another. Both remained standing, pleading to Ghädäniēl.

10

When Surgeon General Shätäniēl learned of the plight of Ädam and Ēve, his face enflamed regarding what his half-brother had done, that he had thrown them out of the safety of the greenhouse and abandoned them in the danger of the wilderness. In the early-morning twilight, Shätäniēl and a few of his power equipment operators sat themselves down in a lärkh and flew to the heights of Three Dog Mountain to inspect the condition of Ädam and Ēve. When they arrived at the two fore-paws of the mountain, Shätäniēl searched for the entrance to the cave by beaming columns of light down and between the paws. Once the entrance was found, Shätäniēl maneuvered his ship to align with the hole. Once aligned, he beamed a very bright light into the opening. Ädam and Ēve glistened in the early-morning brightness. Soothing music and song accompanied the light. Shätäniēl did this so that when Ädam saw the light and heard the music he would think that the light and music were the eternal bright light and soothing harp music of the Garden of Ängleä and be comforted. When Ädam came out and saw them, he immediately bowed to the ground. As he and Ēve saw the light-bringer, or Lucifer, and heard the music, they knew it was not a dream and therefore increased their faith in Ghädäniēl.

After they had risen up and stood trembling at the opening of the cave for a while, however, Ädam said to Ēve, "Look at that great light and the Ängles standing there, and listen to the music and song. However, why do they not come over to us, do not explain to us what they are singing about, or tell us where they have come from, or what the meaning of this bright light is, what their praises are for, and why they have been sent to this place? Why do they not come in? If they are from our Lord Ghäd', they would come over to us and tell us their business."

With zealousness, Ädam pleaded, "O Lord Ghäd', is there another Most High Lord in this world who possesses a bright light with Ängles, who sends them to keep us consoled, and who would accompany them to this place? Look, we see these Ängles standing away from the cave— they are in a great light, playing music and singing songs. If they are from another Most High Lord, tell me, and if they are sent by you, explain to me why you have sent them."

No sooner than Ädam had said this, Mīkhäēl appeared, saying, "O Ädam, do not fear. This is Shätäniēl and his power rangers. He wishes to trick you like he tricked you at first in the great garden with your helper. This time he has come to you disguised as Ghädäniēl within a bright light from the great garden, hoping to enthrall you into praising him and performing his will away from Ghädäniēl."

Mīkhäēl went over to Shätäniēl, uncovering his trickery and showing the true face of Shätäniēl to Ädam— a dark and pock-marked face with dreadful locks.

Mīkhäēl said to Ädam, "O Ädam, Shätäniēl has hidden himself behind this bright masking of light ever since he was banished from his lodging in the abyss of his damnation, and he will be testing you, determining the strengths and weaknesses of your issuance from the springs of the wholly royal spirit of my elder brother, Sīnhäēl. Shätäniēl will also test the same of your offspring in due course. He will be testing you altogether until the fulfillment of the covenant, to your day of maturity at the end of the pentagram of the covenant."

Mīkhäēl bade good riddance to Shätäniēl and his power rangers, and then said to Ädam, "O Ädam, do not be afraid. Your maker and protector, Ghädäniēl, will help you build your trust in his name and number," and then he departed.

Ädam and Ēve remained standing at the opening of the cave. They were not consoled but instead were left confused by what had just occurred.

When morning dawned, they begged to Ghädäniēl for a consolation and then went out from the cave. Their thoughts were toward the great garden-dome in the East and how they were not getting any consolation for having worked there.

11

Shätäniēl peered into his own seven-phase vision-sphere, which received its signal from the hōst falcon ship *Bhōssphoërūsh*, and he saw Ädam and Ēve standing outside their cave. He again gathered together some of his power equipment operators and came upon the cave. When Ädam and Ēve saw them within a halo of luminous mist, they believed Shätäniēl and his Ängles were messengers of Ghädäniēl coming to console them about their having left the garden-dome, or to bring them back into it. Ädam spread his hands, pleading for Ghädäniēl to explain to him who they were.

Shätäniēl spoke instead, saying, "Hear, O Ädam! Let me remind you that I am the firstborn son of the Great Father, Emperor Än. O Ädam, look at the bright Ängles around me. I am here to deliver you to Shämbäēlle, a safe haven in the North, but first you and Ēve must purify yourselves in the pool of sulphur to restore yourselves to your former glory of cleanliness and happiness, so that you can return to Shämbäēlle where the Ängles of Mercy Company dwell, the place from where you were created."

These words sank deep into the thoughts of Ädam and Ēve.

Ghädäniēl, while watching Ädam, withheld an emissary of his own from going to him, because he did not wish to interrupt this test. He wished to observe the strength of Ädam, whether he would be overcome like Ēve had been when they were in the garden-dome, or whether he would fall and then rise up stronger than before.

Shätäniēl called out to Ädam and Ēve, "Look, O Ädam, we are going to the purification pool nearby. Follow us," and the Ängles began to go.

Ädam and Ēve followed them at some distance, and when they arrived down at the pool, they wondered at the clearness and depth of it. They joyously immersed themselves and became disinfected by its sulphur. They then resumed their following of the Ängles, and after they had gone up the side of Three Dog Mountain and come near to its highest head, which did not have any way to step up to the top, Shätäniēl made Ädam and Ēve go up to the top in a column of light so that they could see the wonder of all of the surrounding world, especially Shämbäēlle at the Crest of Säphärōn. Ghädäniēl, however, was now unsure and quite concerned about the situation, especially because Shätäniēl had indirectly laid his hands on Ädam by the use of his powerful column of light to lift them up, which was forbidden of him, and thinking perhaps he might wish to push them off the peak so that the entire wilderness would belong to him alone as his great dominion. Ghädäniēl saw Ädam as meek and without deceit, so he spoke into an oracle directly to Shätäniēl in a loud voice, cursing and reprimanding him.

Shätäniēl and his crew departed, and Ädam and Ēve remained standing upon the tallest head of Three Dog Mountain, where, from as high as they were, they saw below the wide world around them, even Shämbäēlle. However, they soon realized they could not see any of the anonymous Ängles who were with them, and so they wept and begged for forgiveness from Ghädäniēl.

Mīkhäēl came to Ädam and said, "Most High Lord Ghädäniēl says to you: 'O Ädam, learn and understand about Shätäniēl, how he seeks to overcome you with his deceptive tests of your trust in my name.'"

Ädam continued weeping and begging for forgiveness and then petitioned Ghädäniēl to give him something from the garden-dome as a consolation in which to be comforted.

After pondering the request, Attorney General Ghädäniēl gave Captain Mīkhäēl orders to go into the northern corner of the Garden of Ängleä and obtain from there a golden rod of a power ranger.

Mikhail went with his orders to the gate of the garden-dome and said to the burly Knight of the Garder, "Observe my orders. His Majesty, Attorney General Ghädäniēl, has commanded me to go into the garden-dome, to the northern corner, and obtain from there a golden rod of a power ranger."

The knight looked over the orders and said, "Well enough—proceed," and the captain went through the gate, obtained a golden power ranger rod, and returned with the rod to Ghädäniēl.

When Mīkhäēl returned, Ghädäniēl gave him similar orders to go into the southern corner of the garden and obtain from there a token supply of gold saffron, and he went and returned with the spice.

Ghädäniēl then gave Ghäbräēl, the third son of Shätäniēl with Khätäniēlle, similar orders to go into the eastern corner of the garden and obtain from there a token supply of silver frankincense, and Ghäbräēl went and returned with the spice. Although the princes of Shätäniēl fell under the command of Shätäniēl, the princes, even Shätäniēl himself, were bound by wholly royal law and custom to obey the lawful orders of the wholly royal Crown Prince, Ghädäniēl; if they did not obey, they risked receiving the wrath of their grandfather, the wholly royal Emperor Än.

Ghädäniēl then gave orders to Yhūriēl, who was now back on the world, to go into the western corner of the garden and obtain from there a token supply of bronze myrrh, and he went and returned with the spice.

These four elements—a golden power ranger rod, gold saffron, silver frankincense, and bronze myrrh—were gathered from the four corners of the vaulted earth below the crescent dam. The rod was stamped with a representation of a bull and lion—the Seal of Ghädäniël (likened to the primordial sun order of bull to lion)—and would be given to Ädam to help him control beasts and hew-brutes. The gold saffron spice would be given to Ädam for mixing into a potion of love to soothe his sore and weak eyes, because his eyes were afflicted from the cobra spittle and from keeping his eyes open all night from his fear of the darkness. The silver frankincense and the bronze myrrh would be given to Ädam for mixing into potions to soothe other afflictions.

Ghädäniël said to the three princely Ängles, "Mix a measure of each spice with sweet water. When you see Ädam and his helper, Ëve, anoint them by sprinkling the oily water onto their bodies to wash away the troubles of their weeping sores and aching eyes. Give the three spices and pails to Ädam with my instructions on how and when to mix and use them."

Ghädäniël then gave Mïkhäël, Ghäbräël, and Yhüriël, orders to go to the mountain of Khätäniëlle and give to Ädam what they had gathered and made from the four corners of the Garden of Ängleä.

When they arrived at the top of the mountain with the golden rod and three spices and prepared potions, Yhüriël and Ghäbräël sprinkled the potions upon the bodies of Ädam and Ëve, and they received relief from their afflictions. Then, one by one, the princely Ängles each gave Ädam the spice gifts of saffron, frankincense, and myrrh.

When Ädam and Ëve saw these gifts, Ädam rejoiced and wept, because he knew that the frankincense came from within the garden-dome. He knew that the spice was the crystal-fruit that grew under the eternal light which he had been removed from.

Mïkhäël then said, "O Ädam, I have yet another prize for you from Lord Ghädäniël. Stretch out your arms toward me."

Mīkhäēl placed the golden rod of a power ranger
into the waiting hands of Ädam and said, "Most High Lord
Ghädäniēl says to you: 'O Ädam, you have conquered a
great mountain and stand upright upon the highest of
these three peaks. I present to you these three colorful
token gifts of spice in their chests along with this honor
trophy, a wholly royal power rod stamped with my seal to
show the whole wide world that you are my highest-qual-
ity bond issued from the spirited blood of my own son.
Always keep this power rod safe by your side and take it
with you whenever you go walking. You can fend off challengers by grasping and pressing its top to produce a splendor. You are a highly rated security, O Ädam, and you will
perform well and overcome great hardships. You stand
upright here before me as a pentagram Gold Bond. The
oregon you gather from beneath this black and white floor
must be smelted into gold metal like the gold of this, your
wholly royal power rod.

"O Ädam, you are my ghōst-son, a pure reincarna-
tion of the wholly royal spirit of my incarnate son whom I
sired with Khätäniëlle, the chief white-uniformed good
witch of this mountain land. You were created in my image
and likeness. From the beginning to the end of the
covenant, you will reign over the workship of the hew-
brutes who labor as änts in the tunnels below.

"You had asked me for something from my great
garden as a consolation, so I give you this power rod and
three crystal-fruits as gifts to be treasured and kept safe
in your naval. Keep well your trust in my name and number. You will have comfort and solace in knowing that
your spirit will rise up with a new body during the last
days of every sign-age, because I have promised this to
you. Every time your spirit returns in a khrīst, three
princes from the East will return this wholly royal power
ranger rod to you and present you with a fresh supply of
crystal-fruits. They will anoint you again to announce
your return to this mountain of Säphärōn. You will then
remember that säphärōn is for restoring good sight; that

frankincense is for exorcising invisible demons from troubled flesh; and that myrrh is for restoring good feeling to pained flesh. O Ädam, keep these token gifts of my mercy safe. Wherever you tread, keep fast this rod to keep challengers at bay and to remind you of the covenant between us. My second-born son Mīkhäēl will teach you how to best use the power rod. In regard to the three spices, he will explain to you the formula of säphärōn with sweet water, and how to apply it to afflicted eyes, so as to see the light of day. Do not ever again keep your eyes always open in the darkness of the naval; instead, lay your body down and rest your eyes. Michael will explain to you the formula of frankincense with sweet water, and how to apply it to afflicted skin to purify it, exorcising demons from troubled flesh, and then burn a little cone of it to smell its sweet savor and calm your thoughts. Mīkhäēl will then explain to you the formula of myrrh with sweet water, and how to apply it to comfort pain and sadness.'"

When Ädam heard these words from Ghädäniēl through Mīkhäēl, he praised Ghädäniēl. He and Ēve then gave thanks, because Ghädäniēl had given them consolation prizes from the four corners of the vaulted earth in the East.

Other great Lords, the first two sons of Surgeon General Shätäniēl with Khätäniēlle—Captain Shämyazäbäēl and Captain Räphäēl—were also present on the mountain, and they were commanded by Ghädäniēl to lift up Ädam and Ēve and deliver them and their three chested treasures to the cave at the foot of the mountain. Once returned, Ädam and Ēve laid up the chests in a niche of the cave and placed the power rod next to where their shared bed was made. The great Ängles comforted the two and then departed. The chested gifts remained concealed as hidden treasure within the cave.

Ghädäniēl had given Ädam the gold-, silver-, and bronze-colored spices on the third day after he had been driven out of the Garden of Ängleä. These three tokens, kept by Ädam in the niche of his cave, provided him and

Ēve with a little relief from their afflictions and sadness for many years to come.

12

Ädam and Ēve dwelled in the *Cave of Treasure* every night and wandered about every day. For seven days they had not eaten any food nor drunk any water for prolonging their life. During their wanderings they found and ate only weeds and grasses of the field, nothing such as they used to have back in the Garden of Ängleä.

Full of sadness, Ēve said to Ädam, "Ghäd' gave this for beasts and brutes to eat. Our food is what the Ängles eat."

When morning dawned on the eighth day, Ädam said to Ēve, "We begged Ghäd' to give us something from the garden, and he sent his emissaries who brought us a share of what we desired, but it was not the food of everlasting life. O Ēve, it is now proper and just for us to express our sadness in yet another grave manner. We must now impose additional punishment upon ourselves and beg more fervently for forgiveness so that Ghäd' will have pity on us and be gracious enough to give us a share of something from his garden to eat for renewing our youth, some food which is better than the food for beasts and brutes, so that we will not become like them, or so he will give us comfort in some other land than this."

Ēve quickly asked, "What additional punishment? What sort of additional punishment must we do? We must not now impose on ourselves another burden of which we cannot endure, otherwise Ghäd' will not listen to our pleas and will turn the Ängles of his face away from us, because we had broken our promise. My Lord, in regard to the trouble and suffering of which I have caused you, how much additional punishment will you impose on us?"

Ädam replied, "Rise up, Ēve. We will go to the purification pool where we earlier cleansed ourselves. There and then I will tell you about my plan."

Ädam and Ēve departed from the area of the cave and then stood for a while at the shore of the pool of Shätäniēl.

Ädam said to Ēve, "I will go to the river of the West and drown myself for as long as forty days."

Ēve said, "My Lord, yes, you will drown yourself in the river for forty days, and I will drown myself in this pool for forty-five days."

Ädam shouted angrily, "No, Ēve! You are not able to endure as much as I. Do only as many days as I will tell you. Obey my instruction!"

Ēve bowed and said, "My Lord, tell me how many days I must punish myself for bringing this penitence upon you. Perhaps forty-five days is more than I can endure."

Ädam said, "You will stay here at this pool. With the tall rēd grass, make a strong, looping rope of fifty rosy knots to honor the power of Ghäd', and then search along the shore for a rock which you cannot move. Make a strong extension of knots from the loop and make fast its end to the rock by wrapping it around the rock three times and tie it together, then belt the far end of the loop around your waist and grasp a knot. Do not say anything out loud, because you are not worthy to speak to Ghäd'. Step into the pool up to your neck, whisper your pleas to Mīkhäēl or Jäkhäēl, and then drown yourself while keeping your grasp on the rosy knot. If you are not delivered before your last breath, save yourself by grasping the other rosy knots one after another to pull yourself up. Repeat this again and again throughout the day. Do this for thirty-five days. At every rise of dawn, go into the pool, whisper your pleas, drown yourself as long as you can, and then pull yourself up to breathe if you are not delivered by your last breath. Come out of the pool at every fall of dusk if you are not delivered. Always hold fast to your rock with the rosary! In the same manner I will drown myself for up to forty days in the river of the West, five more days than you, or until Ghäd' hears one of our pleas, has pity on us, and gives us our food of everlasting life. If an Ängle does not deliver you by the end, however, stay put on the shore. I will return to you in time."

Ädam gave Ēve further instructions, and after a moment of silence, he said, "O Ēve, take good care of yourself. While in the lake, always grip tightly the roses of your rope, holding fast to your rock. Do not depart from your penitence unless you have verified it is I who has come for you. You will know it is me by the seal of Ghäd' on my golden power rod. Do not trust in words alone; otherwise, you will fall into a trap again."

Ēve remained at the sulphur pool and did what Ädam had instructed her to do, and likewise, Ädam went to the river and repeatedly drowned himself while holding fast to his rock with his grass rosary.

When he was standing in the river, Ädam shouted out, "I say to you: O River of the West, offer to me! Bring me your fish and have them surround me and plead with me, not for themselves but for me, because it is I who has offended Lord Ghäd', not them! He did not keep them away from their food of everlasting life, but I have been kept away from my food of everlasting life!"

After he ceased shouting, a squad of dōghboys from Masonry Company, along with Prince Yhūriēl, gathered downriver at the nearest bend away from the eyes and ears of Ädam. The dōghboys quickly built a barrier which caused the river to calm and the fish to gather and come to the surface around Ädam. The fish raised their noses and opened and closed their mouths repeatedly as though pleading on his behalf. When he saw this as a wonder, Ädam began pleading in unison with them.

After his pleading and drowning for the day, Ädam camped along the river bank and ate fish to renew his strength. Beasts, attracted by the strong smell of dead fish, gathered from all parts of the land and were standing like a wall around him. Each of them raised its nose and made a noise as though it too was pleading on behalf of Ädam.

13

Shätäniēl looked for Ädam and Ēve in the cave but did not find them there. He eventually found Ädam immersed and pleading in the zigzag river and Ēve immersed and weeping in the crater lake. Upon seeing Ēve weep, he began to weep with her. Although Ēve had earlier mated with Shätäniēl in the Garden of Änglea, she did not recognize him because he was again within a halo of very bright light.

He said to her, "Hear, you! Hear, you! Hear, you! O Ēve, come out of the lake and do not weep anymore. Cease the sadness and weeping now. Be glad and rejoice! Why are you and your husband so afraid? I bring you good news of salvation. His Highness has heard your pleas and accepted your penitence. Ängles have made an appeal on your behalf. I have come to deliver you from the lake to the food of everlasting life of which you enjoyed in the great garden-dome, the food which you are now weeping for. Come out of the lake now and I will lead you to your husband, whom I have just seen, and in his joy for his restoration he has said to me, 'Go to my lady in the lake and deliver her to me. Have her come with you to me. If she does not agree to come with you, tell her about the occasion when we were on top of the world, how Ghäd' sent his emissaries who took us and brought us back to the cave, and how we laid the chests of säphärōn, frankincense, and myrrh within a niche of the cave.' O Ēve, I am here now, and I will lead the both of you to Shämbäēlle, to the great cedar forest which is not far from here, where food and water of everlasting life have been prepared for you."

Ēve heard and believed Shätäniēl, and came out of the lake. When she let go of her rosary at the shore, she shook her body back and forth like a broad blade of grass in the wind, and her skin was shriveled like a rotting vegetable. She collapsed to the ground and remained there, unable to move. When Ēve had not been able to move for

two days, Shätäniēl nursed her back to life and led her to
Ädam.

When Ädam saw Ēve, he began to weep. He then
shouted out to her, "O Ēve! Ēve! Ēve! Whatever happened
to my telling you to repent? Why have you disobeyed
again? How were you again tempted and overcome by the
adversary of Ghäd'?"

When Ēve heard this from Ädam, she realized who
it was who had persuaded her to come out of the lake.
Overcome by grief, she again collapsed to the ground. Her
sadness, groaning, and weeping became stronger. From
that day on, the distress of Ädam doubled whenever he
saw his wife suffering.

Ädam shouted to Shätäniēl, "O adversary of Ghäd',
I want you to suffer! Why do you attack us for no reason?
What have you to do with us anymore? What have we done
to you? What offense have we done to you!? I ask you
because you pursue us with deception. Why are you mean
to us? You caused us to be banished from the great garden!
Have we taken away any of your power and glory, and
caused you to be without honor? Did we throw you out like
one of our possessions? Why do you trouble us, acting as an
enemy and hunting us in hatred and jealousy?"

With a heavy sigh, Shätäniēl replied, "O Ädam, my
arrogance and sadness have occurred because of you.
Because of you, I was banished from my beloved sanctuary
in the abyss of my damnation, where I controlled the bolt
of splendor and the locks which hold back the seas from the
vaulted earth. The dōghboys of Masonry, having built a
beautiful lodge for me there, used to surround and greet
me. I was then banished to live and work in the wilderness
of this world because of you. However, I am here for you
now to save you from your painful drowning and assist you
in your venture to live and prosper. I will return you to the
clean chamber of Shämbäēlle at the Crest of Säphärōn, the
place where the bärkhs come and go and the place where
you were created, because it is I who created you, remember? My jealous half-brother, Ghädäniēl, forcefully

removed you from me, and now he has abandoned you, discarded you like one of his possessions."

Ädam was further annoyed and said, "You do not know what you are talking about. What have we done to you? What is our offense against you that justifies you having to do this to us? Understand: You have not been harmed or injured by us. Why do you hunt us?"

Shätäniēl answered, "You are naïve, O Ädam. You do not know what you are talking about. Although you did nothing to me, I entered into this predicament because of you. After I created you, I was banished from my undersea lodge at Eäräith Dam and forbidden to walk in the havens of the East. I created you, remember?

"With a purified fang, I infused the wholly royal blood of Sīnhäēl into an egg of this world to create a new spirit-being. After I performed this bonding of life-stock in the Hall of Noble Silver, according to the perfected incantation by my well-endowed half-sister Khätäniēlle, I carefully placed the egg into her womb. Your face and body became like ours! You exhibited a greater degree of understanding than your predecessor. We kept you there to grow in the sanctuary of Mercy, and then you came to Eäräith Dam. You were the Charge of Affairs, collecting and cooking my food, setting and clearing my table, and opening and closing the town. You even journeyed in a throne ship to meet my father, who reigns supreme as our sovereign monarch on Phaëton. Remember? O Ädam, Ghädäniēl has made you forget your first days with me. When Ghädäniēl realized that you were a perfected creation of mine, he dispatched his son Mīkhäēl to steal you away from me and to make you work for him in the garden house, the great garden house which I created before Ghädäniēl ever arrived on this world.

"Ghädäniēl displayed you in a grand assembly of Ängles and boldly announced: 'Here is Ädam! He is an emanation from my righteous side! By an order in my name, he was created as a new spirit-being, a bonded ghōst to replace Sīnhäēl. He is in our image and of our likeness.

After great trials and errors, I have chosen him to become the new shepherd of the hew-brutes in the great garden-dome, because he possesses a good portion of my righteous wholly royal spirit and has proven himself worthy for the task; he is even highly rated by the emperor. Ädam and his hew-brutes will fully take on the chores of the last king and brutes of the vaulted earth. I, Most High Lord, Attorney General, Prince of Princes, Crown Prince Ghädäniël of Emperor Än, do hereby decree and proclaim my ghŏst-son King of the Vaulted Earth! His divine name is Ädam.

"My half-brother carried on and on about how you are his ghŏst-son, how he created you with the spirit of his son. Do you not remember? A red robe was placed upon your shoulders, and a white collar was placed around your neck, and then a golden ring of jeweled horns was placed upon your head! He proclaimed: 'Upon your shoulders is the wooden yoke of the ox dripping with blood, around your neck is the comforting collar of a lamb, and upon your head are the horns of two crystal-fruits, one representing the ranchers and one representing the farmers. The sole responsibility for the änimals, digging and carrying of earth, even the planting and harvesting, now rests upon your shoulders, around your neck, and against your head forevermore. You, King Ädam, now rule over your lessers. You are now solely responsible for their workship, whether it be successful or offensive. If they disobey in any manner, you will be full of sadness, because your life will be dying on a stake in the middle of a rēd bond fire. O Ädam, understand: You possess the highest upgraded version of the spirit of a hew-brute which has been bonded to the wholly royal spirit of my immortal son, Sīnhäēl, who has sacrificed his spirited young blood and will continue to do so every sign-age to free himself and his former subjects from a horrible death in rēd bond fires because of their fiery rebellion. A good portion of his wholly royal spirit now courses deep within your bones. You, King Ädam, are a purebred aspect of mine!' Ghädäniël then commanded all of the assembled Ängles, 'Bow down before Ädam, King of the Vaulted Garden, whenever you see him. Watch over and protect him as one of my own sons.'

"The assembled Ängles grumbled and murmured. Mīkhäēl was the first to bow down, and then he said to me, 'Lord Shätäniēl, bow down before Ädam. Bow down before the wholly royal ghöst as Lord Ghädäniēl has commanded.' I answered him, 'Go away, Mīkhäēl. I will not bow down to this creature.' Because Mīkhäēl kept insisting I bow down, I said to him, 'Why do you keep insisting I bow down? How can it be proper for me to bow down before him? I will not bow down to an inferior and younger being than myself. I am the senior in the creation! It is I who created this man. Before this man was made, I was already born. Your grandfather the emperor determined and proclaimed me Surgeon General; it is its duty to bow down to me!' When my legion heard this, they agreed with me and also refused to bow down. Mīkhäēl became very angry and demanded I bow down or else. He said, 'If you do not bow down, Ghädäniēl will become very upset and banish you from the haven here in the East, even your lodge in the abyss of Eäräith Dam.' I said, 'If he banishes me from the haven here in the East, even my lodge in the abyss of Eäräith Dam, I will become his nemesis—I will become Most High Lord of the Wilderness!'"

After a moment of silence, Shätäniēl continued to explain himself to Ädam, who was now mesmerized by his words.

Shätäniēl said, "My jealous half-brother, Ghädäniēl, did become upset, and my legion and I were banished from the beautifully terraced earth and my lodge in the deep of the dam. We were banished to live and work in this rough wilderness. O Ädam, understand: My legion and I were banished from our rightful luxury; we had to sacrifice it all because of you! When we realized this had occurred because of you, we suffered immediately with sadness and pain, because we were so accustomed to the joy and luxury there. I then prepared a clever plan. Because Ghädäniēl had commanded you not to partake of

the spiritual tree of eternal life, not to place your serpent
into the rēd zōne of Ēve, I arranged for your first mating
with Ēve there. When you both performed my bidding, this
greatly angered Ghädäniēl and estranged him from the
happiness you brought to him, just as he had estranged me
from the happiness you had brought to me.

"When Ghädäniēl ascended the Mount of *Glōry* for
an assembly of his Ängles, I crept into the garden house
and found Ēve away from you. I showed her the fruit of the
fig tree and explained how its seed could generate a
seedling, which in turn could generate another seed and
another seedling, forever and ever. I explained how the
seed of the fig transfigures itself into a seedling and how
more seedlings branch out and become one grand and eternal spiritual Tree of Life, but only if properly planted and
nurtured in a fertile womb. I explained to her that you possess seed like the fig and that she possesses a fertile womb
like the earth, and that the purpose of your serpent is to
plow and sow your seed into her fertile womb, that her
womb is suppose to swallow the seed like those of the fig
and nourish a seedling like those of the fig. I explained to
her that the sowing of the seed of your flesh by the plowing
of your serpent into the furrow of her flesh would produce
an image in flesh of the both of you together, a seedling of
eternal life for the both of you to possess, that, in this manner, her spirit and your spirit would live forever and ever
in a Tree of Life. This was my solemn promise to Ēve, and
that her and your spirit would live forever and ever just
like the spirit of Ghädäniēl lives within his sons and
within Ädam. Because Ēve was a bit confused, I offered to
show her and she agreed. I climbed up the wall with my fig
in hand, and I bent her down like the branch of the fig tree
and demonstrated the act of mating for her; she opened her
womb and swallowed the seed of my fruit, but not before
swearing an oath to mate with you in the same manner. I
encouraged the male hew-brutes to do as I did, but with
the female hew-brutes instead, and we all intensely
enjoyed ourselves! The female hew-brutes opened their

wombs and swallowed the seeds of eternal life as Ēve and I had done.

"After I gave Ēve further instruction, she quickly ran to the orchard of the fig trees and called out to you to join her there. Ēve desired to explain everything about the fig that I had said to her, even that your fleshy fruit with its seed does not cause death but rather eternal spiritual life like Ghädäniēl. Ēve greatly desired to swallow the seed of your fleshy fruit into her womb. She indeed told you about the knowledge and promise of the eternal spiritual Tree of Life. You understood the wisdom of my words through her mouth, and while believing in my promise, you and Ēve freely engaged in mating beneath the fig tree. O Ädam, you do remember, do you not, Ēve seducing you and you mating with her against the law of Ghädäniēl? O Ädam, by your mating with Ēve, you will become the beginning of a new kind of nation, the root of a wholly royal, pure, eternal spiritual tree of created life, and your kind will accumulate knowledge for better or for worse, just as Ghädäniēl had feared and in accordance with my clever plan. Therefore, your spirit will live forever and ever as a result of my deed with Ēve—I promise you! When Ghädäniēl banished you from the great garden house, he gave you the freedom to choose the fate of your body and spirit. With your newfound freedom, you no longer have to submit to his will—you no longer have to obey his command! He has tossed you away! You are free to choose whomever Most High Lord you wish to watch over and protect you. However, O Ädam, truly understand: There are only two Most High Lords on this world. You must choose between Ghädäniēl and me—Shätäniēl. You should now invoke the name and number of Ghädäniēl if you desire to return to him as a slave in the vaulted garden, or you should invoke my name if you desire to join with me as a free man in the wilderness."

When Ädam heard this long discourse from Shätäniēl, he cried out to the sky, "Father Ghädäniēl, Your Highness! Our life is with you in your great garden! We, your images, desire your eternal light! This land of dark nights is where your adversary hunts us. Vanquish your adversary, he who wants to lead us astray from you. Give us the eternal light of day from your great garden to overcome the dark of night from his wilderness, the eternal light which he himself has lost! Allow us to return to your great garden now!"

Fearing an intervention from above, Shätäniēl quickly departed.

Ädam, still standing immersed in the river, held fast to his rock with his rosary and continued to plead and drown himself, remaining there in his self-imposed penitence. Ēve remained collapsed on the ground, asleep for three days as though dead.

When Ēve awoke, she said to Ädam, "My Lord, you live. Life has been granted to you because you are innocent, having neither committed the first nor second offense. Because of your pleas and the will of the Ängles, the adversary overcame only me. I understand that I have erred and have been led astray again, because I did not obey your command and the command of Lord Ghäd'. I will now depart from you and journey to the West, staying there and eating weeds and grasses until I die, because from this day onward, I am not worthy to eat our food of everlasting life."

Ädam replied, "Be silent, wife. Do not say anything more. My determination has strengthened my body to endure this penitence. Yes, rise up and journey to the West. Whisper your pleas to the Ängles until I have completed my penitence to Ghäd'. I will then come and deliver you."

Ēve departed to the West, weeping bitterly and moaning loudly. She ended her journey at a promontory overlooking a great sea, resting in a grotto there and whispering her pleas...while she was three months pregnant.

14

While still standing immersed in the river, Ädam petitioned Ghädäniēl, "O Lord Ghäd', you are my maker. You commanded the three great Ängles to go out to the four corners of the earth to gather together consolation gifts for me. You approved of my creation with your Ängles of Authority and Mercy by the wave of your hand. You brought me into your great garden to keep it. You explained all of this and more to me through your son the great Ängle Jäkhäēl. At first, I did not know night or day because I was under the eternal light of your great garden, and neither did the light in which I lived ever leave me to discern the night and day. O Lord Ghäd', you brought to me the änimals from your world, the ox, yak, goat, sheep, bull, ostrich, duck, quail, and others which you had also created by your word before I was created. Your will was that I should give them a name, one by one, associating each with a character name from your Ängles, to appropriately title them by their character from my own decision in regard to the calling of their name, and I did as you commanded. You called me your righteous chosen one. O Lord, you made the beasts and hew-brutes subservient to me. You ordered that not one of them should break away from my shepherding and stay in the garden-dome of minions which you had entrusted to me; however, O Lord, they are now all estranged from me—they mind only their own leaders, paying no attention to me. O Lord, you took the essence from my bone and removed a rib from my spirit to fashion a proper helper for me. When I first laid eyes on her beautiful form, I knew who she was and I said, 'This is one of my bone, one of my flesh, a peaceful completion of everything I have ever wanted; therefore, I will call her Ēvening.'

"It was from your good will, O Lord Ghäd', that you had brought a deep sleep over me and quickly brought her out from my side and kept her hidden until she was complete, so that I did not see how she was made, neither could I witness, O Lord, how your goodness and your sons of Mercy are full of awe and greatness. O Lord, in your good will, you gave us bodies with bright skin and made us two as one. By your grace, you filled our bodies with a good portion of the wholly royal spirit of your immortal son so that we would become neither hungry nor thirsty, nor know what sadness is, nor even a fainting like that of death, and neither suffering, punishment, nor exhaustion. You, O Lord, gave us an everlasting life. You commanded us concerning my fruit which resembles the fig, how we were not to partake of it, because you said to me, 'When you partake of it, you will surely die.' You punished me as you said, and I have been dying ever since. You brought us out into a strange land that causes us suffering, exhaustion, hunger, and thirst. Therefore, O Lord Ghäd', we petition you, please give us something to eat from your great garden to satisfy our hunger, and something to drink to quench our thirst. O Lord Ghäd', we have not partaken of food or water of everlasting life since departing your great garden. Our flesh is dried up, our strength is wasted, and good sight is gone from our eyes. O Lord, in our fear of you, we do not dare gather any fruit of the trees here, because when we transgressed at first, you had spared us for a while—you did not immediately cause us to die; however, if we now partake of the fruit of the trees here without your approval, you might perhaps immediately destroy us and wipe us from the face of the world, and if we now drink of this water without your approval, you might perhaps make a sudden end of us, rooting up your righteous planting of us at once. Therefore, O Ghäd', because I have come to this land with Ēve, we beg of you to give us some honey-fruit from your great garden to be satisfied with, because we hunger for the honey-fruit and all of which we lack from it."

Ghädäniēl had again looked into his vision-sphere and seen Ädam in his misery, his weeping and groaning, and his appearing to take his last breath and truly drown himself; therefore, Ghädäniēl sent one of his emissaries to pull Ädam up from the water, who said to him with a herald, "Hear, you! Hear, you! Hear, you! Most High Lord Ghäd of Än, Attorney General, says to you: 'O Ädam, when you were in my plentiful dome, you had known neither hunger nor thirst, neither exhaustion nor suffering, neither leanness of flesh nor any change of your body, and neither soreness of your eyes. However, because you disobeyed my law, and have come into this strange land, all of these afflictions and trials are coming upon you as your punishment. Now, rise up and go to the West. My emissary will guide you to the bank of a high mountain there where Ēve is weeping. Take her back to your naval.'"

Ädam followed the emissary to a headland of many caves near to the Great Sea where Ēve had found refuge, and then he brought her back to the cave in the heights. Upon their return, they collapsed and quickly began sleeping.

15

Ghädäniēl summoned the Knight of the Garder who was keeping the garden-dome secure with his fearsome appearance and firearm, and ordered him to gather two sacks of figs and deliver them to Ädam. The knight obeyed, and when he delivered the figs to Ädam, he tossed the two sacks from a distance because of the fear that Ädam had had of him at the great garden gate, and because of the repugnant odor of Ädam and Ēve. At first, the Ängles had trembled at the presence of Ädam, fearing him. Now, however, Ädam trembles before the Ängles, fearing them.

Ädam stepped cautiously toward the sacks and took one, and in turn, Ēve went and took the other one. As they each lifted their sack, they looked inside them and knew that the fruit was from the trees among which they had transgressed. Ädam and Ēve wept until their eyes were bloodshot.

Ädam said to Ēve, "Ghäd' is so cruel. Do you see these bitter fruits from the trees among which we had transgressed and then lost the eternal light? We now do not know what misery and suffering may come to us from eating these again. O Ēve, we must keep ourselves away from eating these figs. I will ask Ghäd' to instead give us sacks of honey-fruit from the trees of everlasting life."

In this manner, Ädam and Ēve refrained from eating the figs. Ēve sat down, but Ädam went forward and began begging to Ghädäniēl, asking him to give them sacks of the honey-dates instead of the trifle figs.

He said, "O Lord Ghäd', after we disobeyed, we were washed out of your garden-dome and away from your eternal light; you made us come out of it. O Lord, we disobeyed for only a short while, and all of these afflictions and trials have been upon us now for many moons. Do not these many moons rēdeem our short while of disobedience? O Lord, please look at us with an eye of pity and do not avenge yourself of us because of our disobedience. O Lord, please give us our food for living, the sweet dates of the trees of life, not the bitter figs of the trees of death, so that we may eat them and live, and not turn to see sufferings and other afflictions in this wilderness, because you are the Lord of Lords, Lord Commander of the Ängles of Authority and Mercy.

"When we disobeyed, you made us go out through the green door, and you sent a Knight of the Garder to separate us from our food of everlasting life; otherwise, we would journey back through the green door and partake of the milk-goats and honey-dates and live rather than die. We would have known nothing about exhaustion. O Lord Ghäd', understand: We have now endured these many moons and have suffered many afflictions. Make these many moons our full payment for the short while of our transgression."

Ghädäniēl sent Mīkhäēl to Ädam, and Mīkhäēl heralded, "Hear, you! Hear, you! Hear, you! Most High Lord Ghäd of Än, Attorney General, says to you: 'O Ädam, in regard to the land of milk-goats and honey-dates, I will not give it to you until the pentagram of the covenant is complete and your trust of gold in my name and number is fully filled. Only then will I give you the land of milk-goats and honey-dates for everlasting life. The many moons which have passed since you departed cannot atone for the time of your transgression. O Ädam, I give you the bitter fig to remind you of your transgression. Eat it, you and Ēve, because it will sustain your life. I will not turn away from any of your requests, and neither will I disappoint any of your hopes. However, you must endure the term which I have determined for you.'"

Ghädäniēl then withdrew Mīkhäēl from Ädam.

Ädam returned to Ēve and said, "O Ēve, rise up and take your sack of figs, and we will go into the cave."

In the cave just before sunset, they were longing to eat the food, but Ädam said to Ēve, "I am afraid to eat this fig. I still do not understand what will happen to me if I eat it," so Ädam wept and stood pleading again, saying, "O Lord Ghäd', satisfy my hunger without having to eat these figs. I do not understand what will happen to me if I eat them, because after I have eaten them, what will they give me, and what will I desire and ask of you, O Lord Ghäd', when they are gone?"

Ädam continued, saying, "I am afraid to eat it because I still do not understand what will happen to me by it."

Mīkhäēl returned to Ädam and said, "O Ädam, why did you not have this dread, this restraint, this care, or this fear before you decided to disobey the Law of Ghädäniēl, which caused you to come and dwell in this wilderness where your body cannot survive without the food of everlasting life to strengthen it and restore its charge?"

Ghädäniēl then withdrew Mīkhäēl from Ädam.

Ädam and Ēve took their sacks of figs and laid them atop the chests of treasure in the niche of their cave. The weight of the figs was quite great; the fruit in the

garden-dome was much larger than the fruit in the wilderness of Shätäniēl. Ädam and Ēve remained standing and
restrained themselves from eating until morning dawned.

Ädam and Ēve were pleading to Ghädäniēl when
the sun rose, and then Ädam said to Ēve, "O Ēve, come, we
will go to the border of the lowland, to the place where the
river of the West parts into four headstreams. There, in the
same manner as before when we were pleading for some
honey-fruit, we will plead for him to give us the water of
everlasting life, because he has not given it to us in the
same manner as with the fruit."

Ēve agreed, and they both rose up and came to the
border of a lush valley and upon the brink of a brook. They
stood over the Brink of Exhaustion, Ädam pleading out
loud to Ghädäniēl and Ēve whispering to Mīkhäēl, both
begging for Ghädäniēl to look upon them this once to forgive them of their transgression and to grant them their
request.

Ädam pleaded, "O Lord Ghäd', when I was in your
great garden and saw the honey-water which raced
beneath the ground, I partook freely of it and did not
thirst; I did not know thirst because I was always living
rather than dying. When I saw the honey-fruit growing on
the trees, I partook freely of them and did not know
hunger, either. O Lord Ghäd', I am dying. My flesh is
parched with thirst. Please give me the honey-water of
everlasting life from your great garden so that I will start
living again. Of your Mercy, O Lord, send an emissary to
save me from these plagues and trials. If you will not let
me dwell in your great garden, please bring me into a different land, a land of living where I can rest in peace."

Ghädäniēl heard the pleas of Ädam and dispatched
Mīkhäēl back to him, who heralded, "Hear, you! Hear, you!
Hear, you! Most High Lord Ghäd of Än, Attorney General,
says to you: 'O Ädam, in regard to bringing you into a different land, a land of living where you can rest in peace,
there is no other land than this except for the land of my
Ängles. I cannot have you enter any of that land until your

day of maturity arrives and your trust in my name and number is fully filled. I will then take your spirit and soul into my realm and give it the life and rest which you now ask for. In regard to bringing you the water of everlasting life from my great garden-dome to drink and to start living instead of dying, I also cannot give it to you now. When your day of maturity arrives, and after your khrīst descends into the bowels of Three Dog Mountain, breaks open the seven gates of brass and shatters to pieces its shackles of iron, I will then give you the food and water of everlasting life from my great garden-dome, and only then will I, through your khrīst, save your spirit and soul, giving it the rest of eternal life. This will only occur when the final sign-age of assessment and judgment comes, and when and if your trust in my name and number is fully filled.

"'O Ädam, when you were in my garden-dome, these afflictions and trials did not come to you, but since you disregarded my law and mated with Ēve, all of these sufferings have come to you. Now your body yearns for the food and drink to survive—remember this. Now, drink often from the cool, clear, sweet water which falls from the sky and flows before you and beneath you here in the wilderness.'"

Ghädäniēl then withdrew Mīkhäēl from Ädam.

At the Brink of Exhaustion, Ädam and Ēve praised Ghädäniēl, partook of the sweet water of the brook, and then journeyed back up.

16

Returning in midday from their trip down to the Brink of Exhaustion, Ädam and Ēve came over a ridge and saw a large fire near the opening of their cave. They became full of fear and stood still as if frozen.

Ädam said to Ēve, "What is that fire by our cave? We did not do anything in the cave to start this fire. We neither have bread to bake, nor any soup mess to cook there. We do not know the like of this fire; neither do we know what to call it. Ever since Ghäd' placed the Knight of the Garder with a fiery stick which flashed fire in his hand, of which we greatly feared and fell, have we ever seen the like. But now, O Ēve, understand: This is the same fire which had come from the fiery arm of the knight, which Ghäd' has now sent here to keep us away from the cave in which we dwell. O Ēve, it is because Ghäd' is angry with us, and he will drive us away from this place also. O Ēve, we must have disregarded his law in another manner, because he has sent this fire to the cave to prevent us from going back into it. If this is really so, O Ēve, where will we dwell, and to where will we flee before the faces of his adversary, because he will not let us now return into his great garden, and he had deprived us of the good things in there and has placed us in this cave where we have endured darkness, trials, and hardships until at last we had found comfort in there? However, because he has brought us out from his great garden and into this land, who knows what may happen in there, and who knows that the darkness of another land may be far greater than the darkness of this land? O Ēve, if we go to another land, who will know what might happen there by day or by night? Who will know whether it will be far or near? Wherever it will please Ghäd' to put us next, it might be farther from his great garden or where he will prevent us from listening to his words, because we have transgressed again, and because we always make requests of him. O Ēve, if Ghäd' will bring us into a strange land other than this in which we had found consolation, it must be to put us to death, rooting us from off the face of the world. O Ēve, if we are farther estranged from the great garden and from Ghäd', where will we find him to ask him to give us more of the crystal-fruits and seed-fruits of everlasting life? Where will we find him to comfort us a second time? Where will we find him so that he may think of us and the covenant which he made with me?"

Ädam said no more, and he and Ēve kept staring at the flaring fire.

This fire was from Captain Rāphäēl. He had gathered dead trees and dried grasses, brought them near to the cave where the hew-brutes had stockpiled some gold oregon, and set fire to the fuel to separate the gold from the rock. This fire lasted from midday to evening.

Ädam and Ēve were still standing and staring at the fire, unable to come near to the cave from their dread of the fire. Rāphäēl kept bringing trees and throwing them onto the fire until the flames rose higher than the opening of the cave. Ädam could not curse the Ängle, because he knew the Ängles were no longer required to bow down to him since he had been banished from the great garden.

Mīkhäēl arrived and heralded, "Hear, you! Hear, you! Hear, you! Most High Lord Ghäd of Än, Attorney General, says to you: 'O Ädam, this is how you must separate the gold from the rock.'"

Mīkhäēl brought them closer to the fire and gave Ädam further instruction before departing. The fire went on burning as a coal-fire the entire evening. When Ädam and Ēve saw that the heat of the fire had somewhat cooled, they walked toward the cave to go inside, as they had wanted to do but could not because of the heat of the fire; however, they stopped early and wept, because the heat of the rocks began to burn their skin as they walked upon them, and they became very afraid.

Ädam rose up and pleaded, "O Lord Ghäd', look, this fire with its heat has separated us from the cave in which you ordered us to dwell, but now, see, we cannot go into it."

Ghädäniēl heard Ädam and sent Mīkhäēl back, saying, "O Ädam, look carefully at this coal fire. See how different the flame and heat of it is from that which was in the great garden. See the gold within the embers! This purifying fire, along with its smoke, will also keep dangerous beasts away from you,'" and then Mīkhäēl cleared a path through the coals to allow them to safely reenter the cave.

17

Ädam and Ēve stood inside the cave, begging to Ghädäniël the entire night. When the sun came up, they both went outside. Their heads were wavering from their heavy sadness and from not knowing where to go in the day. The coal-fire had died, and Ädam decided that they should explore more of the rēdland in the West. With his golden walking stick in his right hand and the hand of Ēve in his left, Ädam led a trek along the border of the moist and grassy land. Suddenly, however, two ravenous lions came swiftly galloping toward them, one from the right and one from left, wanting to break them into pieces and devour them. Ädam turned his head both ways but then stood still in fear as if quickly frozen. To both their further astonishment, Mīkhäël suddenly appeared and held the two lions at bay.

Mīkhäël said to Ädam on behalf of Ghädäniël, "O Ädam, what are you looking for in this land of the West? Why did you decide to leave your dwelling place in the East? Turn back now to the safe place of the rock-dome and do not ever again venture to this low place."

It was in this manner that Ädam trekked to the low-land and then recovered himself back in the cave.

18

Ēve was showing her pregnancy, but she did not know what it was. She began to feel strange but did not wish to trouble Ädam. She believed Ghädäniël was preparing for her to die on account of her offenses; therefore, she asked Ädam if she could go alone to a cave farther along the heights to the West to plead in solitude to the Ängles for a few days.

Ädam agreed and she departed. Instead of stopping at the cave, however, Ēve continued on in a long journey and stopped at the peaceful place overlooking the Great Sea, the place of the grotto where she had earlier stayed while Ädam was drowning himself in the river during his last days of penitence. She sat down and wept as she gazed out toward the horizon of the sea, and then she whispered her pleas.

When the day arrived for Ēve to give birth, she became upset with pain and cried out to the sky, "O Father, O Lord Ghäd'! Have pity on me! Help me!"

Days and nights passed as Ēve lay weeping and begging. She was not heard by Ghädäniēl, and an emissary from Mercy Company did not come to her.

She finally said in a very soft voice, "Who will tell my Lord, Ädam? I beg of you, you bright ones in the sky, give a message to my Lord, Ädam, during your period of return to the East."

A herald came to Ädam and informed him of the complaint of Ēve, and Ädam said to himself, "O Ēve, once again I fear the adversary of Ghäd' has confronted you."

Ädam was not informed of the true location of Ēve. He straightened himself up and departed from the cave. When he did not find her at the first cave, he surmised that she might have gone farther to the West, to the place where she had gone from him during his drownings in the river, to the place of peace next to the Great Sea. Therefore, Ädam followed the way which he had taken earlier to retrieve her from there, and, when he arrived, he found her in great distress.

When Ēve saw Ädam approaching, she wept terribly and said to him, "My Lord, did you not hear the sounds of my tears? It has been many days and nights that I have been crying toward you. Did the bright ones inform you, since I begged for them to tell you about me? From the moment I saw you, my Lord, my saddened face was refreshed. Please, now beg on my behalf to Lord Ghäd' to listen to me, to look upon me, and to free me from my awful pain, even if it seems fitting for him to send an Ängle of Death to destroy me."

Ädam begged to the sky on behalf of Ēve, and Ghädäniēl heard his plea through the pilot who was watching over and listening to him from the falcon ship *'Hoërūsh*. Twelve Ängles of Mercy Company arrived along with Mīkhäēl, a medical doctor in his own right, and another who was a midwife, both of whom stood at the sides of Ēve. Mīkhäēl stood to her right and touched her on her face and shoulders, and then examined her cervix and breasts to see if she was ready for birthing and nourishing a child.

Mīkhäēl gently said to her, "Ēve, you are honored for the benefit of Ädam, the chosen one and servant of the Most High Lord in the East. As a result of the involvement and many pleas by your Lord, Ädam, I have been sent to give you a potion of love from Mercy. If you had not been brought this potion on behalf of Ädam, you would have grown such a thorn in your side that you would not have recovered from your suffering. Rise up now and prepare yourself to give birth."

Ēve positioned herself as Mīkhäēl had instructed, and she gave birth in great travail to a large boy who was dark and immaculate. After the baby fell into the waiting hands of the midwife, he immediately reached out and plucked a seedling from the ground and gave it to his mother.

The midwife whispered to the newborn, "It is a good thing my Lord did not leave your care in my hands, because I do not wish to help you. You will be an agent of the delinquent and lawless one, a destroyer of the right-eous side of Lord Ghädäniēl. You will represent the adver-sary of Lord Ghädäniēl who pulls up the seedlings of his righteousness and plants the seedlings of wickedness. You will not represent my Lord, who plants the seedlings of righteousness and pulls up the seedlings of wickedness. You will represent the adulterer, who defiled the pure spirit of man. You will be the bearer of bitterness, not sweetness."

Mīkhäēl said to Ädam, "Remain with Ēve until she has done with the child what I have taught her to do."

As the child grew, he ran around everywhere, plucking seedlings and giving them to his mother. Many Ängles described him simply as the Dark-eyed Vassel One—Ibälkhän, or Khän for short—and they all camped in the West, subsisting on food given to them by the Ängles, until Ēve finished nursing.

19

Ädam led Ēve and carried Khän to the cave where they had first dwelled—the Cave of Treasure.

When they arrived, Ädam began to weep and beg, saying, "Father, Most High Lord Ghädäniēl, have compassion on your images, we, the manifestations of your spirit. Allow us a share of something sweet from your great garden to eat for our living, some food which is not bitter like the fig and better than the food for änimals, so that we will not become like änimals."

Ädam and Ēve begged constantly for fifteen days. Mīkhäēl and Jäkhäēl had heard their pleas and were begging on their behalf to Ghädäniēl from inside the acre of his throne ship mount.

Ghädäniēl listened to their pleas and then commanded Jäkhäēl to give Ädam a seventh of the seedlings and farming supplies from the great garden-dome. Jäkhäēl gathered the seventh and secured the load onto reined beasts of burden.

Jäkhäēl ferried all of these provisions by the airy bärkh *Blū Skī*, or *Flying Dutchman*, as it later became known as, and when the last load arrived on the heights, he informed Ädam about what would become of him and his offspring.

Jäkhäēl recited a message from Ghädäniēl: "Plants with thistles and thorns grow where you till; however, you will succeed in growing, harvesting, and cooking food to become satisfied. On my behalf, Lord Shätäniēl will continue to test and manifest the behavior of your Springs of Obedience."

Jākhäēl then presented to them some änimal skins with very rough fur and said, "Shätäniēl and his legion will stalk you, as will dangerous beasts. Therefore, you will cover your bodies with these skins of beasts and adorn them with large thorns to protect yourselves. Also wear spikes and a crown of long thorns. You and your wife will be feared when any of them see you. And you, Ēve, will obey your husband, because he is your Lord!"

Jākhäēl later said to Ädam, "Ghädäniēl had earlier told you that he does not want your wife commanding you, but to obey you. Why have you been obeying your wife?"

Ädam sighed and said, "She is very voluptuous."

Jākhäēl replied, "Yes, indeed, she is very voluptuous. You must watch over and protect her from all lusting eyes. I suggest that you cover her with dark hides from head to toe."

Jākhäēl drove the beasts laden with tools and a diverse collection of seeds and seedlings out through the door of the bärkh and onto the foot of the mountain. He also included separately from Ghädäniēl all kinds of flying and crawling änimals in cages, both wild and tame. Ädam and some of his hew-brutes acquired the reins of the beasts, and then they altogether went to the place of the cave to keep them.

20

Once Khän was weaned, Ädam struggled regarding whether to mate with Ēve again. He was afraid of what Ghädäniēl might do to him if he mated with her again.

One day at sunrise, Ädam said to Ēve, "O Ēve, rise up. We will go up the mountain to the altar and ask Ghäd' concerning a matter."

Ēve said, "What is the matter, my Lord?" and Ädam replied, "I must request Ghäd' to counsel me in regard to mating with you again, because I will not do it without his approval; otherwise, he might make us perish, you and me."

Ēve said, "Why do we need to go up the mountain when we can stand here and make a request to Ghäd'?"

Ädam stayed at the cave, rose up and pleaded, "O Lord Ghäd', you know we disregarded your law and mated without your approval, and from the moment we did, we were deprived of our bright nature. Our body became beastly with hunger and thirst and änimal desires. Command us, O Lord, not to give in to änimal desire without your approval; otherwise, you might bring us to nothing, because if you do not approve of us mating, we will be overpowered by following the counsel of your adversary, and you will make us perish. If not, take our spirits away from us; let us be rid of this änimal lust. If you do not give us your approval in regard to this, separate Ēve from me and me from her, and place us far away from one another. However, O Ghäd', if you place us apart from one another, your adversary will deceive us with his deceptions, destroying our feelings and defiling our thoughts toward one another."

Ghädäniēl heard the pleading of Ädam through his Ängles and sent a messenger who said, "O Ädam, again, if only you had this caution at first, before you came out of my great garden-dome and into the wilderness!"

The three princes who had earlier presented to Ädam the consolation gifts of saffron, frankincense, and myrrh—Mīkhaēl, Ghābraēl, and Yhūriēl—then arrived to provide counsel in respect to his mating with Ēve, saying, "O Ädam, before you can be with Ēve as one flesh, take some gold, make it into a necklace, and give it to her as a gift of betrothal. Then take some incense and a very small measure of myrrh, mix them together with a small amount of sweet water, and present it to her as a fragrant gift."

In this manner, Ädam presented Ēve with a gold necklace, placing it around her neck and dangling it into her bosom, betrothing her with his hands. He then presented her with a fragrant antiseptic gift of incense and an analgesic gift of myrrh, both to anoint herself with. Mīkhäēl then instructed Ädam that he and Ēve must rise up and plead for forty days, at which time Mīkhäēl would return to instruct them further. Ädam and Ēve then stood pleading for forty days, resting only at night.

Mīkhäēl returned and instructed them regarding a sanitizing ritual and a sacred mating rite. Ädam and Ēve cleansed themselves in the pool of sulphur, and then, back in the cave, Mīkhäēl explained to Ädam about his sacred duty to place a pearl of his pure and virile royal spirit into the pure and fertile womb of Ēve. Mīkhäēl next arranged for them to stand side by side, and he gave them further instruction and warnings concerning the sacred wholly royal spirit mating ceremony about to take place. Ädam and Ēve both received the approval of Ghädäniēl and best wishes from his best prince for the success of their mating. Mīkhäēl then administered to Ädam an oath of promise to watch over and protect Ēve, and to remain chaste with her forever and ever; he administered the same oath to Ēve.

Upon completion of their vows of mating, Mīkhäēl said to them, "You must now kiss," and Ēve lifted the skirt of Ädam and kissed him, and then Ädam lifted the skirt of Ēve and consummated the mating right then and there.

It was in this manner that Ädam mated with Ēve again, but this time she conceived from his seed rather than the seed of Shätäniēl.

21

Ädam took an ox with a plow and began to till the rough ground of thistles and thorns, but then Shätäniēl appeared and stood in front of the ox, halting its progress.

Shätäniēl said to Ädam, "My brother has cast you out of Eädam. Well, everything in the earth below the dam may belong to him now, but everything in the wilderness belongs to me; therefore, you belong to me, because I am Most High Lord of the Wilderness, even your creator. If you agree, and you must, you will be allowed to work in this wilderness of mine. However, if you insist that you belong only to my bully half-brother, Ghädäniēl, beg to him now and see if he returns you to the vaulted earth."

Ädam replied, "The earth and the wilderness belong to Lord Ghäd'. I will always plead to him to accept me back into his great garden, but not now, because I am working. Go away, buzzing-fly—leave me alone."

Shätäniēl said, "I do not want you to suffer in your work. I can help you live a happy and productive life. All you have to do to receive my assistance and protection is to solemnly swear an oath confirming that you belong to me."

Ädam said, "I belong to Most High Lord of the Earth and Wilderness."

Shätäniēl was overcome with joy.

Ädam was now in fear, because he realized the implication of what he had just said. He wondered if it were true that Shätäniēl was the Most High Lord of the Wilderness, and he trembled. He expected Ghädäniēl might punish him, but then he was comforted by the thought that Ghädäniēl would probably vanquish Shätäniēl as he had on other occasions, for tricking him.

Shätäniēl said to Ädam, "Well then, solemnly swear in the name of Ghädäniēl to confirm that you belong to the Most High Lord of the Wilderness."

Ädam, in great frustration and anger, swore the oath, believing Shätäniēl would then be vanquished by Ghädäniēl, leaving him alone. He said, "In the name of Ghädäniēl, I solemnly swear that I belong to the Most High Lord of the Wilderness...so help me Lord Ghäd'."

Overhearing this, Ēve rushed to the side of Ädam and said to him, "My Lord, we should beg to Ghäd' now to free us from his adversary. You are in this trouble because of my shame."

Ädam replied, "Ēve, I say once again, because you have repented of your misdeed, I will listen to you because you were created from my side—you are a part of me. We will always rise up together every morning and beg to Ghäd' so that he might free us from his adversary and return us through his great garden gate."

Fearful again of intervention from above, Shätäniēl quickly departed.

22

Ēve gave birth to a girl, whom many Ängles later described as First Bird—Adälläamä, or Adäl for short. A few years later, Ēve gave birth to a second boy, whom many Ängles later described as First Beast—Äbälläamä, or Äbäl for short.

Not long after giving birth to Äbäl, Ēve gave birth to a second girl, whom many Ängles later described as Homely Sleeper—Lūbūddhi, or Būddhi for short.

The first royal family of mankind was living and working altogether on the heights of Three Dog Mountain.

Shätäniēl, as chief scientist of the mission, was very interested in the genetic or spiritual Tree of Life of the hew-man royal family. When Khän and Äbäl matured, he desired that they be assigned a productive task to prove their worth to the mission. As a fair test, he wanted them to be separated not only from the overbearing influence of their father and mother, but also from the influence of each other. He would arrange for Ädam to make Khän a farmer and Äbäl a shepherd and to assign an equal measure of land to each.

Shätäniēl, after consulting the classified Bible of Destinies and Fates, summoned his son Ghābraēl and said to him, "Go and recite to Ädam: 'The Most High Lord says to you: "O King Ädam, separate your two sons from yourself and Ēve and from themselves. Make Khän a farmer and Äbäl a shepherd; I will provide a flock of sheep and goats. O Ädam, understand: Khän and Äbäl must be separated from one another so that one will not influence the other, as a fair test of their obedience. Do not reveal to either of them the reason for this separation, because Khän, as you know, is truly the son of Shätäniël, and you must no longer watch over and protect Äbäl from him for the sake of Ēve. Khän will most likely outperform his brother, but do not feel sad, because I will issue you a replacement son if Äbäl is destroyed.'" Now, Ghābrāēl, go and recite my message to Ädam and have him swear an oath in the name of Ghädäniël not to reveal this plan to anyone!"

Ghābrāēl went and recited the message of Shätäniël to Ädam, and Ädam believed the message was from Ghädäniël, even though Ghābrāēl did not say "Ghädäniël says." Ädam swore in the name of Ghädäniël that he would keep the message a secret; however, he did not keep it secret from his wife, and both felt sad regarding Äbäl, because Khän was very domineering of him.

Ädam assigned to Khän some land to the East below Three Dog Mountain, and to Äbäl some land on the lower eastern slope of the mountain. He taught Khän how to plant and harvest grain, fruit and vegetables, and taught Äbäl how to shepherd and husband änimals. After both of the half-brothers had mastered these tasks, they were taught how to build irrigation canals and durable shelters.

After Ädam taught them how to dig canals, dikes, and ponds, and how to build shelters to store grain and keep flocks, Khän began growing crops and baking bread, and Äbäl began arranging sheep and goats to give birth.

Ädam also taught Khän and Äbäl how to offer gifts of thanks to Ghädäniël. As instructed, Khän offered a tenth of his fresh fruits and bread, and Äbäl offered a tenth of his fresh milk and lambs. Ghädäniël accepted the offerings of Äbäl and ignored the offerings of Khän. Year after year, Khän grew angry and jealous, because only the gifts of Äbäl were being accepted by Ghädäniël. He was also upset about an arrangement by Ädam to take the beautiful Adäl away from him and engage her in a mating rite with

Äbäl, and to take the homely sleeper, Būddhi, and engage her in a mating rite with him. Khän strongly desired Adäl for himself.

23

After a period of drought, Khän observed a flock of sheep grazing in one of his sparse fields and drinking from one of his shrunken ponds. Äbäl was there and seemed unconcerned.

Khän ran to him and shouted, "Get away from my water! Get out of my field! Remove yourself and your flock from my land!"

Äbäl shouted back, "With the way the land is, I cannot control them!" and he would not comply.

Enraged, Khän picked up a stone and threw it straight at Äbäl, hitting him square in the face. Äbäl fell dead. Surprised at what he had done, Khän rushed over and sat down beside him, held the head of Äbäl, and begged him to wake up.

When Khän realized that Äbäl was not going to wake up, he cried out, "Father! Father! What have I done? I have destroyed my brother! I did not mean to destroy him!"

Khän attempted to save the spirit of Äbäl by collecting and placing his spilled blood into his own body. He drank the blood of Äbäl, but he could not keep it within himself and became sick. He was truly naïve and remorseful, crying out even more.

Nearby, Adäl heard his cries, so she rushed over to comfort him. She burst into tears when she saw him holding the bloody head of Äbäl.

When she realized what had occurred, she ran, calling to her father and mother, "O mother! O father!" When they met, she told them what had happened, and then they were all in tears.

Ädam and Ēve shouted, "O my Lord! O my Lord!" and in anguish, they slapped their faces, threw dirt on their heads, and tore their clothes.

They journeyed with Adäl to where Äbäl was killed but could not find his body.

Ädam asked Khän, "Where is your brother?" and Khän replied, "Am I the keeper of my brother?"

On the ground nearby but unseen, two crows cried out, "Khä! Khä!"

Ädam shouted to Khän, "What have you done to your brother? His blood cries out from the ground to the Most High Lord of the Wilderness!"

Ädam rushed over to the cries. When he saw the two crows pecking at the ground, he waived his hands to scare them away. Where the crows were, he discovered the body of Äbäl, murdered, covered in dirt with his blood seeping into the ground. He quickly uncovered the misdeed of Khän, and a group of wild änimals gathered around. As before, when Ädam had been at the river of the West, they raised their noses and made all sorts of noise as though pleading on behalf of Äbäl. Tears of grief fell from Ädam, Ēve, and Adäl, and Khän remained a distance away.

When their tears diminished, Shätäniēl came upon Khän and also asked him, "Where is your brother?" and Khän again replied, "Am I the keeper of my brother?"

Angry at Khän, Shätäniēl shouted, "Do not question me! You have killed your brother and tried to hide your misdeed before me and Ghädäniēl, imagining that we did not see or know of this! You killed your brother for nothing. He spoke the truth to you that he could not control his flock with the way the land is. Both of you should have learned to be thrifty and save provisions for trade. You and your offspring are now forbidden to settle in this place which received the blood of Äbäl from your hand, and you will neither return to the mountain. Your punishment will last for seven of your generations. You will wander as a fugitive in the wilderness of thistles and thorns."

A trembling but bold Khän said to Shätäniēl, "My Lord, Father Ädam caused me to do this, because he is going to take my twinned-sister whom I love away from me and instead give her to Äbäl for mating. My punishment is more than I can endure. Forgive me, My Lord, but you have banished me away from Adäl today, and I will be lost without her. Also, if I wander, I fear some wild beast will destroy me."

Shätäniël had pity on Khän. He decided to put a distinctive feature on his head to help him survive away in the wilderness. A garder quickly fastened the horns of a bull onto a helmet and then placed the helmet on the head of Khän.

Shätäniël commanded, "You will wear these horns until your death. If any dangerous beast should come upon you, these horns will frighten them away. You and your spirit truly belong to me by your misdeed here today."

Shätäniël departed and placed a marker on Khän, betting that he would die at the hand of someone within seven of his generations. In those days, a purebred hew-man could live for thousands of years because of the good portion of wholly royal spirit within every cell of his or her body; the lords of wholly royal spirit live for hundreds of thousands of years, and the upright ape kind indigenous to Phoëton live for only a short period of years. From that day on, Shätäniël relentlessly tested every spirit of mankind, keeping a tally of which spirit-beings were good and which spirit-beings were bad. On his instruction, his captains developed a database consisting of two tables: a Table of the Condemned to record the bad or faulty (evil) ones which would eventually be destroyed in rēd bond fires to the South, and a Table of the Living to record the good ones which would be saved, or rather stored for later use, under a white ice chamber to the North. The spirit of Khän was the first to be entered into the Table of the Con-demned, a list which was colored black on account of the two crows who had witnessed against him. These tables are maintained and protected in a secret place within the haven of the North—the Land of the Living—by the princes of both Shätäniël and Ghädäniël.

24

With tears of grief streaming down his face, Ädam lifted the body of Äbäl from the ground and carried it back to the house which Äbäl had built for his father and mother on the heights of the mountain. However, a terrible odor soon emanated from the body; therefore, Ädam carried it to the cave which he and Ēve had first resided in since their banishment from the garden-dome. He laid the body down inside and rested. After resting, Ädam wrapped the body in cloth soaked with sweet spices and myrrh to mask the odor. In great sadness, he and Ēve stayed inside the cave with the body of Äbäl for many years.

In the meantime, Khän took Adäl without permission from his father and mother. They could not keep him away from his half-sister due to their strong feelings for one another. Khän and Adäl journeyed farther East into the wilderness of Nodimmud, or Nod for short, the Crafter in Mudbrick, an honorary title of Shätäniēl. The ground there was dark and damp and grew many fruit and forest trees. Nod had earlier created another dam complete with a power plant there, a new haven and earth which he could control. It was there in relative luxury from the building of many works where Adäl gave birth to many children by Khän. These children then mated and abundantly populated the land. In his sojourn there, Khän himself created a great city amid the mud which featured great gardens and canals, and great durable shelters for everyone. Many Īgoggles referred to this first city of mankind as Damhouse Irrigated Dwelling Place—Dameäskhūsh. Khän, however, described the city as Land of the Life of Enäkh—Enäkhtiland—in honor of his firstborn son and heir, Enäkh, born by Ädäl.

The seven paternal generations of Khän are as follows: Khän with Adäl sired Enäkh; Enäkh with Adaërha (a sister of his) sired Īrhäkh; Īrhäkh sired Mähänjäkhä; Mähänjäkhä sired Mätthewshälä; Mätthewshälä sired

Lūmäkh; Lūmäkh took for himself two wives (from among
the daughters of Mähällälil, a half-uncle of his): Aidä for
the day and Zillä for the night. Aidä mothered twins:
Jäbälkhän, or Jäbäl for short, who became the lord of those
who live in tents and keep cattle; and Jūbälkhän, or Jūbäl
for short, who became the lord of those who play musical
instruments. Zillä, in her old age, mothered Khōbälkhän,
or Khōbäl for short, who became the lord of those who create things with iron and brass, and she also mothered
Naōmä, a very lovely sister to the brothers.

   As for Ädam and Ēve, they did not mate again
until many years later, when upon the resumption of their
mating, Ēve conceived for a fifth time.

25

   While Ēve was pregnant, Ädam said to her, "Come,
we will take a gift to the table on the altar and offer it up
and beg to receive an acceptable son which we can find
comfort in and join in a mating rite with Būddhi, who has
been waiting a long time to mate. I was promised by the
Most High Lord that if Äbäl were destroyed by Khän, we
would receive a replacement son with a pure spirit, a son
whose color is as ours, who will mate our sleeping Būddhi
and bare enlightened children for our eternal spiritual
Tree of Life."

   They prepared a gift and carried it above the cave
to the altar, which featured a roasting spit made with a
pair of upright longhorns next to the table made with large
stone slabs which Ädam, Khän, and Äbäl had built upon
what Ädam and Ēve had earlier built. While offering the
gift, Ädam begged that it be accepted and that he receive a
son with a pure spirit.

   The very pregnant Ēve said to Ädam, "My Lord, I
wish to go and give birth in the cave farther along the side
of the mountain."

Ädam replied, "Then go, and take Büddhi with you to wait on you, and do not go any farther than the cave this time. Beg to the Ängles to come and assist you in the birth. I will remain here before the body of our slain son."

Ëve listened and agreed. She and Büddhi made themselves comfortable in the cave farther along the heights, and then they began begging to the Ängles while Ädam remained by himself in the burial cave, or Cave of Treasure.

Ädam made another gift, but this time he took it deep within the bowels of the mountain, believing he was away from the eye and ear of the falcon ship *'Hoërüsh*, and away from Ëve and Büddhi. He set up a stone table and offered his gift, begging to Shätäniël to give him a pure-spirited son, an acceptable replacement for Äbäl, as Shätäniël had earlier promised to him. Ädam knew that it was Shätäniël who had earlier spoken the promise to him, and he remembered swearing an oath to the Most High Lord of the Wilderness. Ädam also did not believe that Ghädäniël was the actual creator of creatures of life, even of mankind. He believed in the knowledge of dualism but kept his belief hidden because he greatly feared the anger of Ghädäniël, and he still wished to be received back into the garden-dome of eternal light and living. In this manner, Ädam secretly honored Shätäniël to gain a favor of genesis.

26

Ëve gave birth to a son with perfect body parts and an unblemished skin. His unseen spirit was as pure as it could be for a son from Ädam. His likeness was an expression of his father, and his beauty was like the beauty of his mother. Ëve was comforted when she saw her newborn, and after she remained with him for eight days, she sent Büddhi to Ädam to ask him to come and see the new child.

Būddhi departed and then stayed in the cave by the body of Äbäl in the stead of Ädam. When Ädam saw the perfect body parts and unblemished skin of his son, he rejoiced about him and was comforted.

Ädam gleefully said to Ēve, "Look, I have a perfectly new baby boy, a prince in bright skin for our sleeping Būddhi!"

Many Ängles would later simply describe the child as Foundation, or Seat Spirit, of Mankind—Shäthälmän, or Shäth for short.

After Ädam had seen his son, he returned to the cave and sent Būddhi back to Ēve. He then made a gift of thanks and took it deep within the bowels of Three Dog Mountain, offering it to Shätäniēl and thanking him for giving him an acceptable replacement for Äbäl.

When Ēve had stayed in the birth cave for thirty-five days to honor Mamme, the great white womb-witch Khätäniēlle, she took Būddhi and the child to Ädam, and then they all went down to a nearby spring. Ädam and Būddhi washed themselves of their sadness for Äbäl, and Ēve washed herself and the baby to be clean. Once finished, they returned home and took a gift to the altar above the cave, offering it on behalf of baby Shäth. The gift of thanks was accepted through an emissary, and in return, Ädam received an endorsement and best wishes to them and their baby. After rejoicing, they all went back to the cave.

Ädam did not wish to mate with Ēve for the remainder of his life. He had been given a pure-spirited son to comfort him and Ēve for their loss of Äbäl, and he was also still afraid of provoking the wrath of Ghädäniēl. The only children being born in those days were the dark-skinned ones of Khän and Adäl in the common land below the mountain, and the light-skinned ones of Prince Shäth and Princess Būddhi on the sacred mountain above.

Prince Shäth grew tall and strong and carried on the annual traditions of his father the king, such as repeatedly drowning himself in the river while holding fast to a rock with a rosary and zealously begging to Ghädäniēl to deliver them into his garden-dome of eternal light and living in the East.

27

Many years after he had last mated with Ēve, Ädam was seen by Shätäniēl, who was quite concerned about his separation from Ēve, because the surgeon general was tasked by his father to track and measure the spirits of mankind, to determine which ones were worth saving and which ones were not—which ones may be transfigured into new bodies and which ones may be destroyed in rēd bond fires. The princes of Shätäniēl strove to have Ädam mate with Ēve again, but Ädam kept going onto the roof of the cave every night, sleeping alone there. As soon as the sun would come up in the morning, Ädam would go down into the cave and beg to Ghädäniēl, hoping to receive an honor for his conciliatory deed of abstinence. As soon as the sun would go down in the evening, he would go up onto the roof, because he feared Shätäniēl would have him mate again. Ädam continued in this manner to be apart from Ēve for many years.

When Shätäniēl saw Ädam hungry and begging alone at night, he dispatched a very voluptuous creature to him, one who would later be described by many Ängles as Commanding Ghōst—Lilith—who came in the night and stood before Ädam on the roof.

Lilith, or Lolita, as she was later called, seductively said to him, "O Ädam, I have been watching you in a wondrous vision. While you were living in the cave, I experienced great serenity from you, and I listened to your thoughts. I was comforted by you; however, since you have gone up onto this roof to sleep, I have doubts about you, and I am sad because of your separation from Ēve. When you are on this roof, your thoughts are poured out and your love wanders aimlessly here and there. When you were in the cave, your thoughts and your love were like fire gathered together—they were shown to me by a multicolored Knight of the Garder, and I found pleasure and comfort in them. I also grieve over your children who are separated from you, and I am sad about the destruction of your princely son Äbäl. He was very pure in spirit, and everyone will grieve over a purebred prince. I rejoiced over the consummation of the second emanation of your spirit during your mating for a replacement son, though shortly afterward, I became jealous and sad, because you mated with Ēve, who is my younger, foster-sister, instead of mating with me, who is your equal in the creation. When Lord Shätäniël created you, he also created me at the same time and in the same manner. Do you not remember me from your childhood in beautiful Shāmbäëlle? You and I were created together—we are twins! He created Ēve many years later by removing a rib from your spirit and then placing her with you in the great garden-dome while he kept me, your first true sister-wife. I was very disappointed about you being with my foster-sister instead of me; therefore, Shätäniël made a promise. He said, 'Do not grieve, Lilith. If Ädam ever separates himself from Ēve, I will send you back to him and you will mate with him to bear him children, just as Ēve has given him children.'

"O Ädam, understand: The promise of our creator is fulfilled, because he has sent me here to you! If you mate with me tonight, I will bear you finer and better children than those from Ēve. Moreover, you are still young, O Ädam. Do not end your youth in sadness. Instead, spend the days of your youth in laughter and pleasure, because your life is now short and your trial is great. Be strong, O Ädam, and complete your days in rejoicing. I will take pleasure in you, and you will rejoice with me in an everlasting consummation of this wisdom and without fear. O Ädam, rise up your flesh and fulfill the command of our creator!"

Lilith laid her hands on Ädam. He was aroused by her soft touch, shapely body, unique smell, and seductive words; therefore, he maneuvered himself behind her and attempted to bend her down. Lilith wrestled Ädam down to his back, however, maneuvering herself to be on top of him. She was the firstborn twin and therefore considered herself superior to Ädam. When Ädam realized that Lilith was dominating him so that he could not move, how she had succeeded in mating with him by overcoming him with her strength, he began to zealously beg to Ghädäniël, shouting, "O my Lord Ghäd'! Deliver me away from this she-devil. O my Lord Ghäd'! Save me from this domineering fantasm of the night!"

Lilith felt hurt and humiliated and began also to zealously plea, shouting like a screech owl, "Eä! Eä! Remember your promise! Eä! Eä! Remember your promise!"

She suddenly flew up into the dark sky in a column of light. Astonished at such a sight, Ädam wondered at the power of the name that she had shouted to summon her deliverer. Her screaming incantation was very powerful.

As a result of their mating, Lilith conceived and gave birth to an imperfect, deformed child, and Shätäniël informed her that he must destroy it. Lilith became very angry, confused, and full of sadness. She longed to have a perfect child with Ädam, not only to please her creator, but to please herself. She wished, though, to give Ädam another chance, and Shätäniël agreed, dispatching her back to Ädam in the darkness of another night. Before she returned to him Ädam, however, his days and nights had passed without a message from Ghädäniël. On account of this, and in not seeing any new child of his around, Ädam thought that his encounter with Lilith was simply a dream-vision of the night, and when she reappeared to him and continued to do so for many years, he allowed the succubus to dominate him with great pleasure, relieving him of his beastly passion. In this manner, Lilith kept trying to produce a perfect child, but it was all in vain, because each child born was defective in one way or another, and Shätäniël would have them destroyed. In anger and spite,

Lilith personally destroyed every child she bore, and afterward, she wished to destroy every newborn she could lay her hands on. When Shätäniēl knew of a defective newborn, he would dispatch Lilith to lay her hands of death upon the infant in its crib; this way, he could say that he or an Ängle did not personally destroy the child.

Ghädäniēl revived his interest in Ädam and sent Mīkhäēl to deliver a message to him.

Upon arriving, Mīkhäēl heralded, "Hear, you! Hear, you! Hear, you! Most High Lord Ghäd of Än, Attorney General, says: 'O Ädam, this woman is sent from the rebellious Shätäniēl. Remember, he is not favorably disposed toward you, and he shows himself through this dark she-devil and at other times through other faces. He does this to defile the purity of my righteous wholly royal spirit within you. Remember, he is my adversary! O Ädam, understand: I have saved you before from the tricks of Shätäniēl to show you that I am the commanding Lord of Mercy. Remember, I have determined your fate and the fate of your offspring; you must watch over and protect your spirit, and strengthen your trust in my name and number. I do not wish you harm, and you should never invoke the name of the deliverer of Lilith; otherwise, he will certainly destroy your children in rēd bond fires.'"

Mīkhäēl demanded in the name of Ghädäniēl that Shätäniēl show himself in person, and when he appeared, Ädam became afraid and was trembling before him.

Ghädäniēl himself then amazingly arrived and said to Ädam in a strong voice, "O Ädam, look upon this dark brother of mine. Understand his adulterous behavior and understand that it is he who made you fall from my grace when you and Ēve were in my great garden-dome. You have since strayed many times from the path of my bright son king and into the path of my dark half-brother, Shätäniēl, and from my serenity and rest into his toil and misery. Look at him, O Ädam, he who has said of himself, 'I am your creator!' Can your creator be helpless? Would your creator send a she-devil in his place? Is there anyone more charged than I? Can he be overcome? Look now, O Ädam, and see him restrained by the Ängle of my Law Ministry and unable to move! I command you, O Ädam, do not be afraid of him and instead be afraid of me, Most High Lord, Attorney General! Lord of Lords! Beware and be careful of my half-brother, Shätäniël, in whatever he may do to you, in any of his disguises.

"O Ädam, understand: Shätäniël is the child of a dark concubine, and both are as dark as night. My mother, the fair-skinned Empress Änne, is as bright as day. The impure spirit within Shätäniël is the result of an illegitimate mating. Always remember, he is a fraud and a trickster. My father, who bears the highest wholly royal rank of sixty stars, has determined and proclaimed me Most High Lord, Attorney of Law and General of Business, and I am the Crown Prince of the realm, the legitimate heir who is higher in rank than the rank of forty stars of Shätäniël. O Ädam, you are my security, my bonded ghöst-son, whose primary duty is to trust in my name and number, and therefore, you are responsible to obey my every command. You will resume honoring my titles and the titles of my sacrificed son, Sïnhäël, and resume offering me roasted food and cool drink upon the table of the altar. I will watch over and protect you! You must maintain the perfected balance of springs within your spirit, springs which dwell within every fiber of your body, even your bones. Your spirit was designed to provide me with a domestic hew-man to lord over the domestic hew-brutes, a creature of life capable of understanding and performing commands with honor. Sïnhäël gave his spirited young blood to facilitate your creation and to save his subjects from a destruction of death by rëd bond fires. You, the ghöst-being of Sïnhäël, must be prepared to make the same sacrifice someday. I am the one who decreed that a pearl of wholly royal spirit must be mixed with a pearl of wholly common spirit to create you through my half-sister, Khätäniëlle, the witch of the West. Watch over and protect the Pearl of Great Price within you, because it is the key to your salvation and the salvation of your offspring forevermore."

Ghädäniēl sent Shätäniēl away and then commanded Mīkhäēl to attend to Ädam, whose body was then strengthened and whose mind was then comforted.

Ghädäniēl further said to Ädam, "Go down to the naval and do not separate yourself from your wife. Captain Mīkhäēl will suppress your beastly passion."

At that hour of the night, Ghädäniēl departed from Ädam and Ēve.

In all of those days, Ghädäniēl did not like any of mankind except for Ädam and Ēve, and he would rather they not multiply. He instead preferred the multiplication of the strong ones, the hew-brutes, so as to increase the production of value.

Ädam praised Ghädäniēl. He believed the attorney general had saved him and suppressed his beastly passion; therefore, he came down from the roof of the cave and lived with Ēve as he had done before, ending the many years of their separation.

As for Lilith, Shätäniēl compensated her loss of pleasure from Ädam by continually dispatching her to whomever sleeping male hew-man she wished to dominate in mating. All of her children would come forth from the pre-dawn twilight trysts, and they were called demons by many Ängles. Out of spite to Ädam, however, she continued to destroy every child of a man which Shätäniēl allowed her to lay her hands on.

28

When Shäth was a youth, he knew the difference between good and evil before Ghädäniēl. During a forty-day period every year, he honored his father, Ädam, by imitating his first penitence. He constantly pleaded while drowning himself in the river of the West, holding fast and eating only fish. All year long he spent his nights pleading to Ghädäniēl for an emissary from Mercy Company and for forgiveness of the misdeeds of his mother and father and his brother and sisters, besides himself. He also cleansed himself in a clean pool before preparing and bringing up his gift to the altar every day, more than his father did. As a result of his devout loyalty and these deeds, Ghädäniēl accepted his gifts every day. Ghädäniēl was quite impressed with this particular incarnation of a bond of royal and native spirit. He saw the body and behavior of Shäth as pure and obedient—without offense. In this manner, the disposition of Ghädäniēl toward mankind began to change.

Shäth continued to accommodate the will of his father and mother throughout his childhood, and when Shäth reached the age of puberty, Ghädäniēl confirmed him as possessing a foundation spirit of a ghōst-house of righteous wholly royal pedigree to rule the wilderness of the world. He said to his son Mīkhäēl, "Let Shäth sow the seeds of my righteous wholly royal blood to produce white carnations in support of our mission."

Mīkhäēl relayed this decree to Ädam.

29

After Shäth finished an offering upon the table of the altar, he stepped down to the opening of the burial cave, where he saw a tall, handsome, bright lord who was held in a column of concentrated light and surrounded above by a radiänt disc of light—a throne ship. This lord of light greeted Shäth with a beautiful smile and began to persuade him with pleasant words.

The lord said to him, "O Shäth, why do you live on this mountain? It is rough, full of stones and sand, and the trees have no good fruit on them. It is a wilderness land without homes and towns, not a good place to settle. This entire area is hot, weary, and difficult. I and countless other lords live in beautiful places on a world other than this world. Our world receives constant light, and our condition is of the best. Our sisters are prettier than any others, and your creator wishes you, O Shäth, to mate one of them. He sees that you have bright skin and that there is not one sister on this world who is good enough in body and spirit for you—only five of your kind is living on this mountain. On our world there are a countless number of spirit-beings more beautiful from one to the other. Therefore, O Shäth, he wishes to take you away from here so that you can see our family and mate with whomever you like. You will live near him and always rest in peace. Your spirit will be cleansed; you will be bathed in the splendor of star-fire powder and become as radiänt and weightless as we are, forever and ever, remaining on our world and resting from this world and its misery. You will never again feel faint and weary, nor ever have to raise a child and beg for an emissary of Mercy, because you will not commit any offense nor be swayed by strong feelings. If you will listen to what the Most High Lord of the Wilderness says, you will surely know that you are his creation, and you will mate with one of his daughters, because with us it is no offense to do so, and neither is it deemed beastly passion. On our world, we have no callous and tyrannical lord like Ghädäniël—everyone is a lord! Everyone is bathed in the splendor of star-fire powder—charged, strong, and glorious!"

When Shäth heard this he was amazed and leaned toward believing the lord.

Shäth asked him, "You say there is another world with other spirit-beings more beautiful than the spirit-beings in this world?"

The lord replied, "Yes. O Shäth, understand: You have heard me, and in your listening you have admired them and their ways."

Shäth said, "Your message and the beautiful description of everything amazes me, but I cannot go with you today, not until I have gone to my father and mother and told them everything which you have said to me. If they give me permission to go with you, I will come. I am afraid of doing anything without their approval; otherwise, I will be destroyed like my brother. However, look, you know this place where we stand, therefore come and meet me here again tomorrow."

When the lord heard this, he said to Shäth, "If you tell your father what I have told you, he will not let you come with me. Listen to me: Do not tell your father and mother what I have said to you; come instead with me today to our world, where you will see beautiful things and enjoy yourself there. Celebrate this day among our children, seeing them and taking your fill of laughter and always celebrating. I will then bring you back to this place tomorrow, unless you decide you would rather live with us, then so be it."

Shäth answered, "I am concerned about the feelings of my father and mother. If I hide from them for just one day, they will be distraught and Ghädäniēl will find me guilty of offending them. Besides, they know that I come to this place to offer a gift, and they will not separate themselves from me for more than a short period. I cannot go to any other place unless they allow me. They treat me most kindly because I quickly return to them."

The radiänt one said to Shäth, "What will happen to you if you miss being with them for just one night and return to them in the morning?"

When Shäth realized that this lord would not stop talking and would not leave him, he ran up to the altar and spread his hands, seeking deliverance. An Ängle of Ghädäniēl heard his plea and comforted him and then cursed Shätäniēl, who quickly fled.

Shäth stood still and said silently to himself, "The altar of Ghädäniēl is a place to offer gifts, and he is always there. His column of light will engulf the gift. His adversary will not be able to harm me and not be able to take me away from here."

Shäth came down from the altar and went toward his father and mother, whom he found coming toward him, longing to hear his voice because he had been away for too long. He began to tell them what had happened to him from the lord of the other world. When Ädam heard his account, he kissed the face of Shäth and warned him against the lord, telling him the lord was the adversary of Ghädäniël in disguise who had appeared to him.

Ädam took Shäth to the burial cave, where they then rejoiced. From this day on, Ädam and Ëve never parted from Shäth to whatever place he might go, whether for his offering of a gift or for anything else. This test of obedience by Shätäniël occurred to Shäth when he was a youth. Shäth promised to his father and to Ghädäniël that he would remain pure and obedient for the rest of his days. After this confirmation of loyalty, Ädam wished him to mate, because he feared Shätäniël would otherwise appear to him again and overcome him in another test.

Ädam said to Shäth, "O my son, I wish that you should mate with your sister Büddhi so that she can give you pure and good children who will continue your spirit in this world in accordance with the command of Ghäd'. Do not be afraid, O my son, because there is no disgrace in this. I wish for you to mate with her; otherwise, the adversary of Ghäd' may overcome you with his trickery."

Shäth did not wish to mate Büddhi; however, in loyalty to his father and mother, he did not say a word against it.

30

After Shäth had cleansed himself, Ädam took him into the cave and explained to him his sacred duty to place the pearl of his pure and virile wholly royal spirit into the pure and fertile womb of his wholly royal sister-wife. Ädam had earlier explained this to Büddhi, and after she had cleansed herself, he summoned her to come into the cave. When Shäth and Büddhi were side by side, Ädam instructed them further concerning the ritual of spiritual purity about to take place, and then he gave his approval and best wishes for the success of their mating. He then administered an oath of promise that they watch over and protect one another forever and ever.

Upon completion of their vows of mating, Ädam said to them, "You must now kiss," and they kissed and consummated the mating.

The long wait of Būddhi to mate had ended. She conceived and gave birth to a son whom many Ängles later described as Noble Emanation—Enōish.

Afterward, many brothers and sisters were born to Shäth and Būddhi.

When Enōish matured, he mated with his half-sister, Naōmä (not the same Naōmä as the daughter of Zillä in the line of Khän; many hew-man names were generic, prescribed by the Ängles, who keep meticulous records of the family trees of mankind). Ädam administered the ritual of spiritual purity to them in the cave, repeating word-for-word the same mating rite that he had performed for Shäth and Būddhi. Enōish then sired a son whom many Ängles later described as Vassel One Noble—Khänen.

Khänen matured and mated his sister Mūjälūthew. He sired a son whom many Ängles later described as Great Water Law Commander—Mähällälil.

These purebred men were born and mated while Ädam was still living, and they lived altogether on the heights of Three Dog Mountain.

Many years had now passed since Ghädäniēl had commanded his sons Mīkhäēl and Jäkhäēl to drive Ädam and Ēve out and away from the vaulted garden in Eädam. Mähällälil, the great-great-grandson of Ädam, had matured. He loved pleading to Ghädäniēl, drowning himself, eating fish, helping his kindred, and becoming like his forefathers, until the last day of Ädam came near.

31

When Ädam realized that his last day was near, he summoned Shäth, who then came to him in the cave where he was then living, and he said to him, "O Shäth, my son, bring me your children so that I may honor and speak to them before I die."

When Shäth heard this from his father, he began to weep, and then he departed. He gathered the entire family into three groups, arranging them around Ädam in the corner of the cave where they would sometimes honor and praise Ghädäniēl. Ädam saw them as they arrived and began to weep. When they saw him weeping they bowed and began to weep with him.

They asked him, "Why did you summon us, Father, and why do you lie in your bed here?"

Ädam answered, "O my sons, I am ill and in pain."

All his great sons then asked, "What does it mean, Father, this ill and pain?"

Shäth said, "My Lord, have you perhaps been longing to eat the honey-fruit of the great garden in the East and therefore now lay in sadness? Tell me and I will go find the garden-dome, throw dirt on my head, bow down, and beg and weep with a loud wailing to Ghäd'. He then might listen to me and send an emissary to bring me the honey-fruit for which you have longed."

Ädam replied, "No, my son, I am not hungry. I feel weakness and great pain in my body."

Shäth asked, "What is your pain, my Lord Father? I am not familiar with it. Please do not keep it from us. Instead, tell us about it."

Ädam answered, "O Shäth, my son, listen to me. Your mother and I were placed in the great garden of Ghäd' to lord over the hew-brutes in their digging and carrying the earth from every canal, dike, field, and orchard, and their tilling the ground and harvesting its bounty. We were given every plant bearing fruit to eat except for the fruit of the flesh, which resembles the fruit of the fig tree. I, with the labor of the brutish males, was the caretaker of the vegetables and fruit trees in the North, and Ēve, with the labor of the brutish females, was caretaker of the vegetables and fruit trees in the South. Ghäd' had forbidden us from mating. He did not want us to know about good and evil; otherwise, we would become troublesome. If we did, we would certainly die a spiritual death.

"Ghäd' gave us two of his princely sons, the great Ängles Mīkhäēl and Jākhäēl, to watch over and protect us in his great garden. However, when a regulated time arrived, they and the other lords ascended a great mount to receive counsel from Ghäd'. His adversary Shätän' immediately took an opportunity concerning us. While Ghäd' and his Ängles were away, Shätän' crept into the garden-dome and climbed a terrace wall. He found your mother away from me and tricked her into mating with him, and then her with me. He promised that her life-spirit would not die and instead would gain everlasting life in a spiritual Tree of Life and that her children would inherit the world. Ēve succumbed to his temptation, and she swallowed his seed into her womb. She told me about the promise of the mating and seduced me to mate with her beneath a fig tree. We had just mated when we heard his Ängles descending from the mount nearby. Ghäd' called out for me from the trumpets above, because he could not see me with his many eyes. Your mother and I were hidden from his eyes because we were beneath the low-hanging, broad-leafed branches of the fig tree. We remained there for a while because we did not want to be discovered together. We knew that we had disobeyed his law. Ghäd' kept calling out for me; therefore, I shouted back out of shame, saying, 'O Lord Ghäd', I am here beneath the fig tree!' and he saw your mother and I as we came out, and immediately, he knew what we had done. He became very angry and shouted at me, 'Shame on you! Because you disregarded my law and mated without my approval, you will be punished for seventy of your generations with bodily pains—the suffering of pressure in your

head, eyes, and ears, down to the nails on your toes, and in
every one of your limbs!' Ghäd' commanded this for our punishment and then drove us and the hew-brutes out of the
garden-dome with sprays from sea hoses, banishing us into
this wilderness. These pains of dying are the result of our
great transgression, and they will be passed on for seven
sign-ages through our children. His banishing of us to the
wilderness to experience these torments occurred according
to the plan of our actual creator, the half-brother and adversary of Ghäd'—Shätän'."

32

"O Shäth, my son, listen. I will now tell you what I
saw and heard before your mother and I departed from the
great garden in the East and came to this wilderness in the
West. When I was discovered beneath the fig tree and begging for forgiveness, the great Ängle Mīkhäēl came and
took me up into a wonder, a magnificent bright wheel float-
ing in the black sea above the sky. I was brought before
Ghäd', who was sitting on a magnificent chair. His haloed
face was brighter than fire, so bright that I could not keep
looking at him, but I saw hundreds of Ängles to the right
and to the left of him. When I saw this amazement, I
became confused. Terror affected me and I bent my body to
the floor. Ghäd' shouted to me, 'Look at me or die! You
have disobeyed an order from your maker, Most High
Lord, Attorney General Ghädäniēl! Instead of obeying me,
you obeyed your wife, a helper-bond, who I also made, and
I gave her to you so that you would not want anything else,
but no, you obeyed her and ignored me! I warned you that
if you ever placed your serpent into the rēd zōne of Ēve,
you would die, so now you will die. You and your helper-
bond, along with all of the hew-brutes, will be driven out of
my great garden house and into the wilderness to die.'
"When I heard these words from the mouth of
Ghäd', I laid myself flat on the floor and surrendered to

him in fear, and then I said to him, 'My Lord, Most High Ghädäniēl, Lord of Law and Mercy, please do not let Ēve and I, who are always thinking about your majesty, be driven away from you, and instead keep us in your great garden, because if we die, your images from the spirit of your son king will not strive within us to serve and speak praises to you. Please do not drive us away from your watching over us and protecting us within your great garden, we whom you have perfected with your righteous wholly royal spirit. Please, do not banish us away from your Law and Mercy, we whom you have fed with your food of everlasting life.'

"A message concerning me came surprisingly inside my head! It was the voice of Ghäd', and he said, 'When you were created, you were not only created to replace my firstborn son, Sīnhäēl, but also for the love and pursuit of knowledge. Your spirit, unseen to mortal eyes, was fashioned to make you understand and obey my orders, to make you lord over the workship of your lessers. The righteous wholly royal spirit springs which made you capable of serving me will never be taken away from you. You and your lessers will now toil endlessly in the tunnels of Three Dog Mountain.' When I heard this, I remained flat on the floor and praised him. I said, 'Most High Lord Ghädäniēl, you are the eternal and supreme master, and every creature gives you honor and respect. You are the true Lord of Law and Mercy, highest and purest above every lord. You are the living, countless, Most High Lord, Attorney General Ghädäniēl. To you, Most High Lord of Havens and Earth, the bodies of the spirits give honor and respect. You rule over all of us with your great Law and Mercy.'

"After I praised him, Mīkhäēl grasped me by my hand and took me away from Ghäd' and away from his throne ship. With his other hand, Mīkhäēl held a golden rod of power, the same as I possess. He pointed it into a hole, and suddenly a tunnel of frozen fire appeared. We went across in the coldness of the fire and into his big wheel whirl-winder. He took me back to your mother in the great garden, and we, with the hew-brutes, were driven out like cattle. I received the Book of the Covenant, and then we were carried aloft in a balloon above the river of dead rēds and the desert of ash to this foothill of the mountain.

"The love in our hearts for Ghäd' deserted us, I and your mother, Ēve, along with the first mating rite we shared together—we forsook Ghäd'. Our honor fled from us. We had entered into another land where there was another brutish kind, the Greygōre goon-dogs of Mineore, a kind which did not come from this world. They were of the kind replaced by the hew-brutes in the great garden; these, though they are giants, were the first digger änts in the mountain, who were then replaced by our banished hew-brutes. With their outside assistance from time to time, however, our knowledge has grown and survived. Our kind will enter into an eternal spiritual Tree of Life in great lands.

"Yes, we forsook Ghäd'. From that day on, we learned about death and dead things, like Äbäl. I then recognized and accepted Shätän', the lord who, in league with his half-sister, Khätän', had actually created us. I served him in fear and subjugation. My heart was darkened; I eventually recognized him several times. His Ängles were no longer strangers to me—I finally remembered that I had once served him during my first years, the years before Ēve and I were in the great garden of Ghäd'. I became bitter and sad and slept away from Ēve in those thoughts.

"However, one day I saw three men before me whose likenesses I was unable to recognize, because they were not Ängles of Ghäd'; they surpassed them in their wonder. The men said to me, 'O Ädam, rise up from your sleep of bitterness and sadness and hear about the land and family of Khän, the one born from your wife and to whom has come a joyous life.'

"When I heard this from the tall men who were standing before me, your mother and I sighed within, and our dark creator came up and stood a distance before us. He said, 'O Ädam, why were you and your wife sighing? I am the Most High Lord who created you, the lord who breathed the wholly royal spirit of life into an egg of this world to manifest you as a bonded wise spirit-being.' Sadness descended upon our eyes like night overcoming day.

"Our dark creator had created a son by himself with your mother in the great garden, because he desired my downfall and knew I desired your mother. This son of his was your elder half-brother, Khän. The vigor of our knowledge of Ghäd' was destroyed in us. Without more of his potions of love we became plagued with weaknesses. In this manner, beginning with our original transgression, the length of our lives was greatly shortened. I then realized that we had come under the law and authority of the Ängles of Death belonging to Shätän', those who collect the life-spirits of the dead for measuring and judging.

"My son Shäth, in regard to these Ängleic men whom I had seen earlier, they returned to me not long ago, and I will now reveal to you what they revealed to me. After I finish my days in this generation, a fury will cause a great wall of water to overflow all of the earth below the havens, and everyone living in it will be destroyed, because Ghäd' will cause it to occur without warning, because we kept him from peacefully resting and we obtained forbidden knowledge. He does not want us to seek or desire anything except that which completes our trust in his secret name and number. But he has approved of the destruction of everything, including our children to whom your mother and I have passed on our knowledge, because he considers our children as strangers. However, Ängles of Shätän' will come hidden in a cloud to bring a collection of änimals of whichever kind pleases him, including birds of the sky, and all the kinds of creatures which I had earlier named in the great garden, along with the life-spirits of many others, and he will place them into a great ärkh of wood where they will be safeguarded from the destruction. The entire multitude of our kind, and the rebellious hōst of

Īgoggles called Gregoriäns, with their polluted descendants, will be left behind to perish. Only then will Ghäd'
rest in peace without anxiety, and new safe havens and
fertile lands will be created upon the world.

"O my son Shäth, I will tell you the rest of this
ancient mystery wisdom, even the oath of your sacred
duty. Listen and remember: Ghäd' and Shätän' do not
watch over and protect everyone; they only watch over and
protect those who are pure in spirit and obedient to the
messages of Ghäd'. As I had explained to you earlier,
before you mated with Būddhi, both Ghäd' and Shätän'
wish us to keep our people pure in spirit, generation after
generation. Their plan is to possess a purebred, servile,
trusting people for their mission on this world. They will
eventually reestablish our royal House of Life on this
world, the purebred spiritual Tree of Life which they will
always watch over and protect forever and ever. The disre-
spectful, those of mankind who refuse to love and obey his
law and pollute the pure spirit, will be punished by Ghäd'
through Shätän' will be the one to punish them. Every created living thing will become a subject of Ghäd'. All will
fall under the command of Ghäd' and will not disregard his
law. We will not change our behavior, but we will change
as a result of ignoring his law. In a great assessment, our
creator Shätän', under the Law Ministry, will separate the
corrupt from the uncorrupt, the legitimate from the illegitimate, the mongrels from the purebreds, dividing those
who have strayed from the spiritual path from those who
have kept to the spiritual path. The bodies of the pure in
spirit will then be transfigured to radiate like the Ängles
before him. The offenses of the purebreds will be forgiven
and their spirits will be kept in a clean chamber with purified water, a bathing which our creator uses to keep alive
the spirits and to prepare them for re-embodiment. The
uncorrupted spirits of the world will be afforded a new
beginning.

"When each spirit is examined by the measurer of
Shätän' and Ghäd', and when the final sign-age of assess-

ment and judgment occurs, when his majestic throne ship *Glōry* is seen by all, those of us who chose the spiritual path of disobedience will be collected and cast into rēd bond fires by the Ängles of Death. Those who have received and kept pure the pearl of great price will be joyful, because their spirits will be delivered and saved for a glorious re-appearing of his throne ship.

"O my son, you understand the world. It is full of sadness and weariness, and you understand what has occurred to our people from its trials within it. You are wise, O Shäth; therefore, when I die, my wholly royal authority and law are passed on to you by bestowing upon you an oath of responsibility, an oath of sacred duty, and the receiving and care of the golden rod of splendor. You must carry and keep safe the power rod and swear to stay innocent of corruption, to keep our offspring pure in spirit, to stay just, to keep building our trust in the name and number of Ghäd' and not be overcome by the deceptive tests of Shätän'. You must keep these commands that I give you today, and when you see that your death is near, give them to your firstborn son, Enōish. On that day, instruct Enōish that when he sees that his death is near, he must bestow the royal oath of sacred duty to his firstborn son, Khänen, and Khänen to his firstborn son, Mähällälil, and so on and so on, so that the covenant and our trust in Ghäd' will be fully filled by our descendants before the final end time of the five Great Years.

"O my son Shäth, when I die, you must take my body and wrap it in cloth soaked in myrrh, aloes, and cassia, and leave it deep inside this cave where these and other precious supplies are stored for safekeeping. After my internment, and as I had mentioned earlier, there will be a great flood come over all the earth below the havens. An abundant wall of water will overwhelm all of the land and every living thing within it. Only a few of us will be spared. Before the flood arrives, those of whom it will spare from among your children must take my boxed body with them out of this cave, along with the chested gifts of säphärōn, frankincense, and myrrh. When they have taken it with them, the eldest among them must command his children to lay my boxed body and the chested treasure in the great ship of wood and keep it there until the flood-waters have subsided and they come out. After they are saved, they must take my boxed body along with the chested treasure and lay it to rest in peace within the cap-ital of Shāmbäēlle, at a secret naval which an Ängle of Shätän' will show to them. This will be a place where the Ängles arrive and depart to collect and save chosen spirits.

"O my son Shäth, place yourself now at the head of your people. Be their leader, teacher, administrator, shep-herd, and king. Tend to them. Watch over them in the fear of Ghäd'. Lead them in the pure, spiritual path through the sacred wholly royal spirit mating rite—keep the pearl of the bond of wholly royal spirit safe within them and their children. Command them to honor my first penitence every year, to honor the forty days. Make them understand that they must not be overcome by the tests of Shätän', or he will destroy their spirits in rēd bond fires. Continue the separation of your family from the family of Khän. Do not let them mix or come near to one another either in speech or in deed; otherwise, the spirits of your family will be pol-luted and unworthy before both Most High Lords."

The entire family had now arrived; therefore, Ädam began to bestow his endorsement and honor upon them, first to Shäth and then to the others. He thanked them for allowing him to see them all together on his last day, and then he gave them his endorsement, apprecia-tions, best wishes, and last will and testament.

Ädam turned to Shäth and Ēve and said, "Con-tinue to build our trust in the name of Ghäd', preserve the treasury of gold and the book of the covenant, and the chested gifts of spice, because, as I have said, a flood will sweep over the land, and those of us who will be going into the great ärkh of wood must take with them the gifts with my body. They must then take the gifts with my body to the new resting place of peace and lay it in a secret naval there. In later years, the gifts will be found with my body and plundered. When it is plundered, the gifts must be taken care of with the spoil which is kept. Nothing of it should be destroyed until my spirit returns in a new body from beyond my death. O Shäth, understand: My spirit will be reborn in a flesh-and-blood body which the Lord calls a khrīst, and my khrīst will renew the pureness of mankind at the dawning of every sign-age. My khrīst will plant new seedlings of white carnations in the world, preparing our descendants for the final sign-age of assessment and judgment of the covenant. For the salvation of our spirits, your spirit will also be reborn into a flesh-and-blood body to help me replant the righteousness of Ghäd' in the world. You, my son, will precede my khrīst, gathering and preparing worthy followers. I, as khrīst-king, will return as a messiah and savior to our family, and you as the khrīst-prince will be my appointed administrator to help save the worthy and serve the plan of Ghäd' by reestablishing our pure-spirited reign in the world."

Ädam, tiring, took a brief pause and then said to Shäth, "In the days of our rebirth, the three princes from the East will present to the babe khrīst-king a new supply of säphärōn, incense, and myrrh, verifying to the worthy followers that the babe is indeed the awaited khrīst-king. The princes will bring the säphärōn to represent that the khrīst-king is King of Kings in the world, and the frankincense to represent that the khrīst-king is alive and residing in the world, and the myrrh to represent that the khrīst-king is devoted to the lording over of his nation. Moreover, the säphärōn will represent that the khrīst-king is victorious in the tests of loyalty from Shätän', and the frankincense will represent that the khrīst-king and his worthy followers will abundantly rise up and be transfigured as Saints in the black sea above the sky, and the myrrh will represent that the khrīst-king will tear his face and flay his flesh, and offer up his flesh and blood to Ghäd' on the altar table.

"O my son Shäth, understand: I have now revealed to you a number of ancient mysteries of which the Ängles of Shätän' have revealed to me. Keep safe and secret my command for yourself and for the salvation of our spirits."

33

When Ädam had finished speaking to his family, his suffering with illness became violently painful. He cried out, "I am in agony! What will I do? I am distressed with a pain so cruel!"

When Ēve saw and heard Ädam, she herself cried out, "O Lord above, please give me his pain! I am the one who has offended you!"

Ēve then said to Ädam, "My Lord, please give me half of your pain, because this has happened to you as a result of my own offense."

Ädam said to Ēve, "O Ēve, rise up and journey with Shäth to the head of the River of Petition, to the gates of the haven where Ängles of Mercy reside. When you arrive at the gates, throw dirt on your heads, bow your bodies down, and weep and wail before the Ängles. They might have pity on you both and then might send a messenger to Mīkhäel, who possesses the white-gold Oil of Mercy. Perhaps he will give Shäth a drop to heal me. I might then receive relief from this illness and pain, this khäncer by which I am dying."

Shäth and his mother departed toward Shäm-bäelle, and while they were walking through the high valley along the River of Petition, Shätän' arrived from behind and suddenly grabbed Shäth by his arm, piercing him with a needle. Shäth felt as though he had been bitten by a venomous snake!

As soon as Ēve saw this, she cried out, "Sadly, I am a wretched woman, cursed because I did not honor the command of Ghäd'! All of my descendants will curse me, saying, 'Ēve did not honor the command of Ghäd'.'"

Ēve shouted to Shätän', "Damnable beast! Why have you not been afraid of coming against us, we the images of Ghäd', and have even dared to fight with us?"

Shätäniēl answered, "O Ēve, you are naïve. It is not personal that my anger is directed at you. You are simply a helper bond at the feet of Ädam, who is a bond at the feet of two Most High Lords. Ghädäniēl has deeply and unjustly offended me in regard to Ädam and yourself. Tell me, how are you able to open your mouth to speak? How are your teeth strong enough to bite and eat food? How are you even able to remember yourself as a spirit-being?...You are able to do all of these things and more because of the decisions I made when I created you in the image of Ädam. However, if I now begin kindly to correct your faults, torments, and illnesses caused by Ghädäniēl when he maliciously exposed you to this wilderness, you cannot bear it. Why? Ghädäniēl is not concerned with the wanting and weeping of mankind, but I am, because it is from the spirit of your kind which mingled with the spirit of the Īgoggle-kind that beastly giants have now risen up to rule in the wilderness of this world. Remember how I opened your womb for you to begin your eternal spiritual Tree of Life with Ädam, and acquire knowledge for better or for worse? The spirits of the offspring between the Īgoggles and the daughters of men are greatly polluted—they have become beastly giants! I am trying to solve this mystery."

Shäth said in a raised voice to Shätäniēl, "Ghäd' hates you. Be quiet. Be dumb. Shut up your mouth, you damnable enemy of truth, trickster, confuser and destroyer. Go away from us, we the images of Most High Lord Ghäd', until the day he commands you be brought to justice in the trials of his Judgment Sign-age!"

Shätäniēl said to Shäth, "Yes. As you wish, I am leaving you," and he immediately departed, hurt by the words.

Seeking the mono-atomic white-gold Oil of Mercy to give to the dying Ädam, Shäth and Ēve continued in their journey along the River of Petition toward Shämbäēlle, toward the crest of the high valley of the North— the Crest of Säphärōn. Upon arrival at the gates of

Shērpäppäkh, they threw dirt on their heads, bowed their bodies to the ground, wept and moaned, and begged the Ängles to have pity for Ädam in his illness and pain and to send a messenger with their petition to Prince Mīkhäēl.

After Shäth and Ēve had been begging for days, Mīkhäēl arrived and said to Shäth, "I have been sent to you from Lord Ghädäniēl. He has commanded me to take care of the bodies of your kind. I tell you, O Shäth, you, as a son of Ädam, who is a creature of Ghädäniēl, do not weep and beg for the Oil of Mercy to cure the khäncer of the body of your father, because I tell you that in no manner will Ädam, or any of mankind, receive the Oil of Mercy until your trust in the name and number of Ghädäniēl is complete, which is scheduled for the end time of the final signage of the pentagram of the covenant.

"O Shäth, listen and understand: As your father has already informed you, Ghädäniēl has decreed that your father will be reborn as the khrīst-king and savior of mankind, to serve his mission on this world, to renew the righteous, pure, virile wholly royal bloodline of mankind. You entered into the grace of Ghädäniēl because your behavior has been exemplary. When you are reborn as a khrīst-prince and preparer of worthy followers, you will administer and symbolically drown the followers in the great river of the West in honor of the first penitence of your father, and you will give them each a new name and a new calling. You will be reborn before your father to prepare a pure nation. Your khrīst will be called the baptizier by many. The new you as the khrīst-prince and the new Ädam as the khrīst-king will reestablish the sacred wholly royal rites for the covenant with Ghädäniēl on this world.

"The seal of the khrīst-king and his khrīst-prince will be the representation of the sign-age of the crucifixion of Son King Sīnhäēl. With those whom the khrīst-prince has approved and cleansed, the khrīst-king will be sustained in completing his sacred duty to reestablish the ghōstly wholly royal pedigree of Ghädäniēl and his son, Sīnhäēl, in this world. In turn, the khrīst-king, as a father, and his sons who will become fathers, will gather more worthy followers and approve, cleanse, and anoint the chaste ones to continue watching over and protecting the legitimate wholly royal bloodline of mankind within a the pedigree. The khrīst-king will be called the fisher king, because he will be the king who is fully responsible for the fulfillment of the gold-bonded covenant through the workship of the descendants of the immaculately conceived schools of twin hew-brutes. He will receive the treasured spices to mix with sweetwater to heal the bodies of those whom he deems acceptable before Ghädäniēl. The khrīst-king will also be like a shepherd of choice sheep, and his task will be as a second-chance test of his obedience and trusting in the name and number of Ghädäniēl. He will teach his flock about the legal authority of Attorney General Ghädäniēl and his pure, spiritual path.

"Ghädäniēl will command the khrīst-king to sow his pure seed for his plan to establish an obedient people in new great gardens of safe havens and fertile earths on and beyond this world. The khrīst-king will also reap what he sows. An approved virgin daughter of man will have prepared herself ready to receive his pure seed by cleansing herself in a purifying bath. The khrīst-king will then anoint himself with wholly royal jelly, and they will mate. The khrīst-king will protect his wife so that his son will be born to continue the will of Ghädäniēl. He will have gathered twelve pure-spirited men and engaged them in the sacred wholly royal spirit mating rite with approved virgin daughters of pure-spirited men. The khrīst-king will teach the Children of Ghädäniēl to keep safe and secret the tradition of the sacred mating rite, and he will be solely responsible to ensure that your trust in the name and number of Ghädäniēl is fully filled. If the trust is not complete, the khrīst-king will have until the end of the grace period of half of a Great Year, or 14,400 years, to atone. There will be dire consequences if your trust is not complete by the end of the grace period; if the khrīst-king again falls from the grace of Ghädäniēl, a new covenant of sixty sign-ages will be issued upon him.

"The spirit of Ädam in the khrīst-king, as the most-beloved creation of Ghädäniēl, will be the representative of his Mercy Company in this world. The reborn-Ädam will lead his twelve counselors to a place near the Sea of Noble Salt where the Ängles of Mercy Company will be guiding the reborn-Ädam and his kindred spirits—the Essences.

"Shäth, journey now back to your father, because he will soon die. In six days, his spirit, his essence of life which is invisible to your eyes, will be taken from his body and saved for rebirth. After the Ängles of Death Company have taken his spirit, you will see many wonders in the sky and on the world. You will see a multitude of colorful radiances from sky-wheels and hear a multitude of musical tones from horns. The Ängles will be honoring Ghädäniēl for the pity he has shown to your father."

Mīkhäēl immediately departed, and Ēve and Shäth returned to Ädam with fragrant herbs and spices, like spikenard, crocus, calamine, and cinnamon, instead of a drop of the white-gold Oil of Mercy.

Shäth told Ädam how Shätäniēl had bitten him with venom.

Ädam reacted quickly in anger, saying to Shäth, "What have you done? You have brought a great plague upon us! This, what you have done, and what has been done to you, tell your children about it after my death, because our descendants will be working for Ghäd' and fail as a result of this. They will be tormented in their body and cursing us. They will say, 'Our forebears have caused all of these terrible things to us, those who were living at the beginning.'"

When Ēve heard what Ädam had said, she began to weep and moan.

Ēve later said to him, "O my Lord, tell me, how is it you will die and I will live, or how long have I to live after you are dead?"

Ädam replied, "O Ēve, do not think about this, because you will not wait long after I die. Both of us are to die together; you will be in the place where I will be. When

I die, have Shäth take care of my body, and let no man touch it until a great Ängle of Ghäd' speaks to him about its

disposition, because Ghäd' will not forget my body; instead, he will seek the creature of life that served his purpose. Now, rise up instead and pray to the great Ängles of Ghäd' until I die."

Ēve rose up and went outside and bowed to the ground and said, "O great Ängles of Ghäd', I have offended. O great Ängles of Ghäd', I have offended against Lord Ghäd'. I have offended even against you, his princely sons. I have offended against the Knights of the Garder. I have offended against the fearful and unshakeable throne ship of Ghäd'. I have offended before him, and all offense began through my misdeed in your great garden."

34

When Ädam had finished giving his final endorsements, appreciations, best wishes, and last will and testament to his sons, his limbs became loose, his hands and feet lost power, his mouth became dumb, and his tongue ceased to speak altogether. He closed his eyes and died. His family threw themselves over his body, men and women, old and young, weeping and moaning. Dark clouds obscured the sun. In sadness and distress, Shäth reached above the body of Ädam in a naïve attempt to keep his spirit from departing, and likewise, Ēve searched the ground with her hands folded over her head in a naïve attempt to find the spirit of her husband. Her family wept most bitterly.

Shäth balmed the body of Ädam with sweet spices from trees on and around the mountain. With fine cloth soaked in myrrh, aloes, and cassia, he tightly wrapped the body, boxed it, and laid it to rest in the corner of the cave where the three chests of treasure were kept hidden and safe within a niche. There he also placed a lamp with a fire to be kept always burning, because his father had constantly begged to be returned to the eternal light of the garden-dome of Ghädäniēl in the East. On occasion, frankincense was burned to mask the odor of decay, and to remind visitors that Ädam and his righteous wholly royal family will rise up in abundance and be upgraded into Saints in a haven above the sky. The entire family of Ädam stood there the entire night, weeping and wailing over him until the morning dawned. Ēve, Shäth, Enōish, and Khänen went out and took gifts to offer up to Ghädäniēl, and they came to the bull-horned roasting spit and stone table upon the altar which Ädam had used to offer roasted gifts.

Before they offered, Ēve said, "Wait. We must first ask Ghäd' to accept our gifts and to keep the spirit of his servant Ädam at peaceful rest. We should also ask him to keep us hidden and safe from danger. Let the men plead to Ghäd' and the women plead to the Ängles. Let us *pray*," and they altogether prayed in a circle with their hands held together, enclosing a representation on the floor of the pentagram of the covenant with the boxed body of Ädam set in the middle.

35

A few days after the death of Ädam, Mīkhäēl arrived and stood at the head of his body. He opened the mouth with a tool, cutting and removing flesh, and then drained the blood of the body into a crucible. The spirit of Ädam was within this flesh and blood. With another tool, Mīkhäēl dug deep into the skull and removed the pīnaēl gland. In this manner, Ädam gave up his spirit and soul.

By sunset the next day, Mīkhäēl gave the spirit and soul of Ädam to Yhūriēl, who then carefully placed the sacred relics into a jar of purified water, closed it airtight, and placed his seal of a double cross on its lid.

Ēve was outside the cave pleading on her knees, and Mīkhäēl came to her and said, "O Ēve, rise up from your penance. The spirit and soul of Ädam have left his body."

Ève quickly went into the cave, taking Shäth with her, and they wept over the boxed body of Ädam. She then went back outside and continued her prayers to the Ängles.

After a while, Mīkhäēl again came to her and said, "O Ève, rise up from your penance and observe the spirit and soul of Ädam being delivered up to his maker."

Ève rose up and wiped the tears off of her face with her hand.

Mīkhäēl said to her, "Look up," and she looked up and saw a large flying throne ship with four smaller throne ships preceding it.

It was impossible for any of mankind to describe the magnificence of the throne ships and the faces of the Ängles. When Ève went above the cave, she could see the table of the altar where the spirit and soul of Ädam were resting. There, the large throne ship and the four smaller throne ships had landed. She saw golden censers and three bowls between the large throne ship and the spirit and soul of Ädam. Many Ängles with saffron, frankincense, and myrrh quickly brought them to the table on the altar. They placed saffron in the first bowl, frankincense in the second, and myrrh in the third. Incense was placed in the censers, lit and blown upon, and the resultant smoke veiled the throne ships.

The Ängles bowed face-down on the ground, praising and pleading out loud to Ghädäniēl, "Lord of Lords, Father of All, pardon Ädam of his original shame, because he was created in your image from your spirit—he is your ghōst-son."

Ève saw many bright and fearful Ängles standing before Ghädäniēl, and she cried out loud to her son Shäth down in the cave, "Shäth! Rise up from the body of your father and come to me! You will see a wonder which none of us has ever seen before!"

Shäth did not hear his mother shouting. He stayed by the boxed body of his father.

Mīkhaël went into the cave to get him, saying, "O Shäth, your mother cries out to you. Leave the boxed body of your father now and come out to see the fate of his spirit and soul. Your father was a creature of life belonging to our Lord Commander, and he has had pity on him."

Shäth rose up, went up to his mother, and said to her, "What is your trouble? Why did you cry out to me?"

Ēve replied, "Look over there and see with your own eyes. Seven flying throne ships have opened. See how the spirit of your father lies flat on the table of the altar and all of the Ängles are pleading on his behalf. I heard them say, 'Lord of Lords, Father of All, pardon Ädam of his original shame, because he was created in your image from your spirit—he is your ghōst-son.' My child Shäth, I beg you, what will this mean? Will his spirit one day be delivered into the hands of the hidden father of Ghäd'? Will we be delivered back into the great garden of Ghäd'?"

She then squinted and asked Shäth, "Who are those two in black garments who stand next to the assembly of prayers for the spirit of your father?"

Shäth answered, "They are Sun Lord and Moon Lord! Lord Ghäd' and his son, Lord Sīnhäel! They will take good care of the spirit of father."

Ēve said, "Where are their bright garments? Why are they in black garments?"

Shäth answered, "Their bright garments are nearby, but Ghäd' has commanded that his crucified son wear a customary black mourning garment, as he himself is wearing."

Ghädäniēl went up to the table and quietly said, "O Ädam, what have you done? If you had only obeyed my law, there would not be any rejoicing among those who are bringing your spirit and soul down to the sulphur pool. However, I say to you, O Ädam, I will turn their joy to grief and your grief to joy. During the last days of every sign-age, I will resurrect you to your former appearance and then promote you in the grand conjunction on the chair to the left of me and above your tester, Shätäniēl. He will be brought in to see you as the khrīst-king promoted above him. He will then be reprimanded, and those who follow him will be sorely grieved when he sees you as a khrīst-king elevated above him to rule the wilderness of the world."

Ghädäniēl stayed for a while at the table with the spirit and soul of Ädam.

He said, "O Ädam, Ädam, Ädam. You were told that you were created in a naval of the world, and now you will return to a naval of the world. I promised you that your spirit would be resurrected, that your spirit would be re-embodied. I will raise your spirit above all in a great resurrection of everyone who is pure in spirit."

Yhūriēl collected the airtight jar containing the spirit and soul of Ädam, and then Ghädäniēl stretched out his hand and received the jar.

He held the jar high for all to see, and said to Yhūriēl, "Take his spirit and soul to the white-ice chamber at the Hall of Mercy in Shērpäppäkh, where he was created, and store it there until it is required during the last days of the sign-age."

Ghädäniēl placed the sealed relics back into the hands of Yhūriēl, who would later be described by many Ängles as a measurer of many spirits.

Ghädäniēl said to Yhūriēl, "This flesh and blood will be in your care until the day when I turn its sad spirit into a joyful body. The reborn-Ädam will become my chosen heir in this world to rēdeem and heal my bonded ghōst-children."

An Ängle sounded a horn, and then all of the Ängles who were bowing stood up and cried out in an awful voice. They shouted, "The *Glōry* of Lord Ghädäniēl, from the works of his mission, will be gladly accepted by Emperor Än, because he has pitied Ädam, a creature of life which he has made."

After the Ängles said this, an eagle ship clutched the jar of the spirit and soul of Ädam with one of its six claw-wings and then carried it off to the sulphur pool, where it was immersed three times in a purification rite.

36

Shäth wondered about what had happened with the jar holding the spirit and soul of Ädam when Ghädäniël had spent so much time with it prior to the purification rite.

Mïkhäël explained to Shäth, "Ghädäniël was watching a vision of the past life of your father in great honor to him."

Shäth then saw a marvelous sight. He saw a legion of Ängles in many bright flying throne ships, and they were flashing their lights in various colors and sounding their horns in various tones, identifying themselves.

They were also weeping, and saying in unison, "We honor you, Your Highness, Attorney General Ghädäniël, because you have shown pity on your creature of life."

One of the great Ängles asked Ghädäniël about the laying out of the remains of Ädam. Ghädäniël summoned the lords to assemble with their cards, who each then gathered altogether in their companies upon the world, some carrying in their hands the receptacles of burning frankincense and others carrying megaphones. Ghädäniël came near to the cave of Ädam, arriving in *HMS Glöry*, preceded by the four small-finned wave-guide wheels and guarded by the many mini-finned wheels of the höst. They all came upon the heights and near to the cave where the boxed body of Ädam was resting in peace. As this happened, the flying-finned Ängles sprayed a fragrant sleeping-mist upon all of the trees and grass, rustling the family of Ädam in a great wind. The family of Ädam then slept a sound sleep, except for Shäth, who had returned into the cave to continue his grieving over the boxed body of Ädam.

Ghädäniël turned to Mïkhäël, who was standing next to Yhüriël, and said, "Go to the Hall of Mercy in Shërpäppäkh and bring back three fine white linen sheets and fragrant oil. When you return, pour the oil over the body of Ädam, and then tightly wrap the sheets around the body."

Mïkhäël departed and returned, and Yhüriël and Yhüziël oiled and wrapped the body of Ädam as instructed.

Ghädäniēl then said, "Bring the body of Äbäl forward and change its wrappings with fresh linen. Then rebox them well in the naval."

Before the bodies of Ädam and Äbäl were rewrapped, the Ängles and the chiefs of Ängles walked one by one to pay their respects, viewing the bodies for the last time. They honored the preservation of the bodies of both men.

Mīkhäēl, along with his half-brothers Yhūriēl and Yhūziēl, had boxed the bodies in the cave before Shäth and no one else.

Mīkhäēl then said to Shäth, "Box your dead in the same manner as you have seen here today, until the final sign-age of resurrection has come."

Ghädäniēl and all of the Ängles departed except for Mīkhäēl, and the family of Ädam rose up from their sleep and immediately began to pray. When they had all ceased praying and mourning, Mīkhäēl comforted them, and then they offered gifts to Ghädäniēl and to the caring Ängles on behalf of their father and themselves.

When everyone was finished offering gifts, Mīkhäēl came to Shäth and said, "O Shäth, Shäth, Shäth, as Lord Ghädäniēl was with your father, so will he be with you and your offspring until the fulfillment of the covenant and the promise he made with him concerning the white-gold Oil of Mercy. He said to your father, 'I will send garder Ängles to keep you and your offspring safe until the final day.' As Ghädäniēl had commanded to your father, you must keep the commands which your father gave to you and keep your offspring apart from the offspring of your half-brother, Khän."

Mīkhäēl then flew back to Ghädäniēl.

37

A few days after the funeral of Ädam, Ēve thought she was dying, so she summoned her family to gather by her bedside.

Ēve said to them, "Hear me, O my family, and I will tell you how the adversary of Ghäd' deceived your father, Ädam, and me in the great garden of the East.

After all had gathered, she said to them, "Ghäd' commanded your forefather and I to maintain his great garden. He allotted a portion to each of us. I maintained the southern portion with the Ängle Jākhäēl and the hew-brute females, and Ädam maintained the northern portion with the Ängle Mīkhäēl and the hew-brute males. Shätän' crept into the garden-dome and came to the lot of Ädam. He said to the brutes there, 'Rise up, come to me, and I will give you good counsel to help yourselves,' and they rose up and went to him. He said, 'I hear you are wiser than the beasts, and so I searched for you to give you beneficial counsel. Why do you eat the food of beasts rather than the food of Ädam? Rise up, and together we will cause Ädam to be banished from the garden-dome, and then you may eat the food of Ädam.' The brutes said, 'We fear to do what you wish, for Ghäd' will be angry with us.' Shätän' replied, 'Do not be afraid; you will only be my instrument, repeating to the brutish females what I will say and do to Ēve. Besides this, you can say, "Lord Shätäniēl made me do it." I will teach her how the seed of the fig produces a seedling for an eternal spiritual Tree of Life, and how she and Ädam can do the same, that if his seed is planted in her fertile womb, it will grow into an image of herself and Ädam. I will show her, with the fig, how the seed of Ädam should be planted by his serpent to grow in her womb, and you can simply do the same with your own serpents to the wombs of the brutish females. You will enjoy yourselves and cause Ädam to be banished.' The brutes agreed and followed Shätän', climbing up a terrace and into my portion of the garden-dome. When the Ängles ascended to receive counsel from Ghäd', Shätän' crept near to where I was, singing hymns like the Ängles do. When I heard him below a terrace wall, I leaned over and saw him, and he said to me, 'Are you Ēve?' and I said, 'I am,' and he said, 'What are you and the brutish females doing here in the terraced garden plots of Eädam?'

and I said to him, 'Ghäd' placed us here to keep it dressed for him, and to eat and drink from it.' Shätän' then said, 'O Ēve, you do well, but you do not partake of every fruit,' and I said, 'Yes, we partake of every fruit, except for the fruit of the male flesh, which resembles the fruit of the fig tree, which Ghäd' has forbidden us from partaking; he has commanded us not to touch it, because he said to us, "On the day when you partake of the forbidden fruit, you will surely die."' Shätän' said, 'No. You will surely live forever and ever! O Ēve, I am grieved on your account, because I do not want you to be ignorant and die. Come here, and I will show you the fruit and how your spirit can live forever and ever in a Tree of Life.' but I said to him, 'I fear to do as you say, for Ghäd' will be angry with me as he told us,' and he said to me, 'Do not fear, because as soon as you partake of the fruit, you will become like Ghäd' and live forever and ever; you will bear children and then know good from evil. Ghäd' knows that you would like to be like him; therefore, he became fearful of you and said, "You will not partake of it." No. You should look at this fruit and taste its great glory.' Yet I was afraid to go near him. He then spoke of the eternal spiritual Tree of Life, and said to me, 'Come here, and I will give it to you. Follow my counsel.'

"I went cautiously to Shätän', and then he bent me down like a branch to the ground. He placed his serpent a little way within me. Then he turned himself behind me and said, 'I have changed my decision. I will not show you the glory of eternal life unless you swear an oath to me that you will join with Ädam in this way,' and I said, 'What sort of oath must I swear to you?' From what I remember, I said to him, 'In the name of Ghäd' and his Knights of the Garder, I will join with the fruit of Ädam in this way,' and when he received the oath from me, he placed his serpent all the way into my womb, pouring the poison of his wickedness which is lust, the root and beginning of every offense. In that very moment, my eyes quickly shut and then opened wide with the knowledge of what he had done to me. Afterward, I felt stripped of my honor given to me by

Ghäd'. I cried and said to Shätän', 'Why have you done this to me, depriving me of the honor given to me by Ghäd'?' I wept about the oath which I had sworn. Shätän' then descended the wall and vanished. There, I saw the brutish males with their serpents doing the same deed with the brutish females.

"When I saw that I did not die, I went to the fig trees near to where Ädam was and cried out, 'O my Lord, Ädam! O my Lord, Ädam! Where are you? Come to me and I will show you a great wonder!' When Ädam arrived, I plucked a fig and recited the deceptive words of Shätän' to him, the words which brought the downfall of our kind from the grace of Ghäd'. We stood beneath the canopy of a fig tree, and I began to kiss his fruit. I said to him, 'Do not be afraid, because you will be like Ghäd'; we will mate and I will produce an image of ourselves and live forever and ever.' I quickly persuaded him, and we mated beneath the tree. He wondered at the deed, and then he realized what had been done. He shouted to me, 'Wicked woman! What have I done to you that you deprive me of the honor given to me by Ghäd'?' At that moment, we heard Mīkhäēl sounding the tune of Ghäd' through his horn. We heard the Ängles of Ghäd' singing hymns and coming near to us, and then we saw them touching the flowers of the trees which had just bloomed. Suddenly, Ghäd' spoke in a loud voice from above, calling out, 'O Ädam! Where are you hiding? Can a house hide from its builder?' and Ädam answered, 'O Lord, I am not hiding from you because I do not want to be found; I am simply afraid because I am ashamed of what I have done with my serpent.' Ghäd' said to him, 'How can you be ashamed of what you have done with your serpent, unless you have disobeyed my law, which I determined for you in order to keep you from dying.' Ädam then remembered what I had said to him, that our partaking of his fruit would make him as powerful as Ghäd', and he turned to me and said, 'O Ēve, why have you done this?' and I said, 'Shätän' deceived me through his serpent.'

"Ghäd' went away and then came back. He said, 'O Ädam, because you have disregarded my law and instead obeyed your helper, you will now die in the wilderness of the world. Your labor upon it will be cursed. You will work the ground and it will not give you its strength as here in my great garden. Where you will go, plants with thorns and thistles grow, but by the sweat of your brow, you will be satisfied in eating food. You will then experience many labors. You will cringe from bitterness and not taste sweetness. You will be weary and not receive rest; you will be tired from the heat and stiff from the cold. You will greatly busy yourself but will not be rich. You will grow fat but will not be nourished. The beasts will rise up in rebellion against you, and you will surely die because you did not keep my law.'

"Ghäd' turned to me and said, 'Because you disobeyed me and mated with Ädam, causing him to trespass into your forbidden rēd zōne, turning a deaf ear to my law, you will be in the throes of travail and intolerable agonies. With much trembling of your body, you will bear a large child. At the moment of birth, you may very well lose your life from the sore trouble and anguish. However, you will confess your offense to me, pleading, "O Ghäd', O Ghäd', save me, save me. I will not bend anymore to the fruit of the flesh!" and because of this and from my own words, I will judge you by the enmity which Shätäniēl has planted within you. I see and hear everything!'

"In his wrath, Ghäd' spoke to the brutish males and said, 'Because you have also done this with the forbidden fruit of your flesh, becoming thankless instruments of Shätäniēl and deceiving the innocent brutish females, you are cursed among mankind; you will be deprived of the food which you have been eating and will now devolve to feed on weeds and grass in the wilderness all the days of your life. You will crawl along the ground for your food, and there will be enmity between you and mankind; mankind will bruise your head and you will bruise his heel until the final sign-age of judgment.'

"Ghäd' commanded his Ängles to drive us out through the gate of the great garden and to the dead sticks river. As we were weeping and praying while being driven out, Ädam asked an Ängle, 'Let me stop for a little while so that I can beg to Ghäd' to have compassion on me and pity me, because I am the one who has offended him,' and the Ängles ceased their driving of us. Ädam cried out, 'O Ghäd', forgive me of my misdeed!' Ghäd' then said to the Ängle, 'Why have you ceased driving them out? Why are you not expelling them? Is it I who has done wrong, or have I made a bad judgment call?' The Ängle bowed to the ground and praised Ghäd', saying, 'Lord of Lords, you are just and you have determined a good judgment.' Ghäd' then said to Ädam, 'I will not suffer having you and your brutes mating in my great garden house,' and Ädam said, 'O Most High Lord, before you banish me, grant me some food from the garden,' and Ghäd' said, 'You will not take any food from here. I have commanded a Knight of the Garder with a fiery arm to keep you out of my garden house; you will not eat any of this food for everlasting life. You will now have to deal with Shätäniēl and the conflict he has placed within your helper.' Ghäd' spoke in this manner and commanded that we be banished from his great garden house.

"Ädam wept before the Ängles, and they said to him, 'Ädam, what would you have us do?' and Ädam said, 'Understand: You are driving us out of the garden. I beg of you, allow me to at least take away some fragrant herbs so that I can make an offering to Ghäd' after I have gone out, so that he can hear my pleas.' The Ängles approached Jākhäēl and petitioned on behalf of Ädam, saying, 'O Captain Jākhäēl, will you command that Ädam be given frankincense from the garden?' And Jākhäēl commanded some Ängles to go back a short way and gather sweet spices and fragrant herbs. Jākhäēl did this for Ädam separately from Ghädäniēl, as spices and herbs are not considered food. The Ängles went and gathered frankincense, crocus, spikenard, calamine, and cinnamon. After Ädam received them, we all went out through the gate and were in the wilderness of death.

"Now then, O my children, I have told you about how we were deceived by Shätän'. Watch over and protect yourselves from disobeying the Law of Ghäd'. I will now tell you what Mīkhāēl said to us long after your father and I disobeyed the Law of Ghäd' in the garden. He said to us, 'Because of your disobedience and noise, Ghäd' will deliver his wrath in a great judgment to all mankind, first by a drowning in water, and second by a burning of fire.' By these two things, Ghäd' will punish us and the offspring of the rebellious Ängles. Listen to me, O my children: Because of this, you must make books of stone and write on them everything about my life and everything about the life of your father, everything you have heard and seen from us. When Ghäd' punishes us by water, the books of stone will remain. Then your children should make books of clay and write on them a pure copy of what is written on the books of stone. When Ghäd' punishes us by fire, the books of clay will be baked hard and preserved. We must always pass on the books of our lives, our own testaments and the law of Ghäd', and the book of the covenant of trusting in the name and number of Ghäd', until the day of our rēdemption, to all of our children. Otherwise, they will forget and fall from his grace and not receive his white-gold Oil of Mercy. We owe this to our children on account of our misdeeds. Continue to build our trust in the name of Ghäd'—preserve the treasury of metals and the Book of the Covenant."

38

As she was about to die, Ēve prayed to the great Ängles, pleading to have her spirit taken and placed with the spirit of her husband, Ädam.

She spread her hands to the sky and placed her knees on the ground, and said, "O great Ängles, please give this message of mine to Lord Ghäd': 'O Lord Ghäd', Lord of Lords, do not estrange me, your servant, from the spirit of Ädam, because I was created from his spirit. Instead, deem my spirit worthy to be placed into his place of resting in peace, because in your great garden, we were both together, and even after our first mating, when we were led astray and disobeyed your law, we were not separated. Even so, O Lord Ghäd', do not separate us now.'"

After she had prayed, Ēve gazed into the sky and groaned out loud. She beat upon her breast because her heart was failing and in pain, and she said, "O Lord of All, receive my spirit and soul," and she collapsed and died.

Mīkhäēl came and taught Shäth how to prepare Ēve for burial. The great Ängles Jākhäēl, Yhūriēl, and Ghābräēl also came, and they all together prepared and boxed the body, again teaching Shäth the process of how to lay out every dead of mankind.

The family of Ēve wailed while walking together to the cave to see her for the last time, and they wailed when they carried her boxed body and placed it next to the boxed bodies of Ädam and Äbäl.

When they had wept for four days, Mīkhäēl said to Shäth, "Tell your people: 'Do not mourn for your dead more than six days. Rest and rejoice on the seventh day, because on that day, Ghädäniēl and the Ängles will rejoice over the transmigration of a purebred spirit. An Ängle of Death Company will come and open the mouth of the dead to collect and seal their spirit and soul in a purified jar. Do not ever hinder an Ängle of Death in the performance of his duty. Ängles of Death take spirits and souls away and ensure that they are fully measured, watched over, and protected for the last days of every sign-age.' O Shäth, as you were earlier told, your created spirit is the result of a sacred wholly royal spirit mating rite, a secret incantation to tie the knot of spirit springs, a sacred bond which is eternal and cannot be undone, somewhat like the Īgoggle knot on your sandal strap. The spirit of mankind is a registered and trademarked creation of life which will always belong to him and the wholly royal Empire of Phaëton."

Six days after Ēve died, Mīkhäēl collected her spirit, blood, and pīnaēl gland.

As Mīkhäēl flew away, he said, "Chosen one of Ghädäniēl and Shätäniēl, power and deception is within your spirit forevermore."

Shäth, who was taught writing by an Īgoggle, made books of stone and placed them next to the boxed body of his father in the Cave of Treasure.

39

Shäth and his kindred came down to the cave after praising at the altar. Ädam was the second who rested in the cave, the first being his firstborn son, Äbäl, who had been killed by Khän. The children of Ädam wept over their forefather and offered gifts to him and gifts to Ghädäniēl on his behalf for many years.

Shäth kept his children separated from the children of Khän, who had now proliferated in the Land of Nod below Three Dog Mountain, and where Khän had killed Äbäl. Shäth and his family remained living on the heights to be near the body of Ädam. Shäth, the elder, tall and bright, stood at the head of his people and administered the sacred wholly royal spirit mating rite, and tended to them in innocence, penitence, and meekness. He did not allow any of them to go down to the family of Khän. Shäth and his family were bonded ghōsts of Ghädäniēl, like branded cattle or sheep, though much more closely related. Ghädäniēl considered Khän and his family as unclean creatures of life belonging to his half-brother, who had illegally sired Khän with Ēve. The children of Khän contained adulterated spirit and appeared like pigs in the mud.

The spirit of Ädam had been designed as a purebred mixture. Once incarnated, he was considered a ghōst-being whose spirit possessed an unbreakable wholly royal bond.

Shäth stood night and day before the boxed bodies of his father and mother, pleading for an emissary of Mercy Company in regard to himself and Būddhi and their children. When Shäth would have difficulty dealing with a child, he would ask one of the Ängles in prayer for advice, who would then answer him, because the Ängles were commanded by Ghädäniēl to give the royal family counsel whenever they were properly called upon. Shäth, Būddhi, and their entire family had each been assigned an Ängle to watch over and protect them. It was the duty of these garder Ängles to relay prayers requesting guidance and to ward off life-threatening danger. They were also charged to report back periodically to Shätäniēl about the location, condition, and behavior of each of mankind, keeping a record of each in the database of the havens.

Because Shäth and his family had no concerns other than praises, prayers, songs, and offerings to Ghädäniēl, they did not perform manual labor like Khän and Äbäl used to do. Instead, they dedicated themselves to praising, pleading, singing, and offering to Ghädäniēl. They constantly heard the sounds of the Ängles who were arriving, rejoicing in, and departing Shämbäelle not too far away, or while simply flying on errands.

Shäth and his family did not grow food for their bodies, not even wheat. Instead, they only made gifts and offered them on the stone table of the altar. To survive, they ate the well-flavored fruit of some of the trees growing there which had been planted by Ädam as seedlings from the garden-dome, and they relied on the Ängles nearby who kept bringing them leftover ambrosia and nectar from their banquets as a gift of thanks for their devout service in lording over the workship of the hew-brutes, who had multiplied and were laboring hard inside the mountain, breaking the gold oregon to smelt for the trust in the name and number of Ghädäniēl.

During a forty-day period every year, Shäth would eat only fish, as would his eldest children, in honor and remembrance of the first penitence of Ädam, and they would pray to Ghädäniēl for deliverance to the great Garden of Änglea in the East, of which his father and mother had spoken so much about.

The family of Shäth enjoyed the fragrance of the cedar trees in the North when the wind blew from that direction. They were happy, innocent, and without sudden fear, and there was no jealousy, criminality, or hatred among them. There was no beastly passion or lust, neither foul words nor curses from their mouths, and neither lies nor fraud. There and in those days, the men never swore. Under hard circumstances when men must swear, however, they swore on behalf of the spilled blood of Äbäl the Innocent (Khän being the Guilty). During a large portion of every day, they kept their children and their women in the Cave of Treasure to eat only fish, to pray, and to praise Ghädäniēl. They rejoiced and appointed themselves to final resting places there. They praised Ghädäniēl until the death of Shäth drew near.

Shäth summoned his son Enōish, his grandson Khänen, and his great-grandson Mähällälil and said to them, "Because my end is near, I wish to build a high roof over the sacred altar to keep the rain off of us and off of our gifts to Ghäd'. It must be high enough so that the column of light from the Ängles can enter and collect the gifts, as well as for the aromatic smoke to go out and rise into the sky."

After listening to his wish, everyone went out, old and young, and labored hard to build a high roof over the raised stone floor where the roasting spit and table rested. They expanded the terraced floor and then built a majestic and beautiful roof over it all. By performing this deed, Shäth hoped that the endorsement and goodwill of Ghädäniēl would also come to his family forevermore. He wished to offer a gift to them before his death and that they would make gifts to offer up to Ghädäniēl. They worked diligently through the night and then brought their gifts to Shäth, who in turn took them and offered them up on the table, begging the Ängles to accept them on

behalf of Ghädäniël, to bring an Ängle of Mercy Company
to the bodies and spirits of his family, and to keep them
away from the sudden grasp and stinging bite of Shätäniël.
The Ängles accepted the gifts and sent the endorsement
and best wishes of Ghädäniël to Shäth and his family. An
Ängle also confirmed to Shäth the covenant which
Ghädäniël had made to his father, Ädam, and him.

The Ängle said, "O Shäth, in regard to the
covenant which Ghäd' has made with you and your father,
Ghäd' still intends to have his and your spirit reborn as a
khrīst-king and khrīst-prince respectively, arriving back in
the world during the last days of every sign-age. You as the
khrīst-prince, will precede the khrīst-king and become the
preparer of pure ones. The khrīst-prince will be the baptizier for the khrīst-king, and the khrīst-king will sire the
purest son to reestablish the wholly royal House of Ghäd'
in this world. The khrīst-king will then become a baptizier
himself. He will receive the Oil of Mercy to assist him in
his new calling of bringing mankind back into the spiritual
fold of Ghäd'. Mankind will be like sheep, and the khrīst-
king will be their shepherd and savior. Your spirit, O
Shäth, will prepare them as pure virgins for a sacred
wholly royal spirit mating rite. The khrīst-king will
administer among the flock, approving them in the name
of Ghäd', mating them, counseling them, watching over
and protecting them, and commanding them and their offspring to stay true to the spiritual path of chastity. The
firstborn son of the king will reign in the royal House, and
the firstborn son of the next king will reign after the death
of the previous one, and so on; illegitimate or unworthy
sons will not reign. This is how it is done in the world
above, and so it will be done in the world below."

40

Shäth and his family gathered at the place of the
altar and then altogether came down to the cave containing

the interred bodies of Äbäl, Ädam, and Ēve, the chested token supplies of saffron, frankincense, and myrrh, and sacks of aloes and cassia. Upon arriving before the body of Ädam, Shäth anointed them with oil as a reminder that Ghädäniēl would give them the Oil of Mercy for khäncer upon the completion of the covenant, and then they all together prayed for Ädam before departing. Shäth, however, stayed and lived in the Cave of Treasure for many years and then suffered pains—pains toward death. His son Enōish came to him with Khänen, Mähällälil, and Jährēd, the firstborn son of Mähällälil, and Enäkh, the firstborn son of Jährēd (not the same Enäkh as the first-born of Khän), with their wives and children, to receive the endorsements, appreciations, and best wishes—his bless-ings—and the last will and testament of Shäth.

Shäth prayed to Ghädäniēl for them, gave his blessings, and swore them under solemn oath by the spilled blood of Äbäl the Innocent. He said to them, "My children, I beg of you, do not let any one of you go down from this sacred mountain. Do not make friends among the family of Khän, the impure and illegitimate one. As you know, we flee from him and his uncleanness and wickedness with all of our might, because he killed his brother Äbäl."

Shäth turned to his son Enōish and repeated his blessings to him, and commanded him to stand regularly before the body of their forefather Ädam, to administer the sacred rite of sowing pure and fair seed to chaste and vir-gin daughters throughout all of the days of his life. He also commanded him to stand every day on the pulpit of the altar to teach his people about the words and ways of Ghädäniēl, and how to make gifts to offer up to Ghädäniēl throughout all of the days of his life, and to continue build-ing the trust in the name and number of Ghädäniēl, to pre-serve the treasury of gold and the covenant. Finally, he commanded Enōish that at the end of his days, he must administer the oath of sacred duty to his firstborn son and that he, in turn, must do the same through every genera-tion afterward.

The arms and legs of Shäth became loose, his hands and feet lost power, his mouth became dumb and unable to speak, and then he died. His body was balmed with sweet spices and wrapped carefully with fine cloth and then laid firm to rest in peace at the right side of the body of Ädam in the Cave of Treasure. The Children of Ghädäniēl mourned for many years and offered gifts on his behalf as they did for Ädam.

41

After Shäth died, Enōish became the priest-king of the Children of Ghädäniēl. He explained the words and ways of Ghädäniēl to them and administered the sacred wholly royal spirit mating rite in the cave before the boxed body of Ädam, as his father had commanded of him. By the time Enōish was an old man, however, Khän had fathered a far much larger family than Shäth, because his family had constantly mated until the Land of Nod was filled.

Lūmäkh the Blind, a descendant of Khän, was living in those days and had fathered his son Khōbäl, the one who became the lord of those who create things with iron and brass. Together, they possessed a great number of cattle, and in time, Khōbäl fathered a son—Ädam (not the same as Ädam the first). Lūmäkh was in the habit of sending the cattle out to feed along with his grandson, Ädam, who, in this manner, became a shepherd boy, tending to them. Ädam, however, after coming home in the evening from tending the cattle each day, would weep before his grandfather.

The shepherd boy, Ädam, said to him, "I cannot feed these cattle alone; otherwise, someone will steal some of them from me, or kill me to get them."

There was quite a lot of robbery, murder, and vice among the family of Khän.

Lūmäkh pitied the boy and said to himself, "Truly, when he is alone, he could be overpowered by the men of this place." He gathered a crossbow that he had kept ever since he was a youth, before he had became partially blind, and some large arrows, smooth stones, and a sling which he also had. With these weapons, he went to the field with Ädam and placed himself behind the cattle, while the young boy watched the herd. Lūmäkh the Blind did this for many days.

Meanwhile, Khän could neither settle nor find rest in any one place due to his crime of killing his brother Äbäl. Therefore, he and his close kindred wandered in the wilderness from place to place like fugitives, erecting tents for shelter wherever they went. In his wanderings, he came upon the two wives of Lūmäkh the Blind—Aidä and Zillä—and inquired about him.

Zillä said to him, "He is in the field with his grandson, Ädam, and the cattle."

Khän, wearing the horned helmet that his father, Shätäniēl, had told him to wear to ward off dangerous beasts, went to look for Lūmäkh. As he came into the field, the shepherd boy heard a noise and saw the cattle herding together.

Ädam said to Lūmäkh, "My Lord, is this a wild beast or a robber?"

Lūmäkh said to him, "Let me know which way he turns when he comes up the slope."

Lūmäkh cocked his crossbow and placed an arrow in it, and then fitted a stone in his sling.

When the horned Khän came into the open, Ädam set the arm of Lūmäkh toward the approaching figure and said, "There, he is coming. Shoot!"

Lūmäkh shot his arrow and hit Khän in the side. He then struck him with a stone from his sling. The stone hit him square in the face, right between the eyes. Khän immediately fell and died.

Believing he had felled a beast, Lūmäkh said to Ädam, "Hurry, let us see what kind of beast we have killed."

Lūmäkh and Ädam came to the spot and found him lying on the ground.

Ädam shouted to Lūmäkh, "My Lord, it is our forefather Khän! You have killed our forefather! You have
killed our forefather!"

Lūmäkh was extremely upset and sorry for what
had happened. However, in hearing the boy shout over and
over again, "You have killed our forefather! You have
killed our forefather!" an angry rage with regretful bitterness overwhelmed him, and he tightened his hands into
fists and repeatedly struck the head of Ädam until he died.
Believing Ädam was then pretending to be dead, he picked
up the stone that had killed Khän and struck the boy with
it, smashing his head until he was certainly dead.

Lūmäkh confessed his actions to his wives, saying
to them, "I have killed my grandson, who merely hurt me
with words, and I have killed our forefather Khän, who did
nothing to me. Our Lord punished Khän for his killing by
having him wander with horns on his head for seven generations. Now, with my double killing, I must wander with
horns on my head for seven and seven generations."

Aidä and Zillä divorced themselves from Lūmäkh
and kept their children away from him.

Shätäniēl came to visit, and, in the same manner
as Khän, swore Lūmäkh the Blind under oath that he truly
belongs to him. Shätäniēl gave him a secret brotherhood
name—Master Mayhem. Īrhäkh, the firstborn son of
Enäkh and grandson of Khän, became aware of the secret,
and revealed it to some of the Sons of Ädam who were
dwelling among the sons of Khän at that time.

42

When Enōish was very old, the wives and children
of Shäth, Khänen, and Mähällälil gathered around him,
asking for his blessing.

Enōish prayed for them, gave his blessing and last
will and testament, and swore them under solemn oath by

the spilled blood of Äbäl the Innocent. He said to them, "Do not let any of your family go down from this mountain of sacred oaths; do not let them make friends among the family of Khän the murderer."

Enōish summoned his son Khänen and said to him, "O my son, understand: Set your mind on your people. Teach them the words and ways of Ghäd' to maintain them in their pure spirit, brightness, and innocence. Stand to administer the sacred wholly royal spirit mating rite in your chaste spirit before the boxed body of our forefather Ädam throughout all of the days of your life, and continue to build our trust in the name and number of Ghäd'. Protect the treasury of gold and the book of the covenant."

Within days, Enōish died.

Khänen balmed the body of Enōish with sweet spices, wrapped him in fine cloth, and then laid him to rest in a box at the left side of the body of Ädam in the Cave of Treasure. He made gifts and offered them to Ghädäniēl on behalf of Enōish, following the custom of his fathers.

43

Khänen became the priest-king of the Children of Ghädäniēl, administering the sacred wholly royal spirit mating rite in chastity and innocence before the boxed bodies of his forefathers in the Cave of Treasure, as his father had commanded of him.

When Khänen became very old, he began to experience pain and disease. The entire family gathered around him when he was about to die, and he gave them his blessing and last will and testament. He also swore them under solemn oath by the spilled blood of Äbäl the Innocent.

He said to them, "Do not let anyone from among you go down from this sacred mountain; do not make friends with the family of Khän the murderer. Continue to maintain the chaste spirit within yourselves through the sacred wholly royal spirit mating rite. Continue to build our trust in the name and number of Ghäd'. Preserve the treasury of gold and the Book of the Covenant."

This command was primarily meant for his first-born son, Mähällälil. His father gave him his blessing and last will and testament and then died.

Mähällälil balmed the body of Khänen with sweet spices, wrapped him in fine cloth, and then laid him to rest in a box with his fathers in the Cave of Treasure. He and his family offered gifts to Ghädäniēl on behalf of Khänen.

44

Mähällälil became the priest-king of the Children of Ghädäniēl, administering the sacred wholly royal spirit mating rite before the bodies of his forefathers in the Cave of Treasure as his father had commanded of him. He watched over them to ensure that they did not mate with the family of Khän, until he was very old and fell ill. His entire family then gathered to see him and to ask for his blessing and last will and testament. With tears streaming down his face, Mähällälil sat up from his bed and summoned his firstborn son, Jährēd, who then came to him.

Mähällälil kissed the face of Jährēd and said, "O my son Jährēd, on behalf of Ghäd', I swear you under oath to watch over your kindred, the Children of Ghäd', to maintain their chaste spirit, innocence, and fair color, and to not let any of them go down from this sacred mountain to the family of Khän; otherwise, they and their offspring there will perish with them. Continue to build our trust in the name and number of Ghäd'. Preserve the treasury of gold and the covenant. My son, understand: A great destruction will come to our world on account of their unrighteous behavior. Ghäd' will become very upset and destroy them with a great wall of water which will overflow all of the earth. Sadly, I believe your family will not listen to you and will go down from this mountain and engage in unsanctified mating. They will fornicate and perish with the family of Khän. O my son Jährēd, teach them! Watch over and protect them so that you will not be judged guilty on account of their misdeeds.

"When I die, balm and wrap my body, and lay it to rest in a box with the bodies of my fathers in the cave. Then stand by my boxed body and pray to Ghäd' to keep safe my chaste spirit and to take care of the dead bodies. Also, go deep into the bowels of Three Dog Mountain and pray to Shätän' to take care of the spirits after death. Always pray to both Most High Lords to take care of your family. In regard to pleading to Prince Shätän', however, you must keep the custom secret and keep yourself well hidden from the all-seeing hawk-eye of Ghäd'. Fulfill your sacred duty to administer in chastity and innocence the sacred wholly royal spirit mating rite before them, until you rest in a box yourself. Pass on the sacred wholly royal traditions to your children, the Children of Ghäd'."

Mähällälil gave his blessing and last will and testament to his children. He then lay down on his bed and died like his fathers. When Jährēd saw that his father was dead, he became very sad and wept. He embraced and kissed with his lips the hands and feet of his father, as did his children. The children of Mähällälil balmed and wrapped him, and then laid him to rest in a box by the bodies of his fathers. They mourned the death of Mähällälil for many days.

45

Jährēd kept the commands of his father. He stood on a rock of the altar above his people like a lion perched on a hill above its pride, preaching to them, and then administered the sacred wholly royal spirit mating rite in

chastity and innocence before the boxed bodies of their
fathers in the cave below the altar. He commanded them to
do nothing without his counsel because he feared for them,
that they would go down to the family of Khän and become
like pigs in the mud. For this reason, he kept commanding
them and continued to do so until the end of his life. A
strange thing happened to Jährēd at the end of his days,
however. While Jährēd stood watch over the boxed bodies
of his fathers, Shätäniēl saw him and went to him there,
impressed by his power over the Children of Ghädäniēl,
that his family would not perform any deed without his
counsel. Shätäniēl arrived with thirty Ängleic men but
kept himself hidden. The men were quite handsome, and
the tallest, with a long, fine beard, was the elder among
them. They stood at the entrance of the Cave of Treasure,
and Shätäniēl called out to Jährēd, who came out and saw
them as fine men with snow-white skin and hair, rivers of
blue blood, and roses of red skin. He wondered at their
beauty and snow-white skin and hair, and thought that
they could not be from the family of Khän.

Jährēd thought to himself, "Because the family of
Khän cannot come up to this mountain and none of them is
as handsome as these, and among these men there is not
one of my children, then they must be strangers from a far-
off land. They even resemble Ängles!"

They exchanged a greeting, and Jährēd said to the
eldest among them, "O elder, please tell me about the wonder of yourself and these men who are with you, because
you look so strange to me."

The elder began to weep, and then the others
began to weep with him. The elder said to him, "O Jährēd,
I am Ädam, your forefather whom our creator made first,
and this is my eldest son, Äbäl, who was killed by his elder
half-brother, Khän. This is my second son, Shäth, whom I
asked our creator for, and who was given to me to comfort
me in place of Äbäl. This one is my grandson Enōish, the
eldest son of Shäth, and this other one is my great-grandson Khänen, the eldest son of Enōish, and this other one is

my great-great-grandson and your father, Mähällälil, the eldest son of Khänen."

Jährēd was dumbstruck. He remained wondering at their appearance and at what the elder had said to him.

The elder said, "Do not be confused, O my son. We have been transfigured into new bodies and now live in Shāmbäēlle, the wonderful haven among the cedar trees to the North, a haven which our Lord created before I was made there and then placed in the great garden of the East. When Ēve and I mated against the law of Ghäd', he expelled us from the great garden, and we were left to die here in this cave. Great and sore troubles afflicted me. When my death came near, I commanded my son Shäth to tend to his kindred and to hand down my command and law from one generation to the next until the end of the covenant. However, O my son Jährēd, we live in a beautiful land of the living, while you live here in misery, as your father has told me all about. He reminded me about the great wall of water which will overwhelm the earth below the havens. Fearing on your behalf, I rose up and took my family with me and returned to this place to visit you and your family. I found your family scattered about the heights of this mountain in the heat and misery, and you standing in this cave, weeping. However, my son, as we lost our way while coming here, we found other men and women below this mountain who live in a beautiful country full of trees and fruits and every manner of vegetation which is food for everlasting life. When we found them, we thought they were you, until your father told me they were no such thing. Therefore, my son, understand my counsel now and go down to them, you and your family. You will rest from this suffering. If you will not go down to them in the East, take your family and come with us to the high valley Crest of Säphärōn, the land of the living in the North, where you will live in the beautiful haven of Shāmbäēlle and rest from this trouble which you and your family are now bearing."

After hearing the discourse from the elder, Jährēd wondered, and then went searching around in the cave. In his searching, he did not see any of his family.

Upon his return, he asked the elder, "Why have you not shown yourselves until this day?"

The elder replied, "If your father had not told us, we would not have known it."

Jähred believed his words were true.

The elder asked Jähred, "Where did you just now go?"

Jähred replied, "I was looking for one of my children to tell them I am going with you, and of their coming down to those of whom you tell me about."

When the elder understood Jähred, he said to him, "Never mind this for now, and come with us. You will see our haven, and if the land in which we live pleases you, we and yourself will return to this place and take your family with us. If our country does not please you, however, you will come back to your own place."

The elder urged Jähred to come with them before one of his children came to counsel him otherwise. Jähred left the cave and went with and among the elders. They comforted him until they came to the outskirts of the family of Khän, the Children of Shätäniël.

The elder said to one of his fellows, "We have forgotten something by the entrance of the cave, the garment we chose to dress Jähred with." He then said, "Go back, you, someone, and we will wait here for your return. We will then dress Jähred, and he will be like us: good, handsome, and fit to come with us into our haven."

One of them went back.

When he was a short distance away, the elder called out to him, "Wait. Wait right there until I come up and speak to you."

The one who went stopped, and the elder went up to him and said, "One thing we forgot to do at the cave was to go inside and snuff out the flame of the lamp in front of the bodies. Do this and quickly come back to us."

This one went on, and the elder came back to his fellows and to Jähred. They had come down from the heights, Jähred with them, and they stayed by a waterfall near the houses of the family of Khän, to wait for their fellow to bring the garment for Jährēd.

The one who went back to the cave snuffed out the flame of the lamp and then returned to the group, bringing the garment with him. When Jährēd saw the garment, he wondered at its colorful-striped beauty and grace. He rejoiced in his mind, believing everything the elder had said was true.

While the group was resting by the waterfall, however, three of them went into houses of the family of Khän and asked them, "Can you bring some food today to the waterfall for us and our fellows to eat?"

When the family of Khän saw them, they were wondering about them and thinking to themselves, "These strangers are beautiful to look at, and their snow-white skin and hair is such as we have never seen before."

They went with them to the waterfall to see their companions. They found them so very handsome that they went around, shouting for others to gather together to come and look at these beautiful beings. Then men and women of the family of Khän gathered all around them.

The elder said to them, "We are strangers in your land. Will you bring us some good food and drink, you and your women, to refresh ourselves with you?"

When these men heard the elder speak, each brought his wife, and another brought his daughter, and so on. Many women came to them, every one addressing Jährēd, everyone with dark skin and looking alike. However, when Jährēd saw what they were doing, he took himself away from them and he would neither taste their food nor drink their beverage.

The elder saw Jährēd take himself away from them and therefore said to him, "Do not be so sad, Jährēd. I am the great forefather. Do as I do."

The elder spread his hands and took one of the women, and five of his fellows did the same. They were gesturing to Jährēd that he should do the same.

When Jährēd saw their behavior, however, he began weeping and said silently to himself, "My fathers never behaved like this."

Jāhrēd spread his hands and begged with great fervor and tears. He appealed to Ghādäniēl to deliver him away from their hands. No sooner had Jāhrēd begun to plead than the elder departed with his fellows. Jāhrēd turned around and no longer saw them but found himself standing amid the family of Khän.

Jāhrēd was weeping and said, "O Lord Ghäd', do not destroy me with this family which my fathers have warned me about, because I was beguiled to believe those who appeared to me were my forefathers, but now I have realized that they were minions of Shätän', testing my obedience to you. They lured me by a beautiful description until I believed them. O my Lord, I now ask you to deliver me away from this terrible people. Please send your emissary to take me out from among them, because I on my own do not have the power to escape from them."

When Jāhrēd finished his pleading, Ghādäniēl sent an Ängle who took Jāhrēd away, flying him to the top of a nearby hill, where he then counseled him. The Ängle then showed Jāhrēd him the way back to the cave on the heights and departed.

46

The children of Jāhrēd were in the habit of visiting him every day to receive his blessing and to ask for his counsel regarding everything they did or wanted to do. Furthermore, when Jāhrēd had some work to do, they would do it for him. This time when they went into the cave, however, they did not find Jāhrēd, nor any flame of the lamp. Ängles were hidden deep in the cave and speaking in muffled voices to one another. The family of Jāhrēd thought the dead bodies were speaking to one another!

One said to another, "Shätäniēl has cleverly tested the obedience of Jāhrēd."

Addressing Ghädäniēl through an oracle, an Ängle said, "My Lord, a great test with trickery was brought before Jährēd. We request your permission to deliver him away from the Land of Nod to a safe place."

The Ängles also spoke about other matters and again sounded as though they were the dead bodies speaking. When the offspring of Jährēd heard the muffled voices of the Ängles, they became afraid and stood weeping for their father, because they did not know what had happened to him. They wept for him until sunset and then departed from the cave.

With an anguished face, Jährēd had finally returned, wretched in body and mind and full of sadness from being separated from the dead bodies of his fathers. As he came closer to the cave, however, his children saw him and hurried back. They shouted and hung onto his neck, weeping.

They shouted, "Father! Father! Where have you been? Why did you leave us? You never wanted to leave us before," and said "Father, while you were gone, the flame of the lamp was also gone, and voices came from the bodies."

When Jährēd heard this, he was very sorry and went into the cave. He did not see the flame of the lamp, and he, too, heard muffled voices which sounded as though the bodies were pleading for him. He placed himself upon the boxed bodies, embracing them.

He prayed out loud, saying, "O spirits of my fathers, through your intervention, please have Ghäd' watch over and protect our family from the tests of obedience from Shätän'. I beg of you, ask him to keep me and hide me from his tempting adversary until the day that I die."

Every voice ceased except one, which, just as one would speak to his fellow, said to Jährēd, "O my son Jährēd, offer gifts to Lord Ghädäniēl for having delivered you from the land of darkness, and, when you bring those gifts, make sure you offer them upon a clean table. Beware of the temptations from Shätäniēl—do not let him delude you with his creations of life. He will destroy your spirit if you are overcome by his test of obedience. Should you again find yourself being tested by him, invoke the name of Lord Ghädäniēl, and he will deliver you. Command your people to watch over and protect against Shätän' and to never cease offering gifts to Lord Ghädäniēl. Most importantly, with your hew-brutes in the bowels of Three Dog Mountain, continue to build your trust in the name and number of Lord Ghädäniēl."

The voice, which seemed as though it had come from the body of Ädam, became silent. Jährēd and his family marveled at this and stood pleading the entire night until sunrise. Afterward, Jährēd made a gift and offered it upon a clean table of the altar. On his way up to the altar, he prayed to Ghädäniēl for an emissary of Mercy Company and for forgiveness of his offense concerning the missing flame of the lamp. At the table, Mīkhäēl appeared to Jährēd and on behalf of Ghädäniēl gave his blessing to Jährēd and his family and accepted the gifts. He instructed Jährēd to take a flame from the roasting spit and use it to relight the lamp in the cave to shed light on the boxed body of Ädam. Mīkhäēl revealed to him details of the promise he had made on behalf of Ghädäniēl to Shäth when Ädam was dying. He explained to him about the final sign-age of the pentagram in regard to when the Oil of Mercy for khäncer would be given to the khrīst of Ädam, and he also revealed to him the mystery of the origin of hew-brutes and hew-mans.

Mīkhäēl said to Jährēd, "O Jährēd, I am a son of Lord Ghädäniēl. In regard to the flame which you have taken from the roasting spit to light the lamp in the cave, always keep it with you to give light to the boxed bodies, and do not allow it to come out of the cave until the boxed body of Ädam comes out of the cave. Take care of the flame. Ensure that it burns bright from the lamp and does not come out of the cave. Again, command your people not to mate with the family of Khän and not to learn their ways, because the spirit of Khän is impure and manifests disobedience; he is the son of Shätäniēl the adulterer, not the son of Ädam, who was a spirit-son of Lord Ghädäniēl."

Mīkhäēl also relayed many other commands to Jāhrēd, along with a blessing, and then he departed.

Jāhrēd approached the roasting spit with his family and took a flame from the middle of the sacred fire, and then they, all together, went down to the cave, where he lit the lamp before the boxed body of Ädam and recited to his people all the commands which Mīkhäēl had commanded of him to do. When this encounter with Mīkhäēl occurred, Jāhrēd was of a ripe old age. He continued to teach his people for many years and to administer the sacred wholly royal spirit mating rite; however, the family of Jāhrēd then began to disobey the commands and to do many things without his counsel. One after another, they began to go down from the heights of Three Dog Mountain.

47

Long after Khän had gone down to the land of Nod and his children had multiplied, there was one of them in particular called Jūbäl who was a son of Lūmäkh the Blind. In his childhood, Jūbäl made many types of trumpets and horns, and string instruments, cymbals and psalteries, and lyres, harps, and flutes. He played them at every hour, and from among them were heard beautiful and sweet sounds which ravished emotion.

Jūbäl gathered groups upon groups to play the musical instruments, and when they played, the family of Khän was well-pleased. Jūbäl also made a strong drink out of corn, and with this, he used to bring together groups upon groups in drink houses. He also brought into their hands every kind of fruit and flower, and they drank together. Jūbäl was very proud of his accomplishments. As the knowledge of Jūbäl increased, however, he took iron and made weapons with it. When some were drunk, hatred and murder began among them. One man used violence against another and took his children and mated with them before him. When men saw that they were overpowered by others, and saw others were not overpowered, those who were beaten came to Jūbäl for refuge, and he prepared them to be soldiers. The army of Jūbäl distinguished itself by playing musical instruments before, during, and after a battle.

Offenses greatly increased among the family of Khän, until a man mated with his own sister, or daughter, or mother, or cousin, and others. There was no more distinction of relatives, and they no longer knew what spiritual purity was before Ghädäniēl or Shätäniēl. They badly behaved and greatly angered Ghädäniēl.

Jūbäl continued to gather together groups upon groups which played on the horns and other instruments at the bottom of the feet of Three Dog Mountain. They did this so the family of Shäth would hear them, and, when they did hear them, the family of Shäth wondered and came in groups and stood at the edge of the heights to look down at those below. This occurred for many years. Jūbäl saw people were being won over to him little by little. He learned how to dye garments of diverse colors and patterns for his people, and he made them understand how to dye crimson, purple, and other colors.

The family of Khän, who produced everything and shone in beauty and gorgeous apparel, gathered together in splendor at the bottom of the heights with musical horns and gorgeous dresses. They were having all sorts of fun, even conducting horse races.

Many years earlier, in a wide, bronze-colored meadow called Ärdīseä near the Crest of Säphärōn, two hundred Gregoriän hōst under the leadership of Prince Shämyazäbäēl descended altogether and went down to the family of Khän. The all-male Gregoriän hōst was circling above the sky, accommodating the comings and goings of flying ships, but then agreed to abandon their havens in open defiance of Ghädäniēl to mate and cohabitate with the daughters of men!

The family of Shäth had no longer kept the command of Ghädäniēl. The people relaxed from their ritual drownings in the river and their praying to Ghädäniël and his Ängles at the altar, and they rarely sought counsel from Jährēd. From sunrise until sunset, they kept on gathering together at the edge of a cliff to look down at the family of Khän. They were looking to see what they did, and they saw their beautiful dresses and ornaments. The family of Khän looked up from below and saw the family of Shäth standing like troops along a cliff of the mountain, and they called out to them to come down.

The family of Shäth shouted, "We do not know the way down!"

Jübäl heard what they were shouting, so he thought about how he could bring them down.

The Ängle Shämyazäbäēl, the flamboyänt leader of the Gregoriän höst, came to Jübäl at sunset and said to him, "There is no easy way for them to come down from the cliff, but when they come to the cliff tomorrow, tell them: 'Go farther down to the side of the mountain. There you will find the path of a stream which comes down between two ridges. Come down to us this way.'"

When it was daylight, Jübäl blew the horns and beat the drums as he used to do. The family of Shäth heard him, and they came to the cliff of the heights as they used to do. Jübäl shouted the message from Shämyazäbäēl. When the family of Shäth heard this from him, however, they went into the cave to Jährēd and told him what they had heard. When Jährēd heard them, his face dropped in sadness, because he knew they would disregard his advice and go down to the family of Khän.

Afterward, one hundred men of the family of Shäth gathered together. They said to each other, "Come, we will go down to the family of Khän and see what they do and enjoy ourselves with them."

When Jährēd learned about the one hundred men, his sadness increased and he grieved greatly. He then rose up with great zealousness and went in among them. Jährēd swore to them by the blood of Äbäl the Innocent, "Do not allow any one of you to go down from this sacred mountain, this pure and fair place that our fathers have commanded us to live on and lord over the hew-brutes in the labyrinth of tunnels."

However, when Jährēd saw that they did not listen to his words, he said to them, "My pure and innocent family, understand: Once you go down from this sacred place, Ghäd' will not allow you to return."

He again swore to them, "I swear by the death of our father Ädam and the blood of Äbäl and Shäth, Enōish, Khänen, and Mähällälil, to listen to me. Do not go down from this sacred mountain, because the moment you leave, you will be deprived of spiritual salvation—you will never become a Saint. You will never see an emissary of Mercy, and you will no longer be called Children of Ghäd'; rather, you will be called Children of Shätän'!'"

They would not listen to him.

In those days, Enäkh, the firstborn son of Jährēd, was already grown, and in his zeal for Ghädäniēl, he rose up and shouted, "O you, family of Shäth, small and great, hear me! When you disobey the commands of our fathers and go down from this sacred mountain, you will never again be able to return!"

The men rose up in defiance of both Jährēd and Enäkh. They did not listen to either of them and instead went down from the mountain. They all looked at the women of the family of Khän, at their beautiful figures and their hands and feet dyed with diverse colors, and the swirly tattoos on their faces, and the fire of beastly passion was kindled in them. The descended two hundred Gregoriän hōst had made the women of Khän look most beautiful in the eyes of the men of Shäth, and they had also made the men appear most handsome in the eyes of the women. The women of Khän lusted after the men of Shäth like ravenous wild beasts, and the men of Shäth lusted after the women of Khän until they mated.

After the men of Shäth had finished, they journeyed back and began to ascend the sacred mountain, but they could not go up, because Ängles had placed objects in their path which flashed a very bright and hot light if stepped upon. These mining explosives killed and maimed some of them and prevented them from going up. Ghädäniēl was very angry at them. He regretted their creation because they had shown disobedience by their coming down from the mountain and mating with the people of Khän, whom he considered mongrels, unclean in spirit and disobedient in behavior, not suitable as servants for the mission of Ghädäniēl. These Children of Ghädäniēl, after failing a test of obedience, had given themselves over to Shätäniēl, who could now do whatever he pleased with them, because Ghädäniēl no longer wanted them.

Ghädäniēl said, "My ghostly children have fallen away from my grace, having gone into the Land of Nod by their own free will."

He sent to Jährēd a messenger who heralded, "Hear, you! Hear, you! Hear, you! Most High Lord Ghäd of Än, Attorney General, says to you: 'O Jährēd, understand: These, your kindred who are my ghost-children, have disobeyed my command. They have gone down to the impure people of the damnation of Shätäniēl. Send a messenger to those who are left on the mountain so that they might not go down and lose their spirits, so that they will not fall from my grace and burn in rēd bond fires."

Jährēd wept and asked the messenger for forgiveness from Ghädäniēl. He wished his spirit would be taken now and saved for resurrection in a better world, rather than hear these words from the messenger about the descent of his family from the mountain. He followed the command of Ghädäniēl, however, and preached to his remaining family not to go down and mingle with the people of Khän, but they would not listen to him.

Afterward, another group gathered together, and their spokesman said to Jährēd, "We are going to go watch over and protect our brethren below," as a self-justification to go, and they went down from the mountain. They, too, were unable to return. And so it was with group after group, until only a few of them were left on the mountain.

Jährēd was sickened from grief, and his sickness was such that the day of his death came near.

48

Jährēd summoned his son Enäkh and the rest of the elders.

When they came to him, he prayed for them, gave his blessing and last will and testament, and said also, "You are a wholly royal purebred people, legitimate and innocent Children of Ghäd'. Do not go down from this mountain. Understand: Your kindred went down and estranged themselves from Ghäd' through their abominable lust and disregard of his law. I know by the proven might of Ghäd' that he will not depart from you here on this sacred mountain as a result of your kindred having disobeyed his command and the command of our fathers. O my sons, understand: A great Ängle will come to lead those of you who survive to a strange land, never again to see this place with your own eyes. Let the Ängle lead you to get there. Therefore, set your thoughts on yourselves and keep the law of Ghäd', who is with you. When you have to go into that land which you know nothing about, take the boxed body of our great father Ädam with you, along with the power rod, the Book of the Covenant, and the three chested gifts of säphärōn, frankincense, and myrrh; keep them hidden and safe with the boxed body. The great Ängle will later return to visit with the one of you who is left, the one of you who is to build a great ärkh of wood which is to carry the boxed body of Ädam, the Book of the Covenant, the treasure, and what purity of mankind is left along with their änimals, away from a great destruction by fire and a deluge of water upon the world. When this one of you is saved from the destruction, he must ensure that the boxed body of Ädam and gifts are taken to the haven in the North, to Shämbäelle, and interred within a naval of the capital there, at the Crest of Säphärōn, the new place of resting in peace and the place from where our rēdemption will occur."

One of the elders asked Jāhrēd, "Who is the one of us who will be left?"

Jāhrēd paused for thought and then carefully answered, "The One Who Understands Waters will be the one who will be left. The Ängle Bärräkhäēl, a leader of one hundred of the Gregoriän hōst, will pilot the ärkh, guiding the one and his immediate family in their journey upon the high sea."

Jāhrēd turned to his son Enäkh and said to him, "You, O my son, live in this Cave of Treasure and administer the sacred wholly royal spirit mating rite before the boxed body of Ädam throughout all of the days of your life. Maintain the chaste spirit and innocence of the Children of Ghäd'. Continue to build our trust in the name and number of Ghäd'. Preserve the treasury of gold and the Book of the Covenant at all cost. Do not waiver from this sacred duty."

Jāhrēd said no more. Tears streamed down his face because of his great sadness toward his kindred who had fallen from the grace of Ghädäniēl. After he kissed with his lips the cheek of the One Who Understands Water, the hands of Jāhrēd became loose, his eyes closed, and he died like his fathers had died.

Enäkh and the other elders wept over Jāhrēd, carefully balmed him, and then laid his boxed body to rest in the Cave of Treasure. They stood and mourned over him for many days, and when their mourning was completed, they remained there in gut-wrenching sadness, because the spirit of their father had departed from them and they did not see him alive again.

Enäkh kept the command and law of his father, continuing to administer the sacred wholly royal spirit mating rite in the cave to the few of them who remained obedient, and it is to this particular Enäkh whom many wonders occurred...when he saw Ghädäniēl and walked with great Ängles.

49

The remainder of the family of Shäth descended from Three Dog Mountain to the Land of Nod, and when Enäkh and the other heads of generations saw them leave, they suffered in sadness because of their fall into doubt and total disbelief. Enäkh and the remaining Children of Ghädäniēl wept and sought the emissaries of Mercy Company to watch over and protect those who went down, and to deliver them back to the mountain.

Enäkh continued to pray and offer gifts to Ghädäniēl for many years, and then he became aware that Ängles were going to take him on a journey of discovery, and they promptly did so. He was escorted by Ängles to many wondrous places on the world and in the black sea above the sky. He was even brought face-to-face with Ghädäniēl himself in his throne ship *Glōry*. Throughout his tremendous journey, Enäkh conversed with the Ängles and saw a magnificent sight all around him. They showed him the wonder of the seven-phase vision-sphere, and how it produces a virtual world of width, height, depth, sound, touch, smell, and taste, and informed him about a latter-day people called the Selected Ones, those who would be taken as the best from among a nation of people called the Obedient Ones. This was not a fictional fantasy. He heard everything and understood what he had seen: events which were to occur not during his days but during far-distant days.

Enäkh asked an Ängle to tell him about the Selected Ones, and the Ängle showed him more of the vision-sphere, saying, "In its flight near to Phoëbus, the sun, the flying Phaëton transforms into Phoënix and behaves like a bird on fire, but it is an imperishable star which flies forward from its faraway abode in the darkness to collect and cover itself in gold dust for protection from the searing rays of Phoëbus. It shears the plane of the planets of the sun as it flies in near to an old stone wall whose rocks fall away and tumble near to the path of this world. Phoënix appears to be on fire as it tries to land twice on the stone wall, once upon its arrival and once upon its departure, but it is not destroyed, because it transforms back into Phaëton. It succeeds in collecting and covering itself in gold dust and then returns to its distant abode of everlasting life. During a secret shear, however, when it comes closest to this world, it will greatly disturb this world, as well as being disturbed itself. Ghäd' will descend from the black sea above the sky and walk upon the Mount of Säphärōn. He will arrive with a legion of Ängles and reveal himself to his ghost-children in a vision powered from above. Everyone will be afraid, even the Gregoriän hōst who had circled above this world but then descended in rebellion. From the eastern horizon to the western horizon, everyone will be terrified and shaking. Mountains will quake, and the hills will appear to melt like wax next to a flame. The world will shrivel from increased heat, and nearly everything will die. The final sign-age of assessment and judgment of the covenant will then come to everyone in this world, including the Obedient Ones. Ghäd' will save and give peaceful rest to the Selected Ones, and then everyone remaining will become his subject. The Selected Ones will be happy and honored because the wondrous Ängles of Ghäd' will have enlightened them, transfiguring their bodies to resemble his righteous Ängles. They will be called the Saints of Ghäd'. O Enäkh, understand: Ghäd' will make his throne ship *Glōry* reappear in this world with a legion of Ängles to pronounce judgment on the worth of his bonded creatures of life, to destroy the worthless in rēd bond fires, and to either renew the remainder to toil in the wilderness or to rēdeem them to rest in a haven indefinitely. He will also hunt down any remnant of the fiendish offspring of the Gregoriän hōst, to convict and destroy them."

When Enäkh was seeing and hearing everything from the vision-sphere, he was hidden—none of his kindred knew where he was, where he had been, or what had happened to him. He was entirely busy with the Ängles.

50

Enäkh, the son of Jährēd, said to his firstborn son, Mätthewshälä (not the same as the Mätthewshälä in the line of Khän), "O my son, Ghäd' will soon bring a great wave of water over the earth to destroy the rebellious Gregoriän hōst and their impure and evil-spirited children, along with everyone else, because of their disobedience and noise. He has had enough of the misbehavior, which keeps him from resting his feet upon this world. You are the last priest-king of the Children of Ghäd' on this mountain, because I know that not one of your family will be left here to produce children, neither will any one of them continue to rule over their own children. No pure one of you will be left on this mountain. He Who Understands Water and his family with änimals will be driven toward a strange land, to build a wooden ärkh there and survive the flood."

Enäkh said to them all together, "Watch over yourselves and hold fast to your rock by your fear of Ghäd' and your dedicated workship to him. Keep trusting in the name and number of Ghäd'; keep the Book of the Covenant and the treasure hidden from unclean hands. Ensure the treasury of gold is moved up through the esophagus of the three-headed Dog Mountain, to vomit beneath the capital of the Crest of Säphärōn. Praise both Lady Khätän' and Lord Ghäd' in true obedience and serve them in chastity, innocence, and repentance."

When Enäkh ceased his commands, Ängles removed him in a column of frozen fire. They later delivered him to the twin-city haven of Shämbäëlle, to the hospitality city of Shērpäppäkh, after transfiguring him into a Saint within a resurrection haven above. In this manner, Enäkh found himself living an Ängleic life, an everlasting

life away from the dangers of everlasting death in the
wilderness of Shätäniēl, until Ghädäniēl would have him
die. Altogether, not one of the Children of Ghädäniēl
remained on Three Dog Mountain except the immediate
families of Mätthewshälä, his firstborn son, Lūmäkh (not
the same as Lūmäkh the Blind in the line of Khän), and
the firstborn son of Lūmäkh, described as He Who Understands Water—Knōa—because the remainder of them
went down from the Mountain of Sermon to live among the
people of Khän located in and around the City of
Dameäskhūsh, and they were forbidden from ever returning.

AlienCovenant.com